The Secret Diary of a BENGALI MUM

HALIMA KHATUN

A HAYAT HOUSE book
First published in Great Britain in 2024 by Hayat House.
Copyright © Hayat House 2024
The moral right of Halima Khatun to be identified as the author of this work has been asserted by her in accordance with the Copyright, Design and Patents Act, 1988.
Cover design by Felix Diaz de Escauriaza
All the characters in this book are fictitious, and any resemblance to actual persons living or dead is purely coincidental.
A CIP Catalogue record for this book is available from the British Library

This isn't your average romcom...

Thank you for buying my book and joining me on this author adventure. As a token of my appreciation, I'd love to give you more... so read on to the end for how you can be a part of this very unique series.

16th April, Reflection

"What brings you to this birth reflection session?" the aptly named Bertha asks.

"Birth reflection? Sorry, I thought it was a birth trauma consultation." I shift in my chair, worried that I may have gone to the wrong meeting. I wouldn't be surprised, as it's not even at the hospital where I gave birth. Plus, my brain has turned to cotton candy these last couple of weeks.

Bertha scratches the back of her neck. "We don't really like to use the word trauma, as that has negative connotations. Instead, we prefer to move forward in a more positive light, which is why birth reflection seems more appropriate."

I personally think trauma would be more befitting but keep my opinion to myself.

Baby H2 gurgles in her bassinet. She looks like she might wake up. I'm hoping we can get to the point of this trauma/reflection meeting before we hear some serious baby wails.

"Okay, birth reflection. I just wanted to talk about what happened because I think some of it wasn't right. And I suffered further complications after the baby was born and—"

"Sorry, what do you mean, not right?" Bertha's tone becomes confrontational.

"It's just that, well, perhaps not right isn't the best term. It's just the way things happened. I felt everything was out of my control—"

"Childbirth generally is out of all our control!" Bertha laughs and shakes her head.

"Okay, well, maybe I'm not making my point properly. It's just... I don't know, I thought I should have a birth trauma—sorry—reflection meeting to talk about what happened and see what can be done."

"What can be done? You're two weeks postpartum. I don't think anything can be done now." Bertha looks at the big white clock that is ticking away above my head. My time is running out and there must be someone else after me. Another mum waiting to reflect on her traumatic birth.

"I—I wrote things down, if that helps? I can tell you exactly what happened, which would better explain why I'm here."

"Like I say, nothing can be done now, so there's really no need to rehash—"

"No!" My voice trembles. "I need to share this. I need to be heard."

I rifle through my oversized mum bag, which contains nappies, wipes, some hand sanitizer, a bottle of baby formula and, right at the bottom, my Filofax. It's funny, just a couple of weeks ago, that would take pride of place in my small, neat leather handbag. So much has changed since then.

"Okay... so I wrote this down after I had a chance to process everything. Sorry... I can't find the first bit." I flick through the pages. "Right, here we are. When baby H2 was born..."

Bertha smirks.

"Sorry, H2 is a name we had for her before she was born and it's kind of stuck like a nickname. Bit childish, I know.

Anyway, when I was in labour..." My hands start shaking. "Sorry... I... I mean, when I was going into the beginnings of labour, I was examined twice, then the nurse mentioned she'd done a membrane sweep and I felt it was not appropriate. Then I laboured in such a short space of time, which I think isn't right."

Bertha holds up her hand. "Apologies, I must stop you there. What don't you think was right? Being probed twice, the sweep or labouring quickly?"

"Uh... all of it."

"And what are you basing this on?"

"Erm... how I felt. It didn't feel right." My mouth feels dry. I've built a career based on words and now I can't seem to find any.

I think Bertha notices my chin wobble as she waves her hand in the air and says: "Carry on."

"Thanks. After the examinations, I was sent home. I went back in and, the second time, even though I was holding onto the walls and practically on all fours, they were going to send me home again. It was only when another nurse spotted me and saw me in so much pain that I was admitted."

Bertha looks as though she is about to interject but then lets me continue.

"I ended up labouring on the birthing stool and it was only afterwards I learned I'm more likely to tear in that position."

"Where did you hear that?"

I look down. "The internet."

Bertha rolls her eyes. "Ah, Dr. Google. Okay, go on."

"After that, I was…"

I've lost my place. I'm lost. I'm not sure how this whole ordeal feels like it happened yesterday and another lifetime ago at the same time. I've never known such a feeling.

Bertha looks at her watch.

"The thing is, I'm worried about what long-term effects this will have on me."

"What do you mean?" she asks, her pencil-thin eyebrows furrowed.

"As in…" I speak with a mix of shame and embarrassment, though I'm not sure why. "It's the third-degree tear. I'm worried about the repercussions because I've read about having things like anal fissures."

"You mean anal fistula?"

As Bertha is more knowledgeable about these things than I am, I agree.

"Okay, so it won't be an anal fistula, as that is something that would've been evident straight away. It's not something you develop."

"But the whole thing felt barbaric," I plead.

Bertha sits back in her chair. "I think barbaric is the wrong word."

"Okay, not barbaric but—"

"What did happen was unfortunate," Bertha interjects, resting her elbows on the desk. "However, you have to remember, when you're labouring, people do what they think is best. The fact that you were examined twice is quite routine. There's nothing unusual there. It's unfortunate that you had such a bad tear after giving birth but that's just how it goes sometimes. But look at your baby…" Bertha points towards my newborn daughter, who is sleeping peacefully, for once. "You've got a beautiful baby girl and you should focus on the positive. Forget your birth experience. None of that really matters now. The most important thing is you've created a new life. Your priority is to look after her, not look back."

There's so much more to say but I don't have the vocabulary. Or the energy. "Are you able to examine me?" I ask instead. "I haven't been checked out since a few days after I gave birth, so I don't know if everything down there is... as it should be."

"I won't be able to do that." Bertha sniffs.

"Why not?" I'm offended for my lady parts.

"We don't have the right lighting in here to be able to look at you."

"Alright. It's just... I'm worried that there might be scarring. Also, I'm worried about prolapsing. I've heard a lot about that."

Bertha sits up in her chair, arms crossed. "Look, if you were prolapsing, you would know about it as literally bits would be hanging out. If that's not the case, then you are fine. Any problems, of course you can go and see your GP." She turns to her computer screen. "Is there anything else?"

There's plenty more. I had the most traumatic two weeks of my life. It was a huge ordeal even to get here. It was the first time I've got on public transport with my baby. I avoided the Tube and instead did a merry-go-round using London's less famous DLR service. It wasn't easy. I had to change twice. And after all that, she's asking me if that's all?

"Yes, that's all." Of course, my PR politeness kicks in. What else could I say?

"Great, well thanks for dropping by," she says as though I'm a friend that's popped round for coffee.

The door slams behind me as I exit the consultation room. Now, I have to head out into the cold and get on the DLR again. I hope we make it home unscathed.

THE PLATFORM IS PACKED out. It's way busier than it was on the way there. It is 3pm, after all. I've only got one bottle of baby formula. I hope it's enough for the journey home.

There is another lady with a toddler in a pram and a baby in a sling. I eavesdrop on her phone conversation and deduce that she is Bengali. How does she negotiate public transport with two tiny people? She must be some sort of superwoman. I'm in bits and I've just got one.

As the train slowly arrives, my heartbeat quickens. What if there's no space for two buggies? What if people get annoyed because I'm blocking the path? What if... what if my worst nightmare happens? That I manage to push the pram onto the carriage but can't get on myself and the door snaps shut, separating me from my baby. I tremble at the thought. Has that ever happened before? What is done in that situation? Who would help me? Could they do an emergency stop on the train? Maybe I'll reverse into the carriage. If I go in first and pull the pram behind me, would that be better? But then, what if I get on the train but people shove in and the pram doesn't make it? If I put my hand between the door, would it automatically open, like a lift? Or would I sever a limb? What if the pram falls in the gap between the train and the platform? After all, the tannoy announcement is always warning us to mind the gap. If it's big enough for a human to fall through, could a pram do the same? I grip the handle of the pram tightly, my knuckles straining.

There's so much to think about. A few short weeks ago, I took all this for granted. Hopping on the bus and getting the Tube as I pleased. Apart from the claustrophobia and low-lying worry about being trapped underground, I had it easy. If only I knew at the time.

I don't want to sound dramatic, but it feels like life is over now. At least the life I knew. The bloody baby books were right; things will never, ever be the same again. And honestly, I don't know how I feel about that.

The train carriage slows to a halt and, mercifully, the door opens right in front of me. It's every person for themselves, so I shuffle my way on, ahead of my competitor, the other Bengali lady with the pram and the baby in a sling. Like I say, everyone for themselves. The universe has been kind to me today; there is even a seat at a table. Now, I have to put the pram somewhere. Damn, I wish I had those trendy, foldable prams. My sturdy, bulky gift from mum, for which I am grateful, is taking up lots of space. I can hear the huffs as people manoeuvre around it. It's like road rage without the cars.

One man makes a point of glowering as he sits at the table.

Miserable git.

He doesn't know how good he's got it, getting public transport without a baby in a pram. The lady with the pushchair and baby carrier stands near the door. I feel a hint of guilt about that but everyone else should feel worse. They are able-bodied and without children. Any one of them could've given her a seat.

Bloody London.

The train makes that screeching sound as it moves off. I breathe a sigh of relief. We are on our way home. I made it.

I peer over the bassinet to check on H2. Crap, she's woken up. Probably due to all the shoving by fellow commuters. I rock her gently in the pram, pushing the foam handle back and forth to create a rhythmic motion to complement the gentle movement of the train. She's staring at the ceiling, wide-eyed. Oh no, please don't cry. Please don't cry and cause a scene on the train.

She can't see me. She's in that awful newborn position of being flat on her back, facing upwards. The ceiling of the carriage, with its bright white light, is hardly conducive to soothing a baby that's just woken up. I see her face creasing up. Then she lets out a yelp. An alarm goes off in my body. One that only I can hear. I shush her. She continues, crying louder and louder. I don't know what to do. Should I pick her up? I don't even know how I can without toppling over in the moving carriage. Imagine me falling down with H2 on a packed-out train? I'd die. I'd simply die.

The moody man sat opposite me, wearing a cheap, shiny suit, glances over. Or was that a glare? It wouldn't surprise me given his overall huffiness. What's his problem? Has he never heard a baby cry before? Weirdo.

I need solidarity.

Where's that supermum with the baby in the sling? Oh yeah, she's standing near the door after I barged my way through and took one of the few available seats.

H2's cries are getting louder. I hunch over the pram, shaking along with the carriage, and scoop my arm underneath her back and lift her out. Her head jerks back. Bloody hell, support the neck! Support the neck! I should be better at this. I've had her for two weeks.

I place my feet wide apart and squat down like a sumo wrestler in an attempt to safely return to my seat. She's still doing the baby wail, using all of her lungs to let out a piercing scream. Her mouth is so agape that I can see her tongue shaking with each screech.

With one hand, I reach into my giant mum bag and grab the instant baby formula. I grab the tiny bottle and place it near her mouth. She gags, then moves her face away and continues crying, her tongue quivering with fury. I can't win. I can't win any of this. She won't latch on to the breast and she retches at the bottle. What am I supposed to do? What can I feed this girl?

Suddenly, she stops with her echoey cry and lets me put the bottle into her mouth. Oh, thank God for that.

I take a second to look around. Everyone is doing everything to avoid the novelty of a newborn on public transport. An older lady is looking out of the window. Other people have their eyes closed. Some stare at their shoes. Most face their mobile phones.

The carriage takes a sharp turn. I cradle H2 with both hands and drop the bottle of formula in the process. It falls to the ground and rolls across to the end of a four-seater opposite me.

Fucking hell.

H2 resumes her crying symphony. I can't take it. I want to cry myself. I feel my heart rate quicken. It's everything. Her cries. The stares. The shame. Mostly the shame. The shame I feel because I can't look after my own daughter.

All these people, judging with their eye rolls, don't they know that babies have small stomachs and unpredictable feelings that can only be expressed by crying?

The superwoman with the baby and toddler is looking out of the window. Her toddler son is holding an iPad, while the baby is fast asleep. I wish one of her two would start crying. I could do with the diversion.

There's only one thing for it. I'm going to have to try and feed her myself. I'll need to breastfeed in public, on a carriage full of pissed-off commuters. I can't believe it's come to this. Mum and my prudish big sis would be horrified if they knew but I can't think about them right now. I just need to put an end to this torture. For me and her.

I attempt to be as discreet as possible, loosening my pashmina around H2's head and unclipping my ugly mum bra. First, she gags and then she gives in. Poor thing, she must be exhausted. She didn't ask for this. She didn't ask for any of this. She didn't choose to live in central London. She didn't ask for such a traumatic birth. She didn't ask for a mum who couldn't figure out this most basic thing of how to feed her own baby.

H2 is clamping down with tight gums. It feels like fire but I don't dare take her off. I'd rather endure this than hear her cries.

The cheap, shiny-suited guy rolls his eyes at me. That is definitely in judgment. Dickhead.

H2 seems satiated as she pulls away and is a vision of peace, with watery milk around her mouth. I re-clip my bra, regain some dignity and pat her around the mouth with my pashmina.

Gosh, the pre-mummy me would never use a piece of clothing to wipe anything. The pre-mummy me would've at least had a packet of tissues handy in her bag. The pre-mummy me would've been organised. The pre-mummy me wouldn't be this messy.

The pre-mummy me is gone. I'm not sure if she'll ever come back.

I breathe a sigh of relief as we get to my stop, Watney Market. The spring air cools my head. Now all I need to do is safely get off the DLR, negotiate my way to the lift, then walk home while H2 hopefully stays asleep in the soothing motion of the pram.

Just as I exit the train, it starts raining. Great, I don't even have an umbrella, or a hood. A horde of people rush past me and make a beeline for the lift. Many of whom, I might add, look like they are perfectly capable of taking the stairs.

Even the superwoman with the baby in the sling and the pram does something that is worthy of a round of applause. She takes the toddler out of the pram, keeps the baby in the sling, folds up the pram and carries it with one hand, holding her toddler daughter with the other.

I want to be like her when I grow up.

The lift quickly becomes full and even though people do their best to squeeze themselves into the walls to make space for me and my massive pram, I'm too claustrophobic to join them. Instead, I wait outside for the lift to come back again. I glance over at H2. Her eyes are open, her mouth is trembling. Then, her face creases up in the all-too-familiar way.

Tears again.

Having first felt proud of myself for making my way on the DLR to meet the trauma lady, now I can't help but think, was it even worth it?

17th April, Recollection

Having reflected on the birth reflection meeting, I can say with confidence that it was a load of crap. Instead, I shall turn to Google for solace.

However, it's difficult to find an answer in the vastness of the internet when you don't actually know what you're asking.

I just feel... I don't know... I can't explain.

Deep down, in my innermost layer, I feel that life has ended. Ironic, as I've just given life to the world. And don't get me wrong, it's impossible to quantify the depth of love I feel for this tiny human but, at the same time, she comes with challenges. One being sleep. I don't remember what normal sleep was like before. Proper sleep. Where I'd actually dream. Will it ever come back? Will *I* ever come back?

I think I need to write this stuff down. journalling my feelings has helped me so far in life. From the quest to find a husband, marrying him, negotiating newlywed life, redundancy, being a boss, pregnancy... maybe it'll help me with motherhood. Right now, I need all the help I can get.

Words are therapy, after all. So I need to revisit those experiences I've pushed to the pit of my stomach since H2 came into the world.

Here goes...

Immediately after H2 was born, she was taken away from me.

I lost a lot of blood. 180mls, to be precise. Of course, I was blissfully unaware of this because I just had a baby. She came out crying and was placed in my arms for the first time while I lay on the bed in my giant, Instagram-worthy birthing room. Within moments, several other healthcare professionals came into the room, including one senior consultant. They did their best poker faces, smiling and asking how I felt, while Alison, the midwife who helped deliver H2, couldn't quite keep up the facade. Her face was white with shock. I focused on my new baby and ignored the scene in the corner of my eye where Alison and the other brilliant midwife, Claire, scooped up clots of blood from the floor.

The senior consultant instructed M to hold H2. I was hooked up to various IVs again. I didn't mind so much, as I already had fresh needles in my veins from the labour itself. In some strange way, I felt like a VIP. I was being wheeled around from the birthing unit to the bright white lights of the hospital corridor.

En route, I felt my stomach spin before the copious amounts of gas I had been inhaling came out in projectile vomit. The poor, poor midwives. They cleaned it up and changed me without issue.

God bless the NHS. They are amazing. The things they do without flinching.

We ended up in a dark room. A man in scrubs, who introduced himself as a surgeon whose name I now forget, told me a whole bunch of stuff. His voice was low. His tone sombre. He talked about a third-degree tear. Unexpected blood loss. Emergency stitching. An epidural. Side effects. Fecal incontinence. A year of recovery.

I had to sign a form. I had tubes injected into both arms. My fingers were numb. How could I sign this? What was I signing? I looked for M. He was gone. Another lady was holding my baby.

I asked if I could speak to my husband. They said there's no time.

All I could think was, what would happen if I didn't sign the form? If I didn't undergo this procedure? What was the worst-case scenario? But a bigger thought occurred to me... after going through labour with only gas and air, I now had to have an epidural. Now? Having done all the hard work? Endured all the pain?

The irony.

I asked if M could be in the room while I was being stitched. They said no, it's a sterile environment. Then I wondered what would happen if I died in surgery or became paralysed. What would happen to my baby? Is this how my story would end?

My phone pings. It's M, messaging me from work:
Hey babe, how are my two favourite people doing?
I reply: *We are fine x*
What else is there to say?
I then add: *How are you?*
He replies: *Good. This new boss seems nicer than the old one. He's going to take me and a few others out to lunch.*

Crap. I haven't even asked about his new job. He only started yesterday. To be honest, I wish he was home for longer. I so desperately wish he was with me now. That I didn't have to do this alone. I cried as soon as he went out of the door yesterday. I felt so vulnerable without my safety blanket husband, but he had to go. There was no other choice.

M had been out of work for months, which had caused a huge rift between us. I was constantly on his case about getting a job, so I had no room to complain now that he was employed. Plus, with me barely working, having lost many clients during my pregnancy, we need the money. We have a baby to support.

I look over to M's other favourite person, H2. She is currently asleep, wedged under my arm while I use my spare hand to journal my thoughts on my iPhone notes. Gone are the days of writing down with pen and paper. Now, it's survival. I have to use whatever tools necessary in the most awkward of positions.

I reply to M: *Enjoy lunch x*

I don't mean that. I'm insanely jealous. What I would give to be able to eat without being tethered to a newborn. What I would give to have a hot meal and be able to actually eat it while it's hot. What a luxury that would be.

I close my text messages and re-open my notes. Where was I? Oh yes, what if I die?

H2 moves, startled. I don't know why, I've kept my left arm as still as possible. Despite needing a wee, I daren't move. She opens her eyes briefly. Then she opens her gummy mouth and contorts it into what looks like the beginnings of a cry.

Bloody hell.

Then she closes her mouth and rolls her eyes back to sleep.

I'll take that as a win.

Back to journalling.

Going into the theatre was the scariest thing I've done in my life. I didn't have my husband. I didn't have my baby. I signed away my life.

The anaesthetist saw it in my face when I went into theatre.

"Are you okay?" he asked.

I couldn't even keep my eyes open.

"Fed up?" he asked.

That was a more appropriate question.

"I just want to go home," I replied.

He was as friendly as could be, given that his job was to stab me in the back. He tried to find some commonality, telling me his wife was also from Manchester and he likes it up north. People are friendly there. In between, he muttered to colleagues that he couldn't find the correct place in my spine to inject the epidural. I closed my eyes and prayed, wondering what would happen if he missed the mark. Would I end up paralysed? How often does that happen? I was told it was very rare, one in 1000 or something like that. What if I was the one in that thousand? And, I hadn't even been able to speak to my mum or my husband, or hold my baby one more time.

A nurse came in with a message. Apparently, my baby wouldn't stop crying so they wanted to know if they could give her some formula milk. Oh my God, my baby hasn't eaten a thing. I hadn't breastfed her. She was taken away. I said yes, of course, please feed her! Formula milk was her first meal.

The anaesthetist called another colleague to look at my back. Was it that unusual? I thought I had a regular spine. I took a deep breath. I said another silent prayer as I felt the needle touch my skin.

Then I heard the words I needed to hear. "Okay, that's all done." But there was more. Of course, there was more. "You might be a bit shaky as a side-effect of the epidural and you'll be numb below the waist so you won't be able to move your legs."

It's strange, the most serious condition I've ever had which required the help of a healthcare professional was a low level of vitamin D and iron. Yet, no sooner had I become a mum that I was faced with this.

I can't remember much else of the procedure itself. I was numb. I didn't feel a thing. They quietly talked around me as though I wasn't there. I happily accepted that, wishing I was another being in another body.

Then, I was wheeled out. I caught a glimpse of a window going through the corridor, enough to see that it was pitch black outside. I was in a strange alternate reality where I didn't know what time of day it was, or what day of the week, for that matter.

The room I ended up in was a high dependency unit. That's when I realised that things had gotten real.

When M came through, holding H2, he looked horrified. "You're shaking a lot."

"It's a side-effect of the epidural," I managed to mutter through chattering teeth. "Where did you go when I was signing the forms?"

"Sorry, babe," he replied. "I haven't been to the toilet in 10 hours. I desperately needed the loo. I didn't realise they were going to make you sign anything. Otherwise, I would've held it in longer."

Standard M.

He wasn't allowed to stay overnight. I was left to it. With a drip in each arm and a baby in the clear plastic crib next to me. I couldn't move my toes, let alone feed her. When she cried, I pressed the buzzer to see if somebody would help.

I received a few tuts.

One healthcare worker even said to me: "You're a mum now. You'll have to figure out how to settle her."

Settle her? I couldn't even settle myself with wires and drips and a rattling jaw. The thing is, being in a high dependency unit, there were people in much more critical conditions than me. I was low on the food chain priority. One nurse took pity on me and gave H2 a bottle. This was enough to send her into a deep sleep. I didn't even look at my baby during this time. I was too busy feeling sorry for myself.

I made a half-arsed attempt to put her on my breast, with the help of another health worker. The lady, who was of Indian origin, told me that she birthed all three children by herself, as her husband was unwilling to be with her during labour. She also told me that breastfeeding was supposed to hurt when she saw me wince in pain. Again, I was told, repeatedly, I'm a mum now. This is my lot.

I think I managed to get some sleep that night. In between the noises from the various monitors going off and alarms sounding.

In the morning, the consultant who had stitched me up came around to check my vitals on the monitor next to me. He talked to a colleague as though I was invisible. A faceless, nameless patient. I tried to make eye contact. I was used to being addressed. In work. In life. Everywhere. I wanted to tell him: "Look! I'm a person! I can speak English, too. Can you just say some words to make me feel normal again?"

He finally looked at me and asked if I was okay. How I was feeling, given that I lost so much blood. I said I felt okay, and he went off to deal with another patient. I didn't take it personally. I know he's busy. These consultants are run off their feet.

The kind nurse, who helped me breastfeed H2 the night before, came to look at her and gasped. My baby had done a giant black poop. I didn't know how long she'd been sleeping in it but I remember the feeling of guilt, shame, and failure. That was the wake-up call I needed. H2's number two made me accept what everyone had been telling me - I'm a mum now. I need to get my shit together.

I turn off my iPhone notes. That's enough writing for today. That's enough reliving. I'm tired. More tired than I ever thought I would be. I put the phone to my side and gently ease my body lower so I can lie next to H2.

She immediately wakes up.

19th April, An evening stroll

"Should we go for a walk? It's the weekend, after all!" says M, as if that makes a difference to me. Unlike him, my day is feed, change, repeat.

"Why not?" I say. I guess it's the parental equivalent of a night out.

We go for a familiar walk down Commercial Road, then to Fenchurch Street.

"Shall we go towards the Tower of London?" asks M.

"Sure, Tower Bridge is one of my favourite bridges."

H2 is wide awake, even though it's 8pm. Is it socially unacceptable to have a newborn awake and out on the town so late? I'm not sure what's appropriate. All I can say is, we are the only people pushing a pram. There's not another baby in sight.

The Tower of London, bathed in golden spotlights, never fails to impress me. Nestled among the skyscrapers and modern buildings, this centuries-old castle still remains.

"Should I take her out of the pram and get a photo together?" asks M.

"I'll take a photo of you two. I don't fancy capturing myself looking like this." I stare down at my well-worn trainers.

"What are you on about? You look fine."

"Come on now, we both know that's not true. My face is still puffy like a squirrel and I haven't even brushed my hair.

That girl over there..." I point towards a raven-haired goddess, posing with her back to the camera, looking out onto the River Thames, "she looks fine."

This girl has trained her husband/partner well. He is patiently clicking away while she runs her fingers through her hair, then puts her hands in the air.

She turns around and the first thing I see is a pregnant belly. A very pregnant belly, by the looks of things. Then our eyes meet.

"Bloody hell!"

"What is it?" M asks, clutching H2.

"It's my cousin, Naila. You know, the makeup artist who's also an influencer. Of all the people to bump into."

"The one who married the English guy?"

"Yes! And she's with him right now."

Darren and Naila look at each other as if they're deciding whether or not to acknowledge they've seen us. I wouldn't mind if she ignored us. After all, it's not like we're close or anything. Despite us both living in London and me loving her parents, Uncle Tariq and Auntie Rukhsana, I barely see Naila.

"Shall we go over and say hi?" M asks. "They've not met this little monkey."

"No need. It looks like they're coming towards us."

Naila and Darren walk over, hand-in-hand. Where is baby Ibrahim? Who have they left him with?

"I haven't seen you in ages!" Naila gives me a hug, and her protruding belly presses against my squishy, postpartum stomach. "Me and Darren thought we better get the date nights in while we can. Make use of mum and dad babysitting Ibrahim before the new one arrives." She strokes her belly.

"Salaamalaykum, how's it going?" Darren offers a manly handshake to M, who reciprocates with the one free hand that isn't wrapped around our newborn baby.

I've never seen Darren in the flesh. I've seen his photos on Naila's Instagram. He's impressively tall but I guess I'm comparing him to standard Bengali men's height. He can also pull off a man bun, which I thought most men couldn't, and he's wearing skinny jeans that are borderline inappropriate. Must keep my eyes up.

"Man, is this your girl?" Naila interrupts my appraisal of Darren. "Let's have a look!" She runs her long-nailed fingers across H2's tiny chin. I'm scared she'll maim her with those talons. "Aww man, you do all the hard work and they come out looking like their dad." Naila laughs, throwing her head back.

"So I keep being told," I reply. "When are you due?"

"Not for another four months yet. I know, I've properly popped this time. I can't wait to snap back once the baby is born."

I can hear snippets of conversation between Darren and M. I think they're discussing the sleepless nights. M is saying it's pretty bad. He doesn't know the half of it.

"Anyway," Naila continues, "you should come round. There's a lot more space now we've got a house. There are three bedrooms, so plenty of room for you to stay."

As we live in London, there would be no real reason for me to need to stay at Naila's house. However, I smile politely.

"We're going to grab some food now, if you fancy a burger? We're heading to Tinsel Town, inshallah," says Darren, hands stuffed in his pockets.

M looks to me. I could tell he'd love to have a burger with a mountain of nachos. We used to go to that place all the time. However, now it feels unreachable. We'd have to get there by Tube, it's already late and I don't know when H2 is due to sleep. Plus Tinsel Town is always packed, noisy and full of young people. I couldn't comprehend doing this with H2.

"Another time," I reply, much to my husband's disappointment.

Once Naila and Darren say goodbye and head to the next stop of their date, M asks if I want to eat somewhere.

"No," I reply. "I just want to go home."

21st April, Clock watching

I've never clock-watched so much in my life. In all my years in the corporate sector, fighting the good PR fight, I was never like this. Now, I'm counting the minutes until M comes home. Annoyingly, the more I check the time, the slower it seems to pass.

It's 4.55pm.

With any luck, M will be back around 5.45pm. Now, what can baby H2 and I do to fill the time? She's already done a poo. I've sterilised her bottles for the second time. I put her on the bed, where she lay like a prawn and roared like a baby lion. By roar, I mean full-on crying.

The thing is, in this incredibly early stage of life, babies don't really do much apart from cry and feed. Apparently they do a lot of sleeping too, though I found with this one, it's in short fits and bursts, rather than proper naps.

I know, perhaps a bit of journalling will help.

The day after H2 was born... or was it two days after? It was all a bit of a blur.

Anyway, I was transferred into my own room at the hospital. I seem to have a bit of luck getting special treatment there. However, having my own space was a mixed blessing. My anxiety escalated as there was nobody to ask if everything was okay, if I'm breastfeeding properly, napping her properly. I had a buzzer for help. However, in using it, I felt like I was putting everyone out.

I became rather famous in the hospital, in the worst possible way. I was known as the lady who had a third-degree tear. People would remind me of it, grimacing. Nurses, physios, everyone knew about my torn labia.

It was only when I had a chance to Google that I learnt there is a 1% chance of that happening. Like I say, the worst possible notoriety. I was also the subject of awe, as people were surprised how well I looked given that I'd lost so much blood.

The next couple of days were rough. I was being checked constantly. I couldn't get H2 to latch on properly. And she would be crying for hours in the evening. M finally convinced me to give her another bottle. I asked a member of staff for milk and she looked at me like I was the devil incarnate. Was formula milk really that bad?

It's funny, when I was pregnant, I was so worried about being carted out of the hospital before I'm ready. I'd heard so many stories of women being hurried out due to a shortage of beds. I hadn't considered the alternative- staying, indefinitely, in a room without a window.

I passed the time by attending breastfeeding workshops, which took place at the ward. Other women there had C-sections, or were riddled with other complications. I was in good company. We all sat there, flashing the lactation consultant as we attempted to feed our sleepy babies. What happens on the ward and all that. When baby H2 wasn't sleeping, she'd occasionally latch on. Or so I believed.

However, in the privacy of my room, it didn't go so well. One night, she wouldn't stop screaming. I was desperate and unsure what to do. I walked into the ward, hoping, praying that someone would notice me. However, many other babies were crying, too. Mine wasn't a special case.

She finally slept on M, exhausted. She was on his shoulder while he sat on the chair. For much of that night, I was awake with anxiety. M's method reminded me of all the things I'd been told about dangerous co-sleeping.

Then, I think on day three, there were whispers that I might be able to go home. A nurse came in to take some blood but she struggled.

I'd been injected so much that there weren't really any new places. She told me I had bad veins. I cried buckets. The nurse was surprised that her flippant comment had triggered me so much.

M came in, prompting the nurse to leave, saying she'd come for my blood later.

M, looking confused and worried, put his arms around me while I collapsed into him, sobbing like a child.

I repeated over and over again: "I want to go home. I want to go home. I want to go home."

I close my iPhone notes. I need to lighten the mood.

I know, I'll put H2 down and make a cup of tea.

It's a military operation. I have to be stealthy. I get the baby basket with one hand and carry it to the living room. I bend my legs, as far as my thirtysomething knees can take me and put H2 down, feet first. It's working. It's working! I slowly let her roll onto the mattress.

Damn, I got too confident and her head shunted at the end. She opens her eyes for a second. Shit. Please don't wake up now. Please don't wake up now.

I pat her on her belly, in an attempt to send her back to slumber. H2 slowly closes her eyes again, as though she's exhausted by all this fussing.

My God. That's a first. I've got this.

Not only does H2 let me pour the kettle, she even stays asleep, while I steep the teabag for three whole minutes, ensuring that the tea is as dark as can be, before I dilute it with milk.

I rest my red mug on the coffee table and sit back. It only took me however many days but I'm here. I'm having a brew while my baby naps, just as the baby expert promised in the parenting book.

This is the perfect time to take a selfie. Just to show the world, and mainly my influencer/makeup artist cousin, Naila, that I have nailed parenthood. That I am winning. I turn my phone to selfie mode. Okay, I've looked better. My eyebrows are due another threading session, I'm devoid of makeup and I look parched. It's fine, I can break my golden rule of no filters on this occasion.

I raise the phone to the light, tilting it towards my face to make myself appear delicate and dainty. I could probably add a hashtag. Something like #MumLife. Or, maybe #motherhoodunfiltered, or #motherhoodunplugged. That's another one I've seen people use. Actually, I wonder whether I should pose nearer to the Moses basket. I don't show H2's face on social media, but it's okay to show the basket in the background. It makes the photo seem more authentic. Here's another thought- I could lift her into my arms and have her face snuggled into my chest. Maybe not, that'd just wake her up. Or would it? After all, she prefers being in my arms.

No, I best just lean into the Moses basket instead, looking in at H2 lovingly. That'll do.

I click the photo and don't realise the flash is on. H2's eyes blink open. You've got to be kidding me. I thought babies couldn't see or hear properly at this stage.

Shit, here it comes. The alarmed, piercing cry. I pick H2 up and, with my free hand, examine the spoils of my impromptu photo shoot.

It's not quite the Instagram-worthy selfie I was hoping for. My hair is flying everywhere as I turn to look at the

Moses basket and there is a little chubby fist protruding out of the basket, clenched in anger.

As I hold my baby, I've come to realise some things:

1.   I did not take a good selfie. It was far too authentic.
2.   I will not be able to drink my tea.
3.   I only have myself to blame.

AS I CAN'T HAVE A CUP of tea, I decide that a trip to the supermarket is the best way to kill time before M arrives. He did message something about needing milk and that he'd grab some on the way. I can save him a job and do it myself. That will prove that I still have some uses.

I weave through the supermarket at a hurried pace, racing past the vegetables as I scan for any reduced items. I'm very conscious of my pram banging into shopping trolleys or other shoppers. I picked the wrong time to come. I'm competing with people who've finished work and are grabbing ingredients for the evening meal. It's like a racetrack, with trolleys, baskets on wheels, and my bulky pram, all competing for space in the narrow aisles. I regularly check H2, looking for signs of distress. She seems content, gazing upwards, big brown eyes exploring the world.

"He's a heartbreaker, isn't he?" An old lady, brandishing a cucumber, gazes into the bassinet.

She strokes H2's cheek, while my daughter coos angelically, fingers splayed.

"Thank you. He's a she."

"Oh sorry. They all look the same at the beginning, don't they? All bald and chubby."

"Actually, underneath that red and grey striped hat is a full head of glorious hair. Not a bald spot in sight," I say, feeling defensive.

The old lady rubs H2's arm. I know she's being nice, but it feels a bit invasive.

H2 squirms. I'm not sure whether she's going to poo or cry. Just as her face creases up, the lady looks at me and says: "Enjoy every second. Before you know it, you'll be a grandma, like me."

My inner thoughts scream: *Oh, just be quiet. It's easy for you to say cherish every second when you've had your children and they're so old that they've had their own children. It's hard to cherish every second when most of the time you're in some kind of weird torture situation where you're kept awake for an inhumane amount of time. Why don't you take care of my daughter for a day and then tell me if you cherish every second?*

I stuff down my thoughts, smile at the old lady, and reply: "Of course. I cherish every second."

As she hobbles off, H2 descends into a full-on whine. It's like red mist has come over her. I hate nothing more than the sound of my baby crying in public. I don't know how to stop it, and I feel all eyes on me. A woman struggles to manoeuvre past me with her trolley. She gives me side-eye. Another woman with two older boys looks at me with a lopsided smile. It's a look of pity. I'd rather take the side-eye. I put the vegetables I'd collected in the pram basket back in the nearest fruit box I can find. What was once a neat display of pineapples, now is a medley, including courgette and carrot, thanks to me. I head back home.

"I KNOW IT'S REALLY hard for you and stuff, but... we've got a baby!" says M, just in case I hadn't realised. To further emphasize his point, he parades H2 in front of me as she pulls all sorts of little alien faces. "Look how amazing she is."

I struggle to raise a smile. "I know, I'm just tired."

M's right. She is amazing. I'm not denying that she is the most perfect, cutest thing I've ever seen. But it doesn't negate the fact that she is the hardest thing I've had to deal with. The two aren't mutually exclusive. But there's shame in saying the latter.

M puts his arm around me. "I know you're the one up in the night trying to feed her. She's a little minx, keeping me awake as well. But it will get easier. Have you been out today?"

"I went to the shops."

"Oh good, did you grab some milk?"

"No, she started crying when I was there, so I couldn't get anything."

M rubs H2's head. "You know it's okay if she cries, don't you? That's what babies are supposed to do."

I sigh. "It's hard for me to hear. I think it's different for you. I don't like her being in distress."

M tries not to laugh, though I don't see what's funny. "Does this one look like she's distressed!" He blows raspberries at her tummy. "You're the distressed one."

I turn away and rub my eyes.

"Sorry, babe." M strokes my back. "That was a stupid thing to say. Anyway, I'll pop out and grab some milk. We'll get a little list together because we're out of a few bits. I'll go to the big Tesco."

All I can think is, the big Tesco means a short drive and a longer shop. That'll mean an even longer absence from M. It's hard enough coping while he's at work. When he's not working, I need him here. To be present. To take H2 off my arms. I know that's not fair. Someone's got to get milk.

"And we need more formula?" M asks.

"I think we're running low. I'm also trying to breastfeed her in between."

"Babe, don't worry about that. You had a stressful enough time trying to feed her and that's how we ended up back in hospital in the first place. I'll just get some extra formula."

I say nothing.

M, still holding H2, pulls me closer. "It's okay, babe. It will get better. But listen, I think you should go to your mum's for a bit. It will help you. You'll get lots of support over there. Otherwise, you're just on your own all day."

I still say nothing. Mum hasn't mentioned anything about coming over. Would it be an imposition? After all, it's not just me anymore. It's me, my baby and all the baggage, both literal and metaphorical, that comes with it. Where would we even stay? We couldn't have the box room.

"Just think about it," M continues. "They'll be glad to have you. It was easier when your mum, dad, and sister stayed for a few days after she was born, wasn't it?"

I nod.

"Also, we've got another big job, haven't we?" says M.

"Oh God, what is it? What bigger job could there possibly be than looking after this one?"

M strokes H2's matted, thick hair, which naturally sits in a stylish, albeit spiky, side parting. "We're going to have to say goodbye to her luscious locks."

I sit back. "Oh, yes, the head shave. When are we supposed to do it?"

"Back when she was a week old. My mum keeps banging on about it every time I call home. How we're doing wrong by her and how her hair will be fine and fragile if we don't shave her ASAP."

"I don't see how, given that the midwives said we shouldn't bathe them so soon, let alone shave them."

M rolls his eyes. "It's funny how over centuries babies haven't changed, but the rules around them constantly do." He hands H2 back to me, even though I was enjoying being hands-free for a bit. "Anyway, before that..." M gets up. "I need to pop to the poop station. I've been holding it in since the afternoon."

M heads to the bathroom, taking his mobile phone with him. I know he'll be sat there for half an hour.

22nd April, No laughing matter

"Oh ho," says mum with a chuckle, causing the phone connection to crackle.

Why is she laughing? There's nothing funny about my latest anecdote about H2. Her staying up crying for three hours straight last night is not the stuff of comedy. So why is my own mother, the one who once went through all of this, laughing?

"Have you tried giving her the dummy?" mum asks.

"No, I don't want to do that."

Mum sighs. "You're going to have hard time getting her to sleep without dummy. You end up being the dummy!"

"I don't know, mum. I've read online that dummies can be a problem later as you can't get it off them. So then you have to wean your baby off and it's like starting all over again. It also affects their jaw development and ability to suck, apparently."

I can just hear mum's eye roll. "No talk silly! I give all of you dummy, and you no have goofy teeth! Maybe your teeth *lit-ool* big but okay. You still manage to find husband, no?"

I rub my hand across my mouth. I do have an overbite. I'm not sure if I can blame that on the dummy solely, because nobody else in my family does. And they were all hooked on the pacifier, according to mum.

"What's the madam doing now?" mum asks.

I look down at H2, who is in my arms. She looks so peaceful. Her eyes are closed, long, feathery lashes fanned out. Mouth puckered. And the teeny, tiny nose, with little milk spots, flares lightly as she breathes. I can never get bored of that face. Even if she does keep me awake most of the night and barely sleeps in the day. It's a good thing she's cute.

"Nothing, she's just asleep on me."

Another sigh from mum. "You need put her down. She get used to it and think you be bed. Get her in Jesus basket!"

"You mean Moses basket, mum."

"Moses... Jesus... one of the prophets. What a silly name for baby bed."

"Every time I put her down, she wakes up."

"Try harder."

"I'm trying as hard as I can!"

"Okay, okay. How is the breastfeeding going?"

"I'm still trying. But she doesn't really take it, so I end up giving her the bottle. Then, she pukes the milk out. So, we're just about managing."

"She keeps being sick after bottle? That be no good. Keep trying breast. Otherwise, she be not putting on weight. You don't want to go back hospital again."

"Mum! I know all this. Don't you think I'm doing my best? It's not my fault if she doesn't latch on properly. That's the issue we had in the first place. That's why we had to go into A&E because she wasn't taking enough milk and I was none the wiser. Because nobody tells you how hard it is. Nobody tells you that there might be a problem. You assume it's the most natural thing on earth. I thought nursing her was working and not a single fucking person... not a midwife, nurse, lactation consultant, none of them, said she's not getting milk. Now, I have to do all of it. I have to fucking sterilise bottles every four hours, then I have to give her the bottle only for her to drink a drop of it. Then I have to chuck the rest because it needs to be drank within the hour. In between, I'm trying to get her on the breast and then my own husband doesn't want me to bother with breastfeeding. I don't know which way to turn. I don't know what to do. I don't know who to listen to. And I don't know who is right. All I know is that I am wrong. And everything I'm doing is wrong."

My throat is hoarse. My eyes well up. A tear drops onto baby H2's chubby cheek.

"*Acha*. Alright, my dear. If she's sleeping, why don't you lay next to her in bed for a *lit-ool* bit. But don't go into deep sleep otherwise you might end up squishing her. I've put all of you in the cot. Never had you next to me in bed. Too dangerous. You didn't cling to me either, like your one. I think it's because I gave the dummy-"

"Got it, mum. I got it. Dummy is best. I'll see if I can get some."

"Good. What have you eaten?"

I look over at the kitchen counter, where there is an untouched, cold plate of arabbiata pasta. H2 let me cook my lunch but decided to wake up once I was about to eat it.

"I've not eaten anything yet."

"Oh-ho! She's a cheeky one!" is all mum can say. "What the little madam doing now?"

"Mum, I just told you. She's asleep. On me."

Mum pauses. "Oh, yes yes. You said that, yes. Okay, go eat now."

"I can't eat! I'm still holding my baby!"

Another chuckle from mum. "Cheeky little one."

Isn't mum worried that I haven't eaten? Or is she masking her concern because she knows that over 200 miles away in Manchester, there's nothing she can do? Does she feel guilty for not being able to help? Perhaps she does. I wish she'd stayed longer. I wish dad could just cope with being in my pokey flat for a few more days. I wish they weren't so put out about having to sleep in all sorts of contortions, dad in the single bed in the second bedroom/office, mum and little sis on the air bed in the living room. I know it couldn't have been comfortable. I wish they just sucked it up for a bit longer. I know that's selfish of me to expect it but I have to be selfish right now. Especially as I have to be so selfless as a mum.

"What you have planned for rest of today?" mum asks.

"My friend, Julia, said she'll come over as she's finishing work early today. We'll probably grab some food since it will be the only opportunity to eat before M gets home."

"Good. It be good that you get out. Make sure you give yourself *lit-ool* things to do. It be good for baby to get fresh air but don't go out when it's too cold. Or raining."

I look out of the window of our high-rise flat. It's raining and undoubtedly cold. However, I am determined to get out. I need to do it for myself and for H2. And with Julia coming, it's the perfect excuse to get myself out there. Because truth be told, if it wasn't for her, I wouldn't bother getting dressed, brushing my hair and leaving the house today.

JULIA IS A NATURAL. H2 was whining and writhing just moments earlier. Now, she is beyond content in my best friend's arms, as she is swayed from side to side.

"Babies love motion," Julia informs me.

"They sure do," I say. Though I'd agree with anything Julia says right now.

My arms ache from the constant cradling, and my ears are assaulted by the endless cries. So, to have Julia hold H2 without issue or complaint, for 20 minutes, is like a dream come true. I need to have her round more often.

See, that's the thing they don't tell you before you have kids- how much babies want to be held. It's almost impossible to do anything with them. I don't remember hearing any of this from my older sisters. Maybe I've forgotten? Or maybe I didn't notice because it wasn't my problem? Or maybe every time I saw them as new mums, they were with company, so had infinite pairs of hands to help. I remember holding middle sis' youngest for about 40 minutes when we visited them at their house in Bradford. I only handed her over when I lost the feeling in my forearm.

Julia continues swaying H2, as though they're doing a slow dance. "I'm going to be an auntie," she tells me.

"Really? Is Jemima pregnant?" I ask.

I haven't seen Julia's younger sister in years. She's been forever travelling and even missed Julia's engagement party. I don't hear much about her, either.

"Yes," Julia replies. "She won the baby race! The thing is, she didn't tell any of us straight away. Obviously, mother was fraught with worry given that Jemima lives all the way in Brazil. There is also a small issue that she's not in a relationship."

"Huh? How?" I try to keep a lid on my prim Bengali ways but can't hide my surprise at the idea of Jemima being a mum without a partner.

"How indeed! It's someone she was working with when she was teaching English in a school. They were never a proper item, so it was totally unexpected. However, she's going to go ahead with it and is adamant she will raise the baby over there by herself."

"God, I'm finding it hard enough having a baby in London without my family nearby. And I've got a husband."

Julia exhales. "Jemima has never been one to go by the rules. Unlike me, who ticked every box for mum and dad." She sits down with H2. "Oh well, I guess I'll have to live vicariously through her. And you."

I shuffle across the sofa to sit next to Julia. "It will happen for you."

She smiles tightly. "I know. Let's get the wedding out of the way first, though."

Julia looks down at her feet and plays with a hairball that's attached itself to her sock. God, I'm mortified. Not least because Julia's flat is pristine. Also, because it's Julia. She's never seen me like this. She's never seen my flat like this. The bin is full of nappies. The windowsills are dusty. There is hair, all mine, everywhere. The dishes are piled in the sink, along with a baby bottle that hasn't made its way to the steriliser. The cooker top has greasy pots of various dishes, one of which is unfortunately yesterday's sautéed cauliflower. Ordinarily, I would never have Julia round in such a state. However, I'm desperate for any company from anyone.

I'm half tempted to whip around the flat, hoovering and dusting while Julia has got H2 but then it might seem like I'm taking advantage. After all, she hasn't visited me for free babysitting. Then again, looking at Julia, leaning back blissfully while H2 sleeps on her shoulder, I don't think she'd mind at all.

"Shall we head out?" I ask.

"Yes," says Julia, eyes still closed as she enjoys the dopamine fix from my newborn. "You go get ready, no rush."

I head to the bedroom and begin my military operation:

- Changing bag – check.
- Spare bottle of formula – check.
- Spare, sterilised baby bottle – check.
- Changing mat – check.
- Nappies – check.
- Wipes – check.
- Nappy sacks – check.
- Muslin cloth - check.
- Spare baby grow – check.
- Spare vest – check.

Right, that's everything, I think. I gather all the bits in the bag and come into the living room to see Julia still in a dreamlike state.

"It's the newborn baby smell," she says, intoxicated. "Honestly, they should bottle that stuff and sell it as perfume."

The moment is interrupted by a fart from H2.

She sits up. "She might need a nappy change," Julia declares.

"Oh my God. I'm so sorry, has she pooed on you? It sounded like a wet one."

I'm mortified. H2 has done an explosive poo across my bare legs and on M's work trousers but, she has never shat on a friend. And of all friends to defecate on…

Julia examines her emerald silk shirt. "No, no. I'm unscathed. Though it does smell like there was some follow-through."

I retreat to the bedroom as I think Julia has been traumatized enough, she doesn't need to see me change H2's nappy.

While my friend got off lightly, the same can't be said for my baby's clothes. The contents of her nappy have exploded onto her vest and the inside of her baby grow.

I change her hurriedly, with shaking fingers, as I don't want Julia to be waiting any longer. She might not want to hang around with me much more, if this is what happens when we get together. I put H2 in a fresh set of clothes and carry her into the living room, changing bag slung over my shoulder.

Then I hear another rip. "Oh no you didn't." I glare at my baby. She returns a sleepy smile.

Julia laughs. "Oh, yes she did."

Another full outfit change later and we are in the lift, heading to the lobby. I never noticed how claustrophobic the lift is until I had to take my pram inside. Now, it seems like Julia and I are packed against the walls. For anyone else wanting to join us, forget it.

As we exit the lift, my neighbour, Taslima, is about to go in.

"You're brave," she says. "It's raining outside."

I examine my outfit. I'm wearing the same nursing-friendly wrap top I fell asleep in last night. In my rush to get everything ready for H2, I forgot to put on a coat.

I've only seen Taslima once since H2 was born. She knocked on when my parents came and stayed over, after we'd been discharged from the hospital the second time. She came bearing a helium baby balloon and a card which contained a £20 note. Mum asked her to look out for me. Taslima said she would, before swiftly leaving.

"How is the little lady?" Taslima asks.

"She's good. You must come round sometime," I say, trying to hide my eagerness.

"I will do," Taslima replies. "I've just been really busy with the kids as my middle one's started Arabic and as for Hamza, he's my permanent limpet." She smiles at her toddler, who is busy playing with all the buttons outside the lift. "I'll drop you a text message soon," she says as she's pulled into the lift by her son.

"That's nice. Is she your neighbour?" Julia asks.

"She is and yeah, she's lovely. Before H2 was born, she sent homemade lasagna over."

Julia wrinkles up her nose. "Now I feel bad about turning up with Border biscuits. You know cooking isn't one of my top five skills."

"Never feel bad about Border biscuits. They are the king of biscuits."

As we walk towards the café, I feel lighter. Freezing cold in my thin top and getting drizzled by rain, but lighter. Having Julia by my side makes this whole parenthood thing less anxiety-inducing. It's the same when M comes home from work. I breathe a huge sigh of relief, knowing that there's someone else party to this. Someone I can turn to when H2 is crying. Someone I can look to, even if they can't do anything. It's just moral support. I'd liken it to if you fall over in public by yourself. It's awkward, isn't it? You get up, dust yourself off and go about your business, knowing that any onlookers are trying their best not to laugh at you. However, if you fall over in the presence of a friend, you can laugh and joke together about it. You've got someone to share in the shame. Okay, so that's nothing like parenting but it kind of is. Whatever, I'm sleep-deprived. Nothing makes sense right now.

A motorbike, with an unnecessarily noisy engine, roars past us, beeping as we are about to cross. I stumble back with the pram. He should've stopped. It was a bloody red light! It was our right of way. Idiot. Did he not care that he nearly knocked over a newborn?

"Absolute maniac," says Julia. "Look, he's got company." She points to a line of motorcycles waiting at the lights, engines juddering away.

H2's bottom lip starts quivering. I shake the pram in an attempt to settle her.

I never realised how noisy this road was. How noisy and unfit for a baby.

Julia fills me in about work. How she's up to her eyeballs in caseloads and really wants to jack it all in and go for an easier job. However, the pull of the bigger salary coupled with the need to get a few years under her belt is keeping her chained to her desk. I'm nodding along, not fully paying attention. It's the strangest thing. Pre-kids, I'm talking just a couple of months back, Julia and I would discuss our careers at length.

We would be each other's accountability buddies. Even though we were in completely different fields, her being a family solicitor, and me being a PR consultant. We shared a commonality. We both needed to hustle and find new clients all the time. Now, everything Julia says is going over my hazy head. My attention is on the rows of black bin bags left outside the various shops, restaurants, and beauty salons. One bag has spilled onto the street, revealing its contents of old sandwiches and pies. This never really bothered me before I had a baby. I was acutely aware that I am in a pricey, yet edgy part of London. I liked where we live.

Now, however, I can't help but wonder, am I raising my kid in an urban cesspit?

We head to a very trendy café, which has that East London vibe of being a little bit scruffy. None of the tables match, neither do the chairs. The raw wood floor is barely smoothed out. And the clientele are mostly creatives, working on laptops, or indulging in an artisan coffee.

Julia and I are the only diners with a pram. H2 starts rustling. She's uncomfortable. I think she needs a feed. I get out the baby bottle. I put her in my arms and put the bottle to her lips. The milk feels cold. She looks tiny compared to the gargantuan bottle in her face.

"I really wanted to breastfeed her, but it doesn't seem to be working," I say to Julia, but loudly enough for everyone else to hear.

I feel I need to justify to everyone why my tiny newborn is being fed a huge bottle of formula. I hope they don't judge me too harshly.

"You've got to do what works for you," says Julia. "I was formula-fed and I was fine."

"So was I."

"There you go, then. I read a slogan somewhere on social media that said: 'Fed is best'. I think it's an antidote to breast is best."

"I've not seen that one," I say. "I've only seen endless posters extolling the virtues of nursing. Not to mention people at the hospital being disappointed that I couldn't breast-feed." I think for a second. "Actually, some were disappointed and others were indifferent. It was all very confusing. The lactation consultants were particularly disgruntled about it."

"Disgruntled. They had no right! You had complications! Anyway, it's none of their business how you feed your baby, is it?"

I scratch my head, trying to remember. "It might have been more my paranoia. I'm not sure. A lot happened when I was in the hospital. Anyway, I've got the breastfeeding consultant coming round soon so she'll be able to help me figure this whole thing out."

"Good. And remember, you're doing amazing. Just look at her. She looks so cute with that giant bottle. It's bigger than her face." Julia laughs, though her attempt to amuse me has actually made me feel worse.

23rd April, A close shave

We've had to get the big guns in.

Auntie Rukhsana has come over for the industrious occasion of H2's head shaving. It's been 21 days, you see. We can't put it off any longer. Plus, her head is funky.

"It be very different when my kids were born," auntie Rukhsana says, examining H2's sticky scalp. "Back then, the nurse would give the baby a bath while they were in hospital. I went home with nice, clean, fresh babies." She picks a flake of dry skin off my daughter's head. Actually, it's more like a chunk.

"It's different now," I say, slightly embarrassed. "We were told we shouldn't bathe the baby for the first three weeks, because their skin is so sensitive. It might cause eczema. So we have been giving her a sponge bath to keep her clean." I have to stop myself from screaming: "We're not filthy people!"

Auntie Rukhsana chuckles, picking yet more dry skin off my baby's fragile scalp. I wish she'd stop doing that. "Funny thing, children have been the same since time began, only grown-ups keep changing the rules."

M smiles knowingly. "That's what I said." He then brandishes a razor. "Shall we get started?"

Auntie Rukhsana mumbles lots of prayers under her breath as she holds H2. With an unsteady hand, M takes the razor to H2's head, while my heart rate rises. Unfortunately, the strong, thick Bengali hair doesn't budge. She really does have an excellent mane.

"I might have to trim it first," M decides.

So begins the military operation. M grabs strands of hair while H2, thankfully, sleeps on auntie Rukhsana. I hold my breath until I'm red in the face.

Black locks of hair scatter across the laminate floor, the coffee table, the sofa. It's a good thing everything is wipeable.

M grabs the razor again. He runs it over her hair, slowly and meticulously. Yet, as H2 still has a newly formed, bony skull, it's hard to get a perfect finish.

"Here, shall I do some?" Auntie Rukhsana offers. I suspect it's because her arm is starting to ache.

She is much more swift with the blade, as she's done it many a time before. I'm glad I opted for a woman's razor with a protective film to reduce the chance of any nicks.

"Would you like a turn?" Auntie Rukhsana holds the blade up towards me. "It is something for your memories."

I'd rather not have the memory of slicing my daughter's scalp. However, out of politeness and, given that I've brought nothing to the table so far, I take the razor and do a few polite shaves.

I distract my concern with small talk. I tell auntie Rukhsana how we bumped into Naila the other night. My auntie giggles and tells me how she has resigned herself to a life of free babysitting, especially now there's another grandchild on the way. I try to hide my seething jealousy. I would love someone to take my baby, even just to go to the toilet for half an hour. I can't imagine having an actual date night.

"Naila's baby had much less hair. Ibrahim's hair be fine and brown. You know, because her dad be English. Nothing like this one. She like little hedgehog."

I laugh and swell with pride at the inadvertent compliment. H2 has lovely, thick hair. It will be even thicker once it grows back. Or is that an old wives' tale?

Two hours later and we are done. H2 slept through the entire process. I can't quite believe such a small person has such an impressive head of hair that required a three person operation.

Then it's bath time. I fill the plastic tub with lukewarm water and check the temperature with the help of my new thermometer.

Auntie Rukhsana shakes her head, discards the thermometer, and instead dips her elbows in the water, declaring it to be warm enough.

"Her first bath!" Auntie Rukhsana declares.

"She's had sponge baths in between," I add.

As it's H2's first 'proper' bath, it seems appropriate to take some tasteful photos of her, with a strategically placed sponge to preserve her dignity.

M gazes adoringly at his daughter as he runs water over her little body. He carefully rubs around her belly button, which still has the peg attached to it. Everything involving H2, he does with such love. Whereas most things I do seem like a task. Is it because it's my sole job? Is it because he gets to go to work, have a cup of tea while it's still hot and pee with the door closed? Is it because my parenting role is all-encompassing? I hope that's it. I hope it's not that there's anything wrong with me and my relationship with my baby.

While M dries H2 and auntie Rukhsana excuses herself to pray, I check my phone. The messages from the NCT mums are more frequent as they are all at various stages of new motherhood. Melanie talks about how she got the Tube with her baby for the first time. Claudia says they've got a trip planned to Hong Kong. What? With the baby? Are they insane?

And there's me. I only leave the house when necessary, unless I'm with M. The truth is, I'm too anxious to go anywhere. I truly, deeply hope this feeling passes.

29th April, The lying-down feed

L et's do some journalling...

While much of my birth story was a blur, I will never forget the time H2 and I were finally discharged from hospital.

It was a huge relief to be well enough to go home and be a mum, away from the constant visits from nurses, doctors, and physios. The frequent blood tests, infusions, and all those things that were necessary, but excruciating, painful and stressful.

I followed the instructions of one of the parenting books, which suggested that I show H2 around our very small two-bed apartment. M tried his best to hide his smirk and go along with it. That's why I married him. He rolls along with all my weird shit. And it was weird. Kind of ridiculous. H2 was barely four days old. She wasn't even opening her eyes for longer than a second. She was hardly in a position to appraise our dwelling.

We then sat down for a cup of tea and watched the news on the telly. I leaned into M, my protector. H2 was happily dozing in and out and making random baby noises, while her hands clawed at the sky in jerky movements, like newborns do.

"Blimey," said M.

"What is it?" I asked.

He looked down towards my chest. My boobs were not only huge, they were rock hard to the point of uncomfortable.

"You look like a glamour model," said M.

"How do you know what glamour models look like?" I teased.

M covered his mouth, avoiding the question. "Seriously, though, is that normal?"

"I guess." I shrugged, enjoying the fact that, for the first time in my life, I had an ample bosom.

While bringing H2 home was a dream, bedtime was a nightmare. H2 was constantly crying. She couldn't settle. I couldn't put her down.

I remember nodding off in the sitting position, from the sheer exhaustion of it all. I remember M nagging me, saying we should give her a bottle. We should give her baby formula. Or that we should just let her cry. He was tired, too. He put her in the cot while she cried and cried and cried.

Within seconds, I caved and picked her up. I couldn't do it. I couldn't leave her. My baby had already been through so much, I couldn't let her whimper in the cot, all alone.

I don't know at what point we all fell asleep, but at some point, we did.

And then we were awoken by a knock on the door. It turned out we had a midwife appointment. I had no idea as I'd spent all my time so far in hospital. I couldn't tell you what day it was. I was mortified when they came in and saw the duvet piled up in the corner of the bed, half hanging off. Baby clothes everywhere. Some covered in vomit and piled in the corner. I'm surprised they didn't take H2 off our hands straight away and put her into care.

The two midwives who had come to visit couldn't hide their shock at the state of our bedroom. On the plus side, I was told I looked really well considering I'd lost such a lot of blood. They asked me how I felt. Checked some levels. Examined my tear and informed me it was healing well.

Then they stripped and weighed H2. They told me she was below a certain percentage of weight gain. Or was it lost? I don't remember. But the words I can hear in my ears to this day are the words that came from the midwife after I'd asked what her weight loss meant.

Without flinching, she replied: "She needs to go to A&E."

"Sorry?" I thought I misheard.

"She needs to go to the Accident and Emergency Department because she's lost so much weight."

AT THE RISK OF SOUNDING incredibly sad, I'm excited about the lactation consultant coming over. I need to get the hang of this breastfeeding gig and also, it'll be my first face-to-face adult conversation today. M left in a bit of a huff this morning as H2's incessant crying woke him up one too many times. He has to be on his A-game at his new job, as he's still on probation. He said it's hard for him to be disturbed so often as he has to get up for work. Despite his complaints, I would still happily swap with him. For at least a day.

I attempt to tidy a couple of bits while H2 is dozing in my bed, surrounded by pillows. That girl never really naps for more than 15 minutes at a time. Is that normal? I must ask the NCT mums on the WhatsApp group. I open up my messages to see I've missed a trail of conversations.

Genevieve has had her baby. A little boy and she's called him Oliver. Is she the last in the group to give birth? Or the penultimate one? I've lost track. Oliver is wearing a chunky cardigan with trousers. How has she got him into that outfit? Baby legs are so delicate and fiddly and curled up. After the ordeal of my extended stay in hospital, getting her into the cute little coming home outfit we'd bought early on in my pregnancy, was the last thing on our mind. She ended up in some random baby grow that wasn't covered in sick.

Melanie is talking about her birth. She said she had forceps because the baby was being choked by the umbilical cord.

I wonder to myself whether that is worse than what I went through, like it's some sick, masochistic, motherhood battle.

The doorbell rings, and I usher in the lactation consultant. Hilary is a slim, blonde lady who strikes a balance between seeming friendly and judgemental.

"She's having those big bottles?" she asks as she examines the barely drunk bottle of formula on the coffee table.

Okay, I'm going to settle with judgemental.

"That's what I was told she should have after she lost too much weight. The breastfeeding obviously wasn't working and she really needed to get her weight back up and stay healthy."

"I wouldn't call formula healthy."

Did the hospital really send this woman to see me? She is speaking very much at odds with what every consultant told me.

"The thing is," Hilary leans forward, "formula milk is designed to knock babies out. It's kind of like if you have a massive roast dinner, all you want to do is sleep. So it's artificially making them sleep. That's not what you want. It's not the best thing for her, either." Hilary strokes H2's head as she rests on the sofa. My baby behaves angelically when people are around, so it looks as though I'm complaining for no reason. "Poor thing. You don't want to be milk drunk, do you?" Hilary says in an annoying baby voice.

That's it. The tears are coming. And not from H2 this time.

"Oh." Hillary keeps her mouth agape for longer than need be. Surely I'm not the only mum that has cried in her presence?

I try to clarify things between sobs. "Not a single person told me that I wasn't breastfeeding properly. I was in hospital for three days before she lost all that weight and nobody said a thing. I went to all the antenatal classes. I did an NCT course. I attended the breastfeeding workshops. I even called the midwife hotline when I came home, because I knew something was wrong. I knew it wasn't right that she should be crying this much. I kept getting told that if she's having wet nappies, then it's okay. And she did have wet nappies. So I thought she must be fine. Since then, I've been riddled with guilt. The hospital consultant said she needs to have formula. You're saying she should be breastfed. My husband says I should give up mixed-feeding and stick to bottles. I don't know what to do! I'm trying my best. I didn't expect it to be this hard. I didn't expect it to hurt this much."

"Oh." Clearly, Hilary isn't sure what else to say. "I'm sorry you felt like that. Breastfeeding shouldn't be hard. If it's hurting, then something's not quite happening right."

"Nobody told me that," I say, between more ugly crying. I've clearly lost all sense of etiquette. "I remember when the nurse at the high dependency unit, who was lovely, by the way, said to me breastfeeding should hurt. I thought it was normal. Even when I became engorged, I didn't know what that was. I was just enjoying the fact that I had a nice chest."

Hillary sits up, looking very prim.

"The point is," I continue, "I didn't expect any of this to be this hard and nobody has really shown me the way. Instead, I've received conflicting advice and guilt trips."

"Do you have family nearby? Your mum, perhaps?" Hilary asks.

"No. It's just me and my husband. I have an aunt and uncle in London but they're busy enough with their own daughter, who's got a toddler and is pregnant again."

"Ah." Hilary sighs as though she's found the root cause of the problem. "Don't worry." She rests her hand on my arm. "I'll help you."

Hilary watches while I attempt to feed H2, though it's only a short demonstration as my cheeky baby falls asleep after two suckles.

She tells me how she once left her own daughter in a department store, because she was so tired she hadn't realised she'd gone home without her pram. I told her that is my worst nightmare.

Hilary shows me how to breastfeed lying down, ensuring that I get some sleep, while H2 satisfies her need to be fed round the clock. She also warns me that, as a mum, I'm going to have lots more tears and even more worry. She said she still checks on her daughter now, even though she's 11, to make sure she's breathing at night.

I wish someone had warned me about the worry. I wish someone had told me to make the most of life before H2.

Had I known, I would've, I don't know, maybe enjoyed more lie ins? More date nights? I certainly would've done more of everything that I don't know if I'll ever be able to do again.

Hilary leaves, telling me that I have her number and can be in touch again if I need any further support. What started as a fraught meeting, ended up being very productive. I've learnt how to breastfeed lying down, which might just save my sanity and give me some sleep. For that, I am truly, truly grateful. As for the crying in front of her bit, maybe it needed to happen. Maybe I've just got a pool of tears that need to come out, bit by bit, to release everything that has happened in such a short space of time.

My phone rings. It's mum.

"I was thinking," mum begins, "do you want to come and stay here for a *lit-ool* bit? Just while baby small, I can help you?"

Here they come again. The tears. Because mum has offered something that I really, truly need right now.

1st May, Back to Manchester

No sooner had mum uttered those magical words: 'Would you like to stay over?' M and I bombed it up the motorway, travelling 200 miles up north, with H2.

As we enter my parents' three bed semi, it looks as though mum may have some regrets.

"All this for a *lit-ool* baby?" She chuckles as M unloads the boot like it's a bottomless pit.

"It's all necessary stuff, mum," I say, as my parents' small, modest front room is taken over by a baby bath, bouncer chair, car seat, playmat, changing mat and various other bits and pieces.

"What all this?" Dad asks, exploring the baby stuff strewn all over the floor.

"It's for the baby," I reply. H2 coos in agreement.

"Such a small thing need so many things?" Dad laughs as he manoeuvres his way onto the sofa. En route, he stops to pat H2's leg. "She's not a fair one, is she?"

For a moment, I'm taken back to my own childhood, when I was made acutely aware that I was the darkest of all my sisters. I heard it from aunties, strangers, my own mother. Now, my own father is saying it about my daughter.

M looks at me and shrugs. "It's a generational thing."

"What can she do?" Mum chuckles. "She still be a pretty lady."

I note the emphasis on 'still'. She's still pretty, despite being dark.

Little sis comes downstairs, leaving little room for me to unpack my feelings. "Awww, let's see the bubs- God, that's a lot of stuff," she says, stumbling over the changing mat.

I get it. We may have over-packed.

WHEN M LEAVES AND H2 is held by little sis (I'm already seeing the benefits of staying at mum's) I excuse myself for an extended toilet break so I can journal some more. I'm not sure where I'm going with all this writing but I hope there's some benefit at the end.

When we were admitted to hospital again...

H2 needed to go to A&E because she wasn't gaining any weight. This felt like a failure. A punch in the stomach. Something that was so basic as feeding my child was beyond my capabilities.

On the way to hospital, my phone beeped repeatedly. Messages from my uni friends Reena and Sonali, and my former workmate, Bushra, asking if I'd had the baby yet. I was fielding calls from middle sis. She wanted to come over. They'd apparently filled the car with petrol and were ready to make the journey from Bradford to London that very second. She felt inconvenienced that I wouldn't be in my flat to receive her. She asked what would happen next at the hospital. I told her I didn't know. She asked when I'd be home. Again, I didn't know.

I vaguely remember visiting my sisters in hospital after they had their babies. They seemed like happy, joyous occasions. The noticeboard behind them would be pinned with cards. They'd received fresh flowers and fruit. It was a different time. The etiquette now is that people will visit you at home after the baby is born. Except, nobody expected that I'd be in hospital this long. I didn't expect this, either. I didn't expect any of this.

In the hospital waiting room, I gazed at the fish tank. There was a blue and yellow stripey fish cruising through the water, while the smaller goldfish darted in and out of the fake foliage.

This place brought on so many feelings. One of immense, immense gratitude for the level of care I received. I'd got a gigantic room to give birth in. If I had lived in another country where I would need to pay for my treatment, I would probably be bankrupt given that I'd stayed longer at hospital than the average new mum. I was thankful for the nurses and midwives for the care they provide. God bless the NHS. Then, at the same time, I felt such anger at how my birth story played out. I hated the white lights at the hospital. I hated the sound of the beeping monitors. I hated the fact that a visit here meant that my daughter, or I, were unwell.

I started sobbing when they stripped baby H2 to check her tiny vitals. M cried, too. She was mildly jaundiced. All that wailing, all that fussing. Those times M got fed up and told me she just needs to cry to sleep. She wasn't being difficult. She was hungry. Starving, in fact.

We were in hospital for three more days. This time, there wasn't the luxury of our own room. I was on the ward. The noisy, busy ward. I didn't sleep. One night was so bad because H2 wouldn't settle anywhere besides on me and the hospital wouldn't allow co-sleeping. I walked around with her, helpless, desperate. Every bottle she drank would be vomited out. I went through so many outfits, so much bed linen. We eventually got some sleep. I woke at 8am to find myself in my bed and H2 in her cot, though I have no idea how either of us got to our respective spaces. I imagine that's what it's like to be extremely drunk.

Still exhausted, I allowed myself to close my eyes, only to be woken by the rattle of the cubicle curtain as a lady came over to take my breakfast order.

That's the thing with the maternity ward. If it's not your baby keeping you awake, it'll be everything and everyone else.

That day I had a blind panic. I was about to prepare a bottle of formula, when I suddenly stopped in my tracks, unable to move. I was overwhelmed by this feeling that I couldn't do this. I couldn't be a mum. I was exhausted, panicked, frightened.

Then I heard the rattle of the curtain again. This time it was a woman who I initially assumed was a member of staff. She asked me to fill out a form, then tried to sell me a newborn photoshoot! In my current state? Fuck, no.

Having fended her off, I called M, who had finally gone home after a night sleeping on the chair next to my bed. He came straight over with the extra baby grows I'd requested, only he'd got the 3-6 months size instead of the newborn ones. I didn't shout at him. It wasn't his fault. He was doing his best. We both were.

M saw my distress and called over a midwife to come and have a word with me. She told me, gently, that it is going to be hard but it's nothing I can't handle. She also mentioned that, as I'd been roaming the ward all night, hogging the nurses' station, *and* I'd been admitted via A&E because I hadn't fed my daughter properly, that I ought to really just get on with it. Otherwise, the longer I'm kept in hospital, the more things they'll find and the more questions will be raised. I'm not sure if it was meant like that but that's how it felt. It was like: *get your shit together and show the world you're fit enough to be a mum.*

There was one nurse I was very fond of. She was Eastern European. She was gentle. When I was fed up and frustrated, which was basically the duration of my whole stay, she would come over and whisper: "It's okay, I'll look after you."

She would keep an eye on H2 while I went to the toilet. She fetched me extra bed linen, as she knew I had a sickie baby.

H2 wasn't the only one being examined during this second stint at hospital. Given my traumatic birth, my vitals were checked, too. My blood pressure dipped and peaked. My heart rate was erratic at times. It was also discovered that I was still iron deficient due to the postpartum blood loss.

The pushy saleswoman who wanted to sign me up for some newborn photoshoot visited me two more times. She was really starting to get on my tits. I could barely recognise myself in the mirror. The last thing I wanted to do was immortalise this time with a picture.

My stay was punctuated by WhatsApp messages from other mums from the NCT group who were sharing the first photos of their newborns. I realised I hadn't done that yet, despite being the first to give birth.

There was a girl on the bed next to me. She was younger. Late 20s, tops. She was constantly on her phone, laughing and joking. She had family round. She had a husband come over regularly. Her baby was unwell in the ICU, though you wouldn't know from her demeanour. Or perhaps she was just too naive to realise the gravity of the situation.

A couple more days of shit sleep had left me delirious. More than once, I'd gone to the bathroom and got lost on my way back. Everything looked the same. Each bed had a dark blue pleated curtain around it. Each bay had the same wooden MDF door and magnolia walls. Heck, all the babies looked the same. At one point, my sleep deprivation was so severe that I was convinced that someone was taking my baby. It was another family pushing a cot with another brown baby. But in that moment, I swore she was mine.

Mum, hearing of my ordeal, had come down to London on the train with dad and little sis. When I saw them, tears streamed down my eyes. It was the relief of seeing a familiar face beyond M.

Some stability in this unstable new world. A world I entered so naively, thinking M and I could do all this by ourselves, with the help of a few baby books.

Mum wiped the tears from my eyes and said: "It be okay. Well done, you done it." But the tears kept coming.

We were discharged later that day.

H2 was deemed to have gained enough weight. I was deemed to be a fit enough mother.

H2 was eight days old.

"WHAT YOU DO?" MUM ASKS.

"I'm expressing milk. It will help with my supply."

"Ouch. That look painful. Does it hurt?"

"No, it's just a bit uncomfortable."

Mum sighs. "I feel so sad looking at you doing that. You being drained. Isn't it better to feed her direct?" She looks over at H2, who is wedged between two pillows, having a light nap.

"Apparently I'm meant to do both. She's still not feeding properly so I need to express at the same time. Otherwise, I'll never get her to latch on properly." I feel tears sting my eyes. I blink them away.

"I *doh-noh*. I think you're doing too much. You need rest, too."

"I will rest, mum."

"And can you stop with that milk pump? You look like a little cow being milked."

"Alright, mum."

"And don't keep pillows so close to her head, she might suffocate!"

"Mum, I can see her! She's fine. She'll only sleep if she feels like she's cocooned."

"*Nah, nah.* It not be safe. She need space. And look how tightly she be wrapped. She might hurt her arms."

"No, mum. For the first three months, she needs to be swaddled."

"Let me loosen the arms a *lit-ool* bit."

"Mum! Leave it!" I lean forward. The breast pump falls. The milk spills across the beige carpet. H2 wakes up, screaming.

I put the bottle upright and it tips again due to the uneven weight of the cone attachment. I'll have to deal with it later.

Mum picks H2 up and she immediately settles in her grandmother's arms.

"Look, she be hungry. Try and feed her now."

I put her to my chest. She moves her head away.

"Don't worry." Mum pats my shoulder. "It get easier. You here now. I can help."

And with that, I lean towards mum and let the tears roll freely.

What is it with all these emotions?

7th May, Priorities

The danger of having email on your phone is that you're inclined to check it all the time.

I've just received a message from my client, Raymond. Or should I say rather, I am copied into the email, which was sent to Vanessa, the freelancer I hired to cover me during maternity leave.

It reads:

Amazing work, Vanessa! Nigel was really happy with the piece, even though he was shy about having his photo featured in the magazine. Keep up the good work.

I'm hoping Vanessa's good work isn't better than mine. After all, she's only keeping my seat warm for a year. I wonder whether I should jump in and reply, also congratulating Vanessa, while subtly exerting my authority.

Then, I decide it's not worth it. I literally birthed a baby weeks ago. I shouldn't be checking my emails. All is in hand, and I should be grateful for that. It means I can focus on more pressing matters, such as my baby's increased bouts of crying.

H2 has just vomited out the latest premixed bottle of baby formula. Luckily, I managed to catch most of it on the burping cloth. I am so, so grateful that mum has laminate flooring downstairs. I detested it most of the time when I lived at home. It always felt cold. Now, I am glad for its easily wipeable abilities. At least it saves on mum grimacing away.

"You think it might be colic?" asks mum. "I not really know what it is but I heard people talk about it on Bangla health programme."

"I'm not sure. I'll check." I head to my most trusted resource, Google. The problem is, colic can also be mistaken for so many other things as its symptoms are rather broad.

"Shall we call doctor?" mum asks.

"She's not registered here, mum."

"Oh yes, and if you go hospital, you be waiting hours."

I look at H2. She's clearly upset but I don't think it warrants a trip to the emergency department.

"I know!" Mum has an a-ha moment. "Let's take her to pharmacy. I saw advert saying they can give you a *lit-ool* bit advice. Obviously not as good as doctor but better than nothing." Mum lifts her hands in a weighing motion, as if comparing the advice of a qualified pharmacist, with nothing at all.

I will do anything to stop H2's howling.

"Hold on. I get your father to come, too. Might be help having a man with us. And he not been out all day."

Ten minutes later, we leave the house, walk past my fully functioning, fully serviced, perfectly usable car that I am too scared to drive, and head into a taxi. I am pathetic, I know.

"Why does she keep crying?" dad asks from the passenger seat.

"I don't know." I gently rock H2, as if the car isn't providing enough motion.

"Could you hold her still?" The taxi man stares at me in the rear-view mirror. "A baby that size ought to be in a car seat. Not in your arms." Then he mumbles under his breath: "This isn't Pakistan."

"We're Bengali," dad corrects him, though it doesn't make a difference to this cabbie.

At the pharmacy, there is one customer in front of us, an older man enquiring into verruca treatment. I huff and sigh and cause enough of a commotion for another member of staff to come from behind the wall and serve me.

"Can I speak to the pharmacist, please?" I ask.

"I'm the pharmacist," the young Asian lad replies.

"Oh okay, sorry. It's just my daughter. She keeps crying and arching her back and I don't know what it is."

The boy strokes his thin, neat beard and looks at H2 with kind eyes. "Sorry to ask the obvious but is she feeding okay, or does she need a nappy change?"

I lift H2's bum to my face. No bad smells detected.

"Feeding is not going so well. She doesn't latch onto my breast as I had quite a traumatic birth so she was separated from me. I had a tear and lost a lot of blood, you see."

Mum grimaces and dad has a fake coughing fit, then he starts walking away to examine the haemorrhoid creams on the shelf. Now is not the time for prudish parents. This is a potential medical emergency.

"So... anyway, I was struggling to get her to feed. I made a bit of progress. But she's mixed-feeding. I'm hoping to get rid of the bottle so she can be exclusively breastfed. That aside, I'm not sure why she is still crying."

I hold my daughter over the counter, as though she's a prescription, for the pharmacist to get a better look.

"I couldn't say anything from looking at her. Let me go to the back and speak to a colleague."

As soon as the pharmacist leaves our sight, mum elbows me. "Do you think he be Bengali?"

"What? Mum, I don't care."

"I can't tell. Usually Bengali boys be small and dark. He seems quite tall, too. Do you think he be standing a *lit-ool* bit higher? Sometimes pharmacy counter is higher for them to better see people. I no sure. You go round to take a look when they be busy."

"Don't be ridiculous, mum. My daughter is not well. I've not got time to check how tall the pharmacist is. Plus, I'm married."

"Dooro!" Mum tuts. "Not for you. Obviously, too late for you now you married and old and with baby. And you keep telling everyone about your ripped lady part. No chance of getting man. I meant for your *lit-ool* sister. We need to think about her. We never see any nice looking Bengali boys. The only Bengalis we know live in Longsight. And nobody want to go there."

H2 momentarily stops crying and falls asleep. Poor thing, she must be exasperated by all of this. Either that, or she wants to tune mum out. I wouldn't blame her if that was the case.

"He coming! Quick, ask him."

I ignore mum, and instead listen to the pharmacist, who imparts advice I've heard before. Hold her upright, see if she's gassy. Otherwise, it may be colic, but best to offer another feed. That reminds me, I think I'm out of formula milk.

Mum walks over to dad and says in hushed but still audible tones: "Ask that boy if he's from Bangladesh. Maybe for our youngest."

Dad looks to the ground. "What I ask?"

"I just told you what to ask!"

Mum comes back to me. "Shall we ask your sister to come here?"

"Mum!"

"No, no. I mean to give us lift home. Save £3.50 on taxi fare. Also, while she be here, she can take a look at him." Mum laughs, almost flirtatiously, at the pharmacist. He smirks, looking unsure, as most people do when mum wants to quiz them on their ethnicity.

Despite mum's ulterior motives, I must agree that getting a lift home would be easier.

I get my phone to message little sis, but it looks like she's beaten me to it. She's messaged, saying: *I just got back home and I'm going to take the car to the supermarket. Let me know if you need anything.*

Damn, she sent her message 20 minutes ago. She's probably there now.

"Excuse me." Dad clears his throat. "Are you from Bangladesh?"

The pharmacist looks up. "Sorry uncle, I'm Pakistani."

Well, that's that then.

IN THE COMMOTION OF the wasted trip to the pharmacy, where we left without medication or a potential husband, I completely forgot to tell little sis to get formula milk. I can hardly tell her now, she's just got back from the supermarket.

H2 is still crying intermittently.

"Hold her upright," is mum's order. "Here, let me try."

She takes H2 and cradles her against her chest. This seems to soothe my little one as she stops crying and melts into mum. "Do you want to try breastfeeding her again?" asks mum.

"I tried before but she keeps moving her face away."

"What about milk you pump last night? Do you have any of that?"

I sigh. "I had to throw it away. I forgot to put it in the fridge." My heart hurts at the memory of pouring my liquid gold down the drain.

"Oh yes. I saw the bottles. You have to clean them otherwise you get bacteria on them. Why you not do that now, while I hold her?"

"I'll do it in a minute, mum," I say, trying to enjoy a minute of respite.

When I'm not feeding, I'm changing nappies, or cradling, or cleaning bottles, or expressing. I cannot believe how much hands-on time there is looking after someone so small and immobile.

Little sis enters the room. "Whatcha doing?" She says to H2, stroking her cheek.

H2 purrs back at her.

"Will you take her?" That was a rhetorical question from mum as she passes H2 to little sis. "I've not even read namaz yet. Time is nearly going."

"You already prayed, mum," little sis replies.

Mum looks confused. "I did? Oh yes, I did! Of course, but I should sit and read Quran for bit. I not done that in days as been so busy with..." Mum looks to me. "And can you wash your bottles? They be growing dirty and taking up too much space in kitchen. I need to make chicken later. You don't want chicken juice on your bottles."

"Fine, I'll do it." I trudge my way into the kitchen.

There are three bottles waiting for me, some with the cloudy remnants of breastmilk. I really do need to buy some formula milk.

H2 starts crying. Little sis comes into the kitchen with her. "I'm not sure what to do. Does she need a nappy change?" she asks.

"I don't know. Does she smell?"

Little sis raises H2's bum towards her nose. "Not really. do you think she's hungry?"

The bottle I was mid-scrubbing falls out of my hand. Half of its contents spill out into the counter, while the rest drips into the sink.

There it is again. Bloody tears. Tears from exhaustion, tears from frustration. But mostly, tears from guilt. The guilt that's haunted me since we went back with H2 to A&E.

"Are you okay?" Little sis isn't sure whether to continue cuddling H2 or hug me.

"It's just so fucking hard. I never realised it would be like this. If I did, I wouldn't have had a baby. I'd honestly recommend not having kids," I say between sobs. "Let's normalise being child-free."

"It does seem really hard," little sis sympathises. "I couldn't do it. I can't believe she wakes up so much at night. I can hear her from the other room."

"Oh no. Is it disturbing you?" I feel like I'm putting everyone out with my stay here.

"No, it's fine. I put my headphones in. Anyway, if you want to give her a feed, I can wash the bottles for you. You just need to show me how to do it," little sis offers.

I could give her a hug. All my life, little sis has been the one in need of help. A lift here and there. Help with filling out forms. Now, she is the one stepping up.

"The problem is, I don't think she's getting much from breastfeeding. So, I'm still topping her up with formula. And... I've run out of formula!" I burst out crying once more.

This is ridiculous. I'm ridiculous. Helpless and hopeless.

The thing is, in London, everything was to hand. Running out of milk wasn't a huge deal as I could walk with H2 to the big Sainsbury's. Here, at my parents' house, I feel like I've lost all my independence. The nearest supermarket is a drive away and, as I've barely driven in London, and I certainly haven't driven with a baby in tow, I just don't have the confidence to do it. The thought of negotiating traffic, finding a parking spot, taking the car seat out, attaching the car seat to the pram... I can't imagine executing such a military operation without making a huge fuck up.

I never knew by having a baby, I would lose all my independence and sense of self. This isn't me.

"Where do you need to get the formula from?" asks little sis.

"I'm so sorry," I say. "I'm so, so sorry. I shouldn't be sending you out this late in the evening."

Little sis shrugs. "It's alright. I go to my friends' in the evening sometimes, when dad's gone to sleep. Just tell me what you need and I'll get it."

I wipe my eyes and take H2 from my younger sister's arms. "It's the ready-made formula. They look like little bottles that already have the milk in. Not the powdered box thingy. I think you have to drive to a big supermarket for it."

"That's fine. I'll take mum. Actually, I won't. She makes me nervous driving."

"Me too. When I used to drive, that is. Also, since you're going, could you get me some salt and vinegar crisps?"

Don't judge me. I'm having a hard time.

8th May, Tears, tears and more tears

Crying has become my default state. I've cried in front of mum, M, every health worker I've encountered, and anyone else who wants to see some ugly tears.

Now is the turn of my in-laws.

My father-in-law becomes bashful. "It be nothing. Baby healthy, so what problem?" he asks, with half an eye on his Bengali documentary about tea gardens. "Look how she is now." He reaches his hand out to take baby H2 from my arms.

I happily pass her over.

My father-in-law reveals a gappy smile. He's forgotten to put his false teeth in again. H2 seems to bring out a playful side of him that I've never seen before. As the other grand-children in the family are older, baby H2 is a novelty. He looks at her, making cooing sounds and being more animated than ever. All the while, H2 lays asleep, mouth agape.

"She be so small," my mother-in-law exclaims. "Does she have enough milk? Are you giving bottle?"

"A bit. I'm actually trying to breastfeed but it's hard as it didn't work out first." More tears fill my eyes. What the actual hell is wrong with me?

"Never mind," my mother-in-law offers in consolation. "Bottle better, anyway. Breastmilk won't be enough for them."

M's younger brother comes into the room upon the sound of crying.

"You alright?" goes his usual greeting.

"Yeah, I'm good."

My father-in-law looks like he's struggling to hold H2 for much longer, especially now that she's woken up from her 10 minute nap and is wriggling around.

My mother-in-law takes over. "There she is. You are the newest one, aren't you? Look at her, she's got everything of yours," she says to M. "You're like twins!"

M beams proudly. "Even down to the bald head now!"

M's mum strokes H2's head, which is patchy in places.

"You want rice? Eat something. I made chicken and beef and there's some fish." M's mum urges.

"I'm not that hungry," I say, before realising she is asking her son, M, not me.

"We'll eat in a bit," says M.

In a bit? How long will we be staying for? I thought it was a quick sip and see. Though I shouldn't be so on edge visiting my in-laws with a newborn. After all, she surely wouldn't ask me to peel any onions or bash any ginger in my raw, postpartum state, would she?

"Okay, I put extra rice on." M's mum lowers H2, who's gone back to sleep, down onto the sofa, putting a floral sausage pillow on her side to prevent her from falling. My baby doesn't even flinch. Not one single jerky movement. Why doesn't she sleep so undisturbed for me? It's like she already knows better than to mess with my mum-in-law. Sensible.

"Come in here," says M's mum, ushering me into the kitchen.

No freaking way. No way is she asking me to help with cooking, is she? I follow her in nervously.

"Would you like tea?" she asks.

Phew. She doesn't want to make a spontaneous batch of samosas, kebabs or soy fita.

"I'm okay, thank you," I reply.

My mother-in-law boils the kettle for herself. "I know you no like fish but try some. It's good for breastmilk."

"I will do."

I hear H2 rustling and then comes the familiar baby cry.

Dare I say, I'm relieved. If she doesn't nap for me when I'm at home and I could sit around doing nothing, she damn well shouldn't be napping here.

I take H2 into the small room at the back of the kitchen, which houses a fridge, a chest freezer, a linen basket, a washing machine, a drum containing rice and other bits and bobs that don't have a place elsewhere in the house. M's mum follows closely behind.

"You have bottle?" she asks, scooping some rice from the big plastic drum into a stainless steel cooking pot.

"No, I'm going to breastfeed her."

My mother-in-law nods her head from side to side. I can't tell if it's disapproval or indifference but I haven't got time to analyse her.

"Nobody will come into the room, will they?" I ask, suddenly aware that I'm not at home so can't have my boobs out freely.

"No, no. Just be us at home."

My mother-in-law goes to pray upstairs as I've taken her usual spot in the back room. M's dad is in the living room watching the news and I'm not sure where M is. He always finds a reason to disappear when he comes to his mum's.

I loosen my blue and green stripey scarf around H2's head and latch her on. To my relief, she starts suckling and it doesn't hurt. That is progress.

The door swings open, M's little brother bursts in, then quickly turns back without saying a word.

My God, I hope I didn't flash him.

"Err... can I get some milk when you're done?" he asks from behind the door. "From the fridge?"

I'm glad he clarified that he wants the shop-bought, full fat milk, and not the watery stuff I'm feeding my daughter.

"Yeah sure. Won't be long," I reply, to the sound of my younger brother-in-law running out of the kitchen, no doubt traumatised by what he may or may not have seen.

H2 is such a slow feeder. She suckles. Then she unlatches and rests her perfectly puckered mouth on my bosom. Then she suckles again. I can never tell if she's had enough. I'm also not sure how long I should be holed up in the back room at M's parents' house. People need to access things like the fridge, or the second bathroom. I use my little finger to loosen her gummy grip on me. Of course she starts crying. Of course my mother-in-law comes in just at that moment, like she's been waiting behind the door.

"Oh, she still hungry. Do you want to give a bottle?"

"No, I'll try to feed her some more."

My mother-in-law shakes her head. "Breastmilk be watery. It won't make her full. Maybe give her a bit of bottle."

I inhale deeply to calm my nerves. "It's okay. She'll settle."

This time, I'm pretty certain it's a look of disapproval from my mother-in-law as she leaves the room. I'm not sure whether H2 has given up on the milking or she's satisfied but she falls asleep, nonetheless. I think it's our cue to go. I'm not comfortable here with the potential of people walking in and out and the questions around nursing.

M's little sister comes down once I've finished feeding H2. She looks awkward, as she often does, as I re-fasten the cup of my bra.

"Sorry, it's going to be a boob show while I'm here," I say.

She laughs and her eyes dart from side to side. She is a woman now. She'll have to get used to it.

"Do you want to hold her?" I ask, as H2 wakes from her micro-nap.

She looks at me, surprised, as if she wasn't expecting this rather normal offer.

"Yeah, okay. But I'm a bit nervous about dropping her. I haven't held a newborn in years, since my big brother's kids were born."

"Here... I'll help you."

M's little sister sits next to me, arms out and ready for action. I ease H2 onto her. Both seem uncomfortable, with my baby writhing around, while her auntie holds her as if she's a wobbling jelly.

"Do you want to hold her upright? My little sister seems to find that easier."

"Are you sure? Is that safe?" M's little sister looks even more nervous, if that were possible.

"Yeah, it's fine. In fact, it'll strengthen her core. As long as you support the head."

After trying this new position, H2 nestles into M's little sister's well-perfumed top.

"See, you're a natural."

M's sister gently strokes H2's back. I think both are enjoying the current situation. "I'm happy to hold babies for a bit," she says. "I couldn't take care of them for long. Is it true about the sleepless nights?"

I exhale. "You have no idea."

All the back stroking induces a burp, which triggers some creamy vomit, which H2 expels onto M's little sister's shoulder. She looks disgusted.

"Sorry about that. I should have given you a burping cloth. I also should've mentioned, it won't be just a booby visit but a sickie one, too."

I HATE TO SAY IT (ACTUALLY, I'm not that hateful) but I am relieved to be leaving my in-laws' house. I'm not sure what the etiquette is in this current situation. I mean, am I expected to help out a bit? Or do I just sit around with the baby? What do I do? My brain is too fuzzy for all the over-thinking, therefore I'm ready to go back to my mum's house where I can get waited on, hand and foot, without second-guessing anything.

As we leave, M announces. "We will bring mum to London with us, for a few days, when we head back. Is that okay?"

What? When was that agreed? My mother-in-law has never in my five years of marriage, ever visited us in London. It's always been the other way round.

M's mum looks at me, waiting for a response.

"Lovely," I say, because that seems like the only appropriate answer.

9th May, A mixed bag

It's a mixed bag being at my mum's. On one hand, I am truly, utterly grateful for the support. Mum has been running me Dettol baths to help heal my stitches. She has made sure I've had plenty of dairy, milk, yoghurt, and orange juice. Most of all, and most amazing of all, mum has helped me establish breastfeeding with gentle encouragement. I've spent hours upstairs in her room, trying to get H2 to feed properly, which is something I didn't have the patience or understanding to do while I was in London. And I sure as hell wouldn't have been able to do it at my mother-in-law's with the constant nudging about bottles of formula.

That said, and I feel bad even thinking this, but mum is ever so slightly annoying. The constant opinions on everything I do can be a little intense.

"Okay, put her down now. She get too used to you!" is mum's response to me cradling H2 while she sleeps.

See what I mean?

"This is the only way to get her to stay asleep," I say.

"No, no! I put all my babies down and you turned out fine. If you keep doing that, she think you be bed."

I gently lower H2 down in her Moses basket. Inevitably, she starts wriggling. Then, mum performs magic by gently patting on H2's belly and the cheeky little bugger goes straight back to sleep! Bloody H2.

"You have to learn to do things around her and put her down. It's okay if she cry *lit-ool* bit. Then she understand that you not bed. She need to learn this because you will have to do things on your own over there."

"I know, mum."

"And you need rest, too! You had hard time in hospital. You need to look after yourself, not just baby. Why you no take shower before your friend come?"

"I'm not sure there'll be time. Sophia will be here any minute." Mum's made me paranoid. "Why? Do I smell that bad?"

Mum steps back. "No, I just be saying. Your friend is quite fancy, no? Maybe you change top to look bit less cheap and skanky?"

Mum's eyes lower towards my milk-stained nursing top. I probably should get changed.

Here's the thing that nobody tells you about breastfeeding. It makes you absolutely reek. I don't know if this is a short-term thing or it'll be this way for as long as I nurse H2 but I've never sweated so much in my life. I'm offending myself.

Mum takes H2 while I put on a fresh top over my gross sweaty armpits, though it doesn't seem to help. It's kind of like wallpapering over a huge hole in the wall. It's only masking the underlying issue.

Through the window of my old bedroom, I see our neighbour, Mrs Barker. She's standing outside her sky blue front door, in a thin pink shirt. It's unusually chilly outside. I wonder if she feels it. She's holding a teddy, much like the last time I saw her.

I come downstairs to the sound of H2 crying.

"Mum, you said you'd watch her. I was only gone two minutes."

"*Acha!* She be fine. I got jobs to do. Need to fry onions for chicken. Get rice on. Can't hold baby all day, like you."

I scoop up H2 and turn towards the window, hoping the view outside our cul-de-sac will cheer her up. Though, by all accounts, our front drive, which is too small for a car and is besieged by weeds and dandelions, isn't very scenic.

Mrs Barker is still standing outside her house, teddy in hand.

"Does she always stand outside like that?" I ask mum.

"Who?"

"Mrs Barker."

Mum looks confused.

"Our neighbour of about 30 years?" I add.

"*Oh-ho*, that Mrs Barker. I *doh-no*, she waiting for daughter I think. They visit more now."

"You mean since she was diagnosed with dementia?"

"Heh? Who have dementia?"

"Mrs Barker, mum. You told me she's got dementia."

Mum looks into the distance in search of an answer. "I can't remember."

Dad comes into the front room. "*Eh-heh,* I wanted to watch the news."

"My friend's coming over," I say. "Can you watch it in the other room?"

Dad was just about to sit down. "Okay, I go." He strokes H2's cheek and mumbles as he leaves: "She's not a fair one, is she?"

With that casual colourism imparted, the doorbell rings and mum returns to the kitchen to get on with her many jobs.

OF COURSE, SOPHIA LOOKS radiant. Of course, she doesn't have a hair out of place. Of course, there's not a hint of sweat on her person.

It's not fair that she has to see me like this, that I have to be like this. I sit far away from her so she won't realise the extent of my stench. H2 lays happily in her arms, angelically half asleep.

Sophia has come bearing flowers. I'm not sure if that's the best thing because children can be allergic. However, I don't say anything as it would seem rude.

"How have you been?" she asks.

I look down at the cold, laminate floor, pleading with the tears to stay lodged in my eyes. I don't need another crying show. Not in front of Sophia. I blink them away.

But it's Sophia. She's been through it. "I know how hard it is," she says.

"The birth was pretty horrible."

"Oh hon, I remember you messaging me about the third degree tear. It made me wince." Sophia stretches out her bottom lip, just in case her words weren't cutting enough. "She's worth it though, isn't she? So cute."

H2 turns her head towards me. I don't know how something that is so beautiful can cause so much pain. Or something that is so hard can feel so good. It's the ultimate dichotomy.

A stray tear rolls down my eye.

"Are you okay, hon?"

"Not really," I say.

Sophia shifts herself closer, inching across the sofa. I wish she wouldn't. "I know how you feel. It's funny how time makes you forget but I was in exactly the same place you are right now, when I had baby Imran. I had that same look in my eyes. The bewilderment. Like you don't know what you're doing and everything is overwhelming. That's why I ended up having talking therapy and-"

"I'm okay. I don't think I need anything like that." My pride kicks in, as it always does. "It's just a lot. I'll get used to it. It's all the hormones. The breastfeeding and pumping to increase my supply, then bottle feeding-"

"Hold on." Sophia raises her hand. "If you're breastfeeding, why do you need to pump to increase your supply?"

"That's what the breastfeeding consultants said. At least I thought they did."

"If you're pumping, then when are you feeding her?"

"I don't know. Every few hours, maybe? Do I not need to pump then?"

"I think it's more of an either/or thing. If you're breastfeeding regularly, that will naturally increase your supply. You don't need a pump. Most people express milk because they plan to bottle feed them or they can't breastfeed. For example, if they're going to work. I don't think you need to do all that at this stage. No wonder you're exhausted. Just focus on the breastfeeding."

Damn. That's what mum's been telling me since I got here.

"I wish I knew from the beginning. It would've saved a lot of... everything." I blink away yet more tears.

What is actually wrong with me? I seem to cry at the drop of a hat.

Sophia leans forward. "Bear in mind, there are services out there if you need help. And there's no shame in it. I know in my community we don't talk about that stuff but baby blues are a real thing. Don't go through it alone."

I sit up and straighten out my top. I notice it's bobbly. I really need to update my postpartum wardrobe.

"I won't be alone. And I'm fine. I just need some sleep."

"Neither of mine slept through for the first year. I remember how knackered I was all the time. But, eventually, you get into a routine. Then, slowly, it gets better. Suddenly, six months have gone and you're weaning them. Eventually, they start walking around and don't need you so much." Sophia places her hand on my arm. "It doesn't feel like it now but it will get better."

Another tear breaks free, rolling down my cheek. I quickly wipe it away. "I'm sure it will."

11th May, A travel buddy

"You pack everything you need?" asks mum.

I look at the now empty front room. "I think I'm all good."

Don't cry... Don't cry... I've got this. H2 is nearly six weeks old. I can totally handle looking after her without mum. Each passing day, she grows bigger and stronger.

Mum turns to me. "Do you want to stay another week?"

"Wait. What?" I search mum's face for signs of jest but she looks deadly serious. "I can't. The car is packed and she has her six-week check-up in a couple of days."

Mum nods. "*Acha*, of course. Yes, time to go back." She comes closer and puts her arm around me. "Remember, you be okay. She's doing well now. She be feeding properly. You're better. Remember, plenty women have babies in worse situations. You be okay."

M comes back from loading up the car for the hundredth time. "All good?"

"All good," I reply, surprised at my composure, given that I've been a sobbing wreck of late. Mum's words have given me the boost I need. "There's just one thing left. I need to collect my child."

I go to the living room to find dad holding H2. His wrinkled hands are clasped around her bottom, while her face is snuggled into his beard.

Dad's not one to show much affection, or emotion, or expression but, since I've been here, he has gleefully picked up H2 at every opportunity, even when she wasn't crying.

"You go so soon?" he asks.

Mum walks in and is about to scold dad as usual but stops herself as she is all too aware there are people in the house that aren't blood relatives. "They need to go. Long journey ahead," she says in a more gentle tone than I am accustomed to.

I hear the toilet flush and my mother-in-law's footsteps in the hallway.

Oh yeah, we have an extra guest.

I'm still not sure how to gauge things. Surely, she's not going to expect me to host her? I'm hoping she's a help, not a hindrance.

"Is the bride ready?" my mother-in-law asks, referring to H2. It's a weird Bengali thing to jokingly call a baby, or a young child, a bride. I guess it's like calling her a princess? I don't know. I don't make the rules.

I take H2 out of dad's grasp, as he reluctantly releases his grip. My little sister's come downstairs now, in a respectfully long, green cardigan as my mother-in-law is in the house.

As everyone waits at the door, I do my best not to cry.

It will be okay. Just like mum said, I will be okay.

Despite my inner affirmations, a sneaky tear forms in my eye as we drive off.

"She's such a good girl," my mother-in-law says as we join the motorway. "She must like to travel. All babies do. They fall asleep with the moving car." She beams at her newest granddaughter from the front passenger seat.

However, she's spoken too soon, as H2 starts wailing. I try the shush-pat thing but it doesn't work. Instead, H2 kicks her legs and flails her arms robotically in protest.

"She must be hungry," my mother-in-law concludes. "Did you pack bottles?"

"No, I'm mostly breastfeeding her now."

"Are you?" asks M.

"Yeah it's working."

"Hmm," is his response.

"That's why she be hungry. Breastmilk all watery. Shall we stop at shop to get bottles?" She looks to her son.

"What should I do?" M asks me over his shoulder.

"Nothing," I reply. "There's no point getting bottles now. It will confuse her. I'll just shush her back to sleep."

A few minutes in and she's still screaming. Poor thing is using all her lung capacity, while I'm losing all my patience.

My mother-in-law says: "She got good lungs!" Her and M share a giggle together.

Am I the only one who doesn't find this funny? My daughter's crying sends pain signals to my brain.

"When we get onto a straight stretch of motorway, I'll take her out and feed her."

"Okay," M replies. "I'll stay in the left lane and drive slowly."

I carefully scoop H2 out of the car seat. I'm sure I'm breaking the law. I hope there are no police patrolling the road. I latch her on and she's quickly pacified. I breathe a sigh of relief.

After a few minutes, H2 is knocked out. I gently place her back in her seat. She startles and starts crying. Bloody hell! Not this again.

"*Eh!* She still hungry. Get bottle!"

"We don't have any bottles ready," I reply.

"You should've packed some," my mother-in-law says.

I say nothing.

She looks to her son for support. "Will they sell bottles at service station?"

M looks in the rearview mirror for my reaction. I shake my head. He ignores his mum and continues driving.

I place my knuckle in H2's mouth. It sounds weird as hell but I read somewhere that it could be used as a pacifier. She clamps down on it hard with her gums, making me clench my own teeth in pain. After a couple of suckles, she rejects my knuckle. I don't blame her. I don't know when I last washed my hands.

"You're going to have to leave her to cry," M shouts above the wailing. "Then she'll learn to settle."

"I can't," I shout back, trying and failing to console her with yet another knuckle.

Beneath the crescendo of crying, I hear my mother-in-law mutter: "Mum's milk no fill baby up. That's why bottle be better."

It's going to be a long journey home.

ONE EXPLOSIVE POO, hours of on-and-off crying, lots of meddling from my mother-in-law and two service station stops later and we are on the homestretch.

As we roll into our apartment car park, it begins to rain. Brilliant. We have to walk across the car park in the rain with my newborn baby. M holds H2 at the door and lets my mother-in-law slowly make her way in first. What the hell? Shouldn't he be rushing my tiny baby in first? What's wrong with him? I push down my feelings of anxiety as he finally crosses the threshold with H2. If she gets a cold after this, I will not be happy.

Pascal is on duty at the concierge tonight. "How is the lovely lady doing?" he asks.

M goes over to show H2, all swaddled in her blanket.

"What a beautiful young woman. Just like her mother. And grandmother."

My mother-in-law blushes.

Once in our flat and semi-unpacked, M orders me to lie down. "Me and mum can sit with her."

I go into the bedroom, which goes against all I envisioned when my mother-in-law would come and visit. Still, if my husband says I need rest, I really ought to listen.

I shut my eyes. Please come, sleep. Please wash over me, waves of sleep. I've forgotten what proper sleep feels like. Instead, it's replaced with a semi-awake state, on constant alert to make sure H2 is okay. It's like I'm her bodyguard as well as her mother.

I can hear M and his mum, laughing and chatting in the living room. M isn't remotely tired, as he's had two weeks of uninterrupted sleep. He and my mother-in-law are having the best time with my daughter. I hear the TV come on. M is flicking through the channels and, from the sounds of it, settling on Bangla TV. The loud, high-pitched tones of the programme is giving me a headache. I can't imagine what it's like for a tiny baby. At the very least, it'll make her think it's daytime, therefore time to stay awake. They shouldn't be encouraging H2 to be so lively at this hour. If she doesn't sleep, how the hell am I supposed to?

"What time do you call this?" M asks who I assume is H2. "Wide awake at 11 'o'clock?"

Bloody hell! Is that what time it is? She really does need to go to sleep. Or she'll be overtired and up all night. Then who'll pay the price for that? Me!

That's it. I'm going in. Plus, I don't want my mother-in-law to be whispering more things about the virtue of formula milk in my husband's ear.

"Did you get some rest?" M asks as I enter the room.

"Not really. I have to take her to bed. If I don't, she'll be overtired."

"This one wants to stay for chat!" my mother-in-law says. "You want to eat some rice? I brought curry over."

It's only then that I realise I'm famished. The service station chips we had was hours ago.

"Okay, shall I heat some up? Will everyone eat?"

"*Nah, nah.* It be too late for me. You eat," she says, looking at her son. "I brought ayr fish and some shutki."

Is she serious? She's only made curry that M likes. She knows I don't like fish, especially stinky fermented fish.

"I'll just take her to bed," I say to M and disappear into the bedroom before anyone has a chance to say anything.

H2 is not playing ball. The little minx. It's like she wants to show me up. I'm desperately trying to get her to sleep by feeding her into a slumber. Yet she's wide-awake and looking around. If I wasn't so eager to fall asleep so I don't have to sit with M and his mum in the living room, I'd find H2 adorable right now. But, as it stands, I don't.

My mother-in-law hovers near the doorway, giggling. "She's not ready to sleep, is she?"

I ignore her and continue to shush and feed H2 to sleep.

Eventually, my mother-in-law gets the hint. As I see her walk away with a slight limp, I am overcome with guilt, remorse and, most of all, fatigue.

13th May, Six-week check

I am officially the world's crappiest host. Since my mother-in-law has been staying with us in London, I haven't been able to cook anything as I've had a baby attached to me at all times.

M has been ordering takeaways while his mum finished the fish curry that she thoughtfully brought over to eat with her son. I made a half-arsed attempt at making pesto pasta straight from the jar. There wasn't much enthusiasm for it.

I wish she'd come at a different time. I wish she visited before H2 was born. That way, I could've been the dutiful daughter-in-law and made her a chicken curry. I'm not in the headspace now. Even when I've made a cup of tea, I've done it begrudgingly. I feel like I'm the one needing to be looked after. Beyond H2, I haven't got the scope to take care of anyone else.

Anyway, I mustn't grumble. I'm out in the fresh air, walking to H2's six-week health check.

Once summoned to my appointment, I'm glad to see Dr Fraser, the GP that first delivered the good news that I was pregnant. His smile is still in sharp contrast with his severe widow's peak hairline. Seeing him today, however, presents another problem. Aren't I supposed to be examined in this appointment, to check everything is as it should be?

"How are you doing?" Dr Fraser asks.

"I'm fine," I lie. It's not worth mentioning that I'm drained from H2's cluster feeding and so tired I might die.

"I see you've had a few appointments back in the hospital. You went back in because she wasn't feeding?"

A lump forms in my throat again. Those bloody lumps. I swallow it down. "I did but we're okay now, I think. She's exclusively breastfed and hopefully she's gaining weight."

"Well, let's have a look at her." Dr Fraser instructs me to put H2 on the bed and undo her baby grow. She is gargling and smiling at him, which is a new thing she's learnt. It's borderline flirtatious.

I keep my fingers crossed that she has gained weight and the breastfeeding is working. If it hasn't, M will put the pressure on to give her the bottle. And my mother-in-law will pull an epic *I told you so* face.

"Right, so she's 9lb, which is just about right. She is gaining weight nicely."

I feel my shoulders drop and my chest relax. She's okay. It's working.

"Right, that's all good. She'll be weighed again in a few weeks' time and then you've got her vaccinations, if you choose to, coming up at eight weeks. We'll send you a letter for that." He turns back to his screen.

Okay, so this is awkward. "I'm just wondering, are you meant to do an examination at the six-week check? Of me?"

Dr Fraser looks blankly. "We don't need to. Unless there's anything in particular that's been worrying you."

That's the problem with not knowing your own body. I don't know what's normal and I'm too scared to look at myself. "No, nothing in particular. I just wasn't sure whether I'm supposed to be seen because I had quite..." my voice lowers and I suddenly feel very Bengali, "a bad tear."

Dr Fraser pushes his glasses up his nose. "No, if there's any problem, you can tell your health visitor when she's next due."

"Yes... yes, that's fine," I reply, with a mix of relief that I don't have to expose myself to a male GP and also confusion as I thought that was one of the main things that had to happen today.

"Right... all the best, mum."

That's it. I'm a mum now. I guess my health goes on the back burner. At least H2 has been putting on weight. Silver linings.

I COME HOME TO FIND my mother-in-law napping on the sofa. H2 is still asleep, so I don't take her out of the pram and instead keep her in the kitchen, near the window, in the hope that the breeze will help her have a long sleep.

I fill the kettle with enough water for both M's mum and myself. I feel bad that she's been so bored here that she's given herself a day nap. I'm also envious that she gets to sleep at will. When will that happen for me again?

As the kettle brews, she wakes up. "What you do? Did you have your appointment?"

"Yes, it all went well. She's putting on weight. So the breastfeeding is working."

"Good, good. I fell asleep as I no know what to do. I called your big brother-in-law. I'll be going to theirs later and leave for Droylsden from there."

"Okay." I pour two mugs of tea while relief pours out of me. I don't even bother with a fake protest, asking her to stay a bit longer. It's been shit for her and weird for me. There is an imbalance here. At her house, she has her kitchen, her rules. She's got her routine. Here, she doesn't have her things and we don't even have the commonality of having M around in the day, as he's at work. So we're just bumping into each other the entire time.

H2 wakes up while I'm adding milk to the tea. I take the barely brewed cup to the coffee table and pick up H2. She settles immediately on my lap.

"Put her down. I get her back to sleep. Leave it with me," says my mother-in-law, like a woman on a mission. Let's see what she's got planned.

She takes H2 from me, lays her on the sofa and puts two thick, fleecy blankets either side of her and, to my horror, a heavy blanket on top. I'm sure that was outlawed years ago. It's warm in the flat. It's the middle of May! Now is not the time for heavy blankets, especially on a newborn. I've read they can die from being too hot.

My mother-in-law pats H2 several times and, as if by magic, she goes back to sleep! Do grandmas have magic hands or something? She goes to the bathroom while I look at H2, smothered by blankets. My mum anxiety goes through the roof. Wake up, wake up. My thoughts turn to stories I've heard about Sudden Infant Death Syndrome. I can't take it. I go over and lower the blanket. She wakes up, looking pissed off at me.

Rinse and repeat.

My mother-in-law comes back to find me holding H2.

"Little lady got used to you now," she says. "That's it. You no be able to do anything because she always want to be held."

Not for the first time since I've become a mum, I feel like I'm doing something wrong.

My phone rings. It's M's sister-in-law.

"Assalamu-alaykum. How is the princess doing?"

I've noticed in all this new mum business that everybody asks about the baby. H2 has gold standard treatment, being weighed, checked and monitored, yet hardly anyone enquires after me. It's like I don't exist anymore.

"She's fine," I reply. "A bit clingy, that's all."

"Oh dear. They try to be like that. Honestly, they do it on purpose. You keep her down. She needs to get used to the cot and not always being on you. My eldest got spoilt like that. We were living with my in-laws and everybody was around to hold her. Second time round, once we had our own place, that was it. My youngest barely got picked up. Eventually he got used to staying in cot." My heart sinks. I don't want H2 to get used to not being on me. I don't want her to think she's on her own. "Anyway, take the rest when you can. But I called because I want to speak to *maa*. Is she around?"

I pass the phone to mum. My mother-in-law tells her other daughter-in-law how my baby doesn't sleep and keeps her awake at night. How she wants to be held. How she doesn't leave me time to do anything. That's why the flat is messy and I can't make proper food for her son, my husband. In all my years of marriage, I've never heard M's mum bitch about me. If this is how she talks while I'm in earshot, I wonder what she says when I'm not around.

Though I'm only hearing one side of the conversation, I can deduce that my sister-in-law has cooked a feast for M's mum to eat when she goes over. My mother-in-law says she shouldn't have made so much. She then smiles at me.

M's sister-in-law always shows me up. She's from Bangladesh, so can speak mother tongue fluently and confidently. She cooks like a chef. And she always puts her best face forward for my mother-in-law. I can't imagine her having ever been raw and hormonal and slightly down.

M will be home soon. He'll take his mum to stay with his older brother and fantastic sister-in-law at their place in Luton. My mother-in-law has only been here for a couple of days. I wish I could've been nicer, more accommodating. I add this guilt to the pile that is already wearing me down, hoping I don't break under the pressure.

23rd May, My hot flat

Of all the times for middle sis to come and visit me, I wish she hadn't chosen now. I'm not looking my best, my head is all over the place and the flat is a shit tip.

I keep reading in the mum forums how it really doesn't matter what your house is like when the baby is born. This is the time for everybody to host you. Take care of you. Nobody is going to judge.

However, now that middle sis, her husband and three kids are in our small flat and I can see her appraising the dusty windowsills, pokey kitchen, and the humidity of this flat, which is like a greenhouse in the summer, I am feeling judged. Even if it's unintentional.

"Are they always doing building works here?" She is referring to the constant drilling outside.

In this part of London, there's always a new high-rise going up. Next door is accommodation for international students. Further down into Aldgate, there are more apartments being built to house the many people that keep squashing into the capital. Why on earth did we decide to rent in central London? Why didn't we do the sensible thing and move to the suburbs before H2 was born?

"You can't even close the window in this heat," my brother-in-law helpfully adds.

He then provides some additional commentary about how you don't get much for your money in London, compared to Bradford, where they have an expansive house, complete with an open-plan kitchen-diner that is bigger than our entire flat.

Still, they brought gifts. My adorable, youngest niece proudly presents us with a cellophane wrapped gift basket containing clothes, teddies and toys. She places a fluffy yellow chick next to my baby.

H2 is more animated now. She smiles for everyone and turns her head at the sound of anything, including the incessant drilling and hammering outside.

"Can I hold her?" my eldest niece asks.

"Sure," I hand her over, relieved to take the weight off my hands.

I make the short walk to our kitchen to see if M needs help brewing up.

"Do you want to plate up the biscuits?" he asks, as he takes the teabags out of the now blackened tea. My brother-in-law likes it extra strong and extra milky. Like a builder.

I search the cupboards to find that there are no biscuits to be offered. Damn. Did I eat them all? Surely not. I look at the other culprit.

"I think I might have had the last of the shortbread," says M. "I'll go and get some from the shop."

"Hold on." I check the carrier bag of goodies my sister brought over. Thankfully, there is a chocolate cake among the treats.

"Is the game about to start?" asks my brother-in-law. Obviously, he's talking to M. I wouldn't have a clue if the game started or finished.

"It's about to." M grins, glad he's got a fellow football fanatic in the flat.

Life hasn't changed so drastically for M. He still gets to watch the entire 90-minutes of a football match, longer if there are penalties.

While the men and kids watch the game, my sister and I head to the bedroom with H2.

"You'll find you're a much lighter sleeper now," says middle sis. "And you'll be like that forever."

That's not helpful.

"It's all a bit of a blur. Do you ever feel like yourself again?" I ask.

"I don't want to lie to you, girly, but life is never really the same. They're part of you now. Even now, I sleep with one eye open. It's just how it is. It's always the way for the ladies."

I hear some cheers from the living room. Liverpool must have scored.

"Why is it so much easier for men?" I ask.

Middle sis sighs. "Where do I start? We birth the kids. We're the ones that stay at home and look after them. They do the work. They earn the money. And even if you both worked before, something's got to give, unless you want your kids in full-time childcare. Even then, you do most of the work, like the cooking and cleaning and school admin."

I look at H2, who is blowing raspberries at middle sis. "It's so unfair."

Middle sis puts her arm around me. "Don't be upset. It is hard, but you get used to it. And look at her! Look at this life you've created."

Middle sis is right. I have created life. And H2 is more amazing than I could've imagined. But in the pit of my stomach, in the deepest layer of my soul, I can't help but wonder... is it okay to love something so much but hate everything that comes with it?

2nd June, Play groups

"That's a good look," M tells me as he's about to leave for work.

"I'll have you know, in very recent history, women made a deliberate choice to wear tracksuit bottoms with heels. Therefore, I'm unintentionally stylish." I examine myself in the full-length mirror on our wardrobe. "Can you tell I slept in this top last night?"

M comes closer and sniffs my shoulder. "Not really but if you're going to be facing the outside world, you might as well get changed. It will improve your chances of making mum friends."

I yawn. "That's assuming I can keep awake long enough to even hold a conversation."

M goes over and kisses H2 on the sole of her chubby foot. "I was talking to Paul, a guy at work, and his baby was a nightmare sleeper, too. The only thing that worked for them was leaving the baby to cry. Then they get used to sleeping in the cot."

I look at H2, all tiny and innocent.

"Maybe not right now," M adds. "But something to think about when she's a bit older." He lifts H2 by the armpits. She throws her head back in delight. "You hear that? You better sort yourself out. If you keep this up when you're bigger, we're gonna use tough love."

H2 looks at her dad with an adorable smile. It's as though she already knows he's a softie, so she needn't take his threat seriously.

With that wisdom shared, M heads out the door, while I look for a nursing-friendly top. If it hasn't got a zip, buttons, or can be easily pulled up or down, I can't wear it.

My phone rings. It's big sis. She never calls this early.

"I just realised I can't call you little lady anymore. You've got your own little one now," says big sis.

"You can still call me little lady. I'd like to keep some semblance of my old self. Anyway, when will you come and visit?"

Big sis sighs. "I'll have to see, lady. It's hard for your brother-in-law to get time off from the business. Especially as he's short-staffed in the restaurant right now. It might be easier to catch you at mum's during the school holidays."

I look around the bedroom. The duvet has fallen to the floor, H2 is playing on her tummy, and by the looks of things, has puked on the bedsheet. I knew I shouldn't have put her on her front so soon after a feed. Perhaps it's best big sis sees me at mum's rather than bearing witness to the puke show/shit show that is currently my home.

"How you getting on?" asks big sis.

"I'm okay. I'm going to a mother and baby playgroup shortly and I'm debating whether to have a 10 seconds shower or just run a wet wipe under my armpits before I leave."

"Is the fella home to watch the baby?"

"No, he's just left."

"You're best off wiping your pits, then," big sis concludes.

"I agree. It's the breastfeeding, it's making me sweat buckets."

"That's an odd side-effect. Though I wouldn't know, I gave my three kids bottles. I couldn't get the hang of breast-feeding. Is she sleeping through yet?"

I knew that million dollar question would come up at some point.

"Not yet. She's only tiny."

Big sis gulps as though she's just drank some water. "Ah yes. It'll come. By the three-month mark she should be set-tled and you'll be able to get some sleep. Meanwhile, sleep when she naps. Anyway, I just called to check in. I figured you'd be up early now you've got a baby."

"Erm, yeah, I was up this time before I had a baby. You know, for work?"

Big sis tuts. "Yes but not when you started running your own business, surely? You had a lie in then, didn't you?"

"No, I worked regular office hours."

"Blimey," says big sis. "And there was me thinking you didn't have much work on."

I want to explain to big sis how I actually worked a lot harder when I ran my own business, because I had to find clients. I had to do my own marketing. I had to fill the pipeline. I was a business owner, creative director, adminis-trator and saleswoman. However, I realise that there is lit-erally no point in saying this to big sis, who hasn't worked properly since the day she got married, over two decades ago. I don't have the strength to argue my case.

We say our goodbyes and I look for a pack of baby wipes for my under arms. Don't judge me.

I WALK TO A MOTHER and baby rhyme time session that's five minutes down the road. I never even knew it existed before having H2.

En route, I spot a couple of mums walking in the same direction, pushing small, thin-framed prams. It must be nice to have a mum friend. Despite joining the NCT group when I was pregnant, I'm yet to meet with the other mums. We're constantly pinging messages on the group WhatsApp but it's usually questions, moans or the occasional bragging. Melanie sent a picture of a baby bottle containing 100ml of her breastmilk. She said the midwife called her a milk machine. It wasn't very helpful as I can barely express an ounce.

Once I get to the group, myself and other mums are invited to sit in a circle while the session lead, Leanne, sings a 'hello' song. We all have to wave at the respective babies but it's not reciprocated as most babies aren't at waving stage so just stare at us. The babies that can wave are busy crawling around and exploring the silver balls, beanbags, and plush toys. I might have the youngest one here and I'm scared that these more mobile babies could knee H2 in the head.

We say hello to Leo, Carter, Ismail, Jodie, Nooria and a few other names I forget.

"Come on, let's get up and do some musical roundabout," says Lianne with more enthusiasm than I've seen from anyone in my entire life.

Then they start dancing. I kid you not, the mums get up and do some kind of mum dancing in a circle. Right on queue, they twirl as well. What kind of fresh hell is this? I can't dance around a circle, twirling. I barely dance.

I can't do this. I just can't. This isn't me.

20 MINUTES LATER, IT doesn't seem so bad. So far, I've wound the bobbin up, I pulled and pulled and then clapped three times. I then repeated the process. Then I pointed to the ceiling, to the floor, to the window and then to the door. This was followed by a raucous triple clap again. I think I went really method with it.

H2 is blasé as anything. She couldn't give a toss as to what I'm doing. Instead, she is focusing on forcing out an explosive poo.

"How old is he?" asks the lady next to me.

It must be the blue baby grow and bald head. "She's a she. And she's eight weeks old."

"Sorry, I'm always mis-gendering babies. Most of the time people think my Rohan is a girl."

Rohan is dressed in a sunflower-coloured jumper and has eyelashes for days. Yep, I can see why people would think he's a girl. He's chubbier than H2, with baby-soft skin. Not that I'm comparing but all the other babies seem to have silky skin, as babies should, whereas my little girl's complexion isn't quite so smooth. Her arms and legs seem dry, too. I must apply more coconut oil.

Hold on... is Rohan asleep? How could anyone sleep amongst all the racket?

His mum laughs. "This boy can fall asleep at the drop of a hat. We never get a full session in the playgroup."

"Where did you get such a sleepy baby from? And how come I couldn't get one?" I ask, half joking and half bitterly jealous.

"God knows. I'm sure I'll draw the short straw in other ways. Plus, the first trimester was rough. He didn't sleep through the night for the first eight weeks."

The first eight weeks? Does that mean H2 could suddenly turn it around?

"I'm Chandni, by the way." She holds out her hand. "I very rarely attend mother and baby sessions as he's too busy napping. And the times I do go out, this happens. He fell asleep during his swimming lesson, can you believe?"

I look at H2, who is observing everything around her. This kid is so alert. Every rustle, every rumble, she arches her head back as far as she can, to see what the fuss is about.

"You know what they say," Chandni adds, "the babies, who don't sleep, turn out to be highly intelligent."

I don't know who says that but I choose to believe this wholeheartedly. There's got to be some positives of prolonged sleep deprivation.

Chandni is a first-time mum as well. She shows off some silver strands of hair, nestled within the black, to prove how stressed out she is.

"Now we are at the six-month mark, it's all fun and games. I started feeding him things like baby rice and carrot purée."

"Is he feeding well?" I ask, admiring his chunky thighs that are straining against his light green shorts.

"It's going good. He loves food. I'm also glad to be at the stage, because it means we're a step closer to him turning one. Then, I can say that I've kept my baby alive for a year!"

"I thought it was just me that was always worried about killing my baby." I laugh.

"No, you're not alone. I'm constantly paranoid about things like that. I'm terrified I'll leave him in the supermarket one day. It's a big responsibility, being in charge of a tiny human."

"This one is in charge of me," I say, as H2 kicks me in agreement.

It turns out that Chandni doesn't live far from me. We walk down Commercial Road together and share stories of motherhood. She is an accountant and plans to go back once baby Rohan is one and her maternity leave is up. She asks about my plans. I tell her I'll be looking to get a nanny and, as I work for myself, I can work around H2. I decide to omit the fact that I actually have no idea how and when I'm going to do this. I tell Chandni I have hired a freelancer who is picking up the slack while I'm on maternity leave. I choose not to mention that she's only servicing the one client I have left. Chandni is in awe of my career, at least the filtered version I've shared with her. She says her job feels boring in comparison. I bet it pays well, though.

I wonder whether it's easier to work for someone else, to stay in the corporate sector. I wonder whether needing to go back to work by a certain time, going back to your same job, salary and colleagues, simplifies things. Me, with all my choices, has left me not knowing what to choose. I don't know when to go back to work. Right now, even the most basic of decisions, such as how many baby grows to pack when heading out of the door is just about all my mind can handle.

I don't ask for Chandni's number as it would be far too keen. I hope I get to see her around again, though. She mentioned there is another playgroup near Stepney Green. I make a mental note to attend.

I think that's what I need to get through this newborn phase. Cram in as many mother and baby sessions as I can. At this stage, it's about 10% for H2 and 90% for me.

As I enter the lift to my flat, I bump into my neighbour, Taslima.

"I've been meaning to get in touch with you," she says, sounding out of breath. "I'm just going to pick up my kids from the mosque now but are you around on Tuesday?"

"I am," I reply. "Just knock on my door whenever." I hope that doesn't sound too desperate but she really is welcome to come round any time.

"Okay, I'll message you beforehand, to make sure you're free."

We safely arrive into our flat unscathed. H2 didn't have a tantrum on the way home. I didn't get flustered. She's starting to rustle now. I think she might be hungry. As I sit on the sofa feeding her, I feel like I've got this. For the first time in two months, I feel like it's okay. There's not a sense of drudgery in getting through the day.

I know I shouldn't rely on the company of others to determine my happiness but isn't that what life is? Finding pockets of joy, friendly conversations, a joke and a laugh and some good company to help you through it? It seems to be working for me right now.

I look at the time. It's 3.30pm. Only about three hours until M finishes work.

"THIS IS THE FIRST TIME I've come home to find you smiling," says M, putting his arm around me. "Have you had a good day?"

"It's been alright. I went to the mother and baby session. It was a bit weird. Lots of singing and some dancing but it was good to meet other mums."

"I'm glad to hear it. I always feel sad when I see you looking upset when I come in. I know how hard it is for you."

I sink into M. "It is easier when you're home. I won't lie."

"I'm here now. So don't worry. I just need to go poop and shower and then I can take her off your hands."

Okay, so that's going to add another 45 minutes to an hour, but, for once, I'm not annoyed with him.

12th June, Feeding trouble

H2 has been crying non-stop for the last hour. She's red in the face and keeps arching her back. I don't know what's wrong with her. I don't know what to do.

I tried breastfeeding her. She suckled and settled for a minute and then started crying again. I got so desperate I gave her a bottle but she immediately spat it out. What am I supposed to do? I am alone with a screaming baby I can't pacify.

I wonder if the neighbours can hear us. I hope not. They're probably not even in. Unlike me, most people that live in these flats are young professionals, child-free and living their best life.

I know, I'll call Taslima. She lives on the same floor so it's hardly an inconvenience for her to check in. I dial her number. She promised to come around last week but she never did. She didn't even call me or send a message. I'm not sure why she's being so rubbish.

My call goes straight to voicemail. She must be busy.

I need to do something. I don't even want to take her out like this. I look exhausted, she's crying her head off. What will people think? They'll deem me incompetent at best, or a terrible, terrible mother at worst.

I call the only blood relatives I have in London.

"Salaamalaykum, my dear niece, what are you doing? And how's the little one?" asks auntie Rukhsana upon answering the phone.

"We're okay. Actually, not really. She keeps crying. I don't know why."

Auntie Rukhsana giggles, though this isn't a laughing matter. "Is that right? Are you crying and stressing out your mummy?" she says in a baby voice as if H2 can understand.

H2 stops to listen for a brief second because she's nosey. Then, she resumes crying and contorting her body, like she's in pain.

"You no worry. Babies cry. That's their job. Is she hungry?"

"I don't know. I have just fed her. I even gave her a bottle but she puked it all out. I don't know what to do. Can you... sorry... but can you come over?"

"I can't. I've got Naila's boy here."

I tune out H2's crescendo of crying to hear Ibrahim, a happy toddler, chatting gibberish in the background.

"You just walk around with her for *lit-ool* bit. She'll be okay, babies cry. You need get used to it."

Auntie Rukhsana keeps saying babies cry but should they cry like this?

I hang up.

That's it, isn't it? My beloved auntie has her own daughter that takes priority. Her own grandchild that she needs to look after. M won't be back from work for hours. I have to do this by myself. I walk around with H2 in the living room. I whisper prayers, sing nursery rhymes, try anything to soothe her.

I can no longer call the midwives as I've passed that level of care and now am with the health visitor. Aha! I'll try her.

The phone rings, rings and rings. Then it goes to voice-mail. Bloody hell. What am I going to do? I take H2 near the window to let her see the city. She coughs a little, like the smoke is choking her lungs. I move her away. It's times like this I really wish we were back up north. Near my mum. She'd know what to do. She'd help me because I am her daughter, her priority.

Uncle Tariq and auntie Rukhsana have been fantastic ever since I moved to London. I've been over whenever I wanted. Eaten them out of house and home. However, I would swap all that kindness for just one visit from my auntie to help me with H2 but it's not possible, is it? I've got to figure this out myself.

My phone rings. It's my neighbour. Finally.

"Did you give her a bottle?" she asks after hearing the constant wails.

"I did but it's not making any difference."

"It's probably the bottle that's making her worse, actually. I never bottle-fed any of mine. I think it's lazy mums that bottle feed them right at the beginning. It's too much for the poor babies. It makes them feel sick," says Taslima.

I want to say I had to bottle feed her at the beginning. Instead, I reply: "Oh, okay. What do you think will help her now?"

Taslima huffs. "Just persevere with the breastfeeding. Also, open her baby grow buttons and rub her belly a bit. That might help. She might be constipated or gassy. That can happen when you bottle feed but listen, I've got to go. I have a ton of things to do so just keep doing that and inshallah she'll be okay."

Taslima hangs up, having been put out by my neediness. I undo H2's baby grow and rub her gently. It does precisely bugger all. She keeps crying. I walk with her around the living room. She keeps crying. I rock her in my arms. She keeps crying. I put her near my chest and offer her a feed. She keeps crying.

I hold her by the arms and look her in the eye. "What do you want?" I shout. "What do you fucking want?"

H2 stops crying, startled. I pull her in close.

"I'm sorry. I'm sorry. I'm sorry. I'm sorry," I say repeatedly, stroking her head. I am an awful, awful mother.

I hear her panting in my ear. She's exhausted. So am I. I look at her tiny face. She searches around, looking pained, then cries once again.

HOURS LATER, THE CRYING stops. I have resorted to skin-on-skin contact, stripping her to her nappy and me down to my bra. We sit on the bed, out of puff.

I go on social media to find the same death, destruction and inhumanity that has been playing on a loop since H2 was born. Images from Palestine, Yemen, the Congo and Sudan. I immediately scroll past the horrific footage and feel guilty all over again. Guilty for having the privilege to turn my eyes away because it's not happening to me. Guilty that by a pure accident of birth, I am faced with first world problems such as struggling to get my baby to settle, while these people, these other people of colour, don't know what they'll eat or if they'll live to see the next day.

My Instagram feed simultaneously shows me pictures of influencers, enjoying date nights, as well as small children who have lost limbs. I squeeze H2 tighter.

THE PHONE RINGS. IT'S middle sis. After some pleasantries, I can no longer hold it in and start sniffling down the phone.

"Oh, are you crying?"

The sniffling turns into an ugly sob. "Sorry, it's just so hard."

"Awww, girlie, you'll be alright. You can do this," says middle sis. "Remember, we've all been through it. All our kids didn't sleep. My eldest was an absolute nightmare, she still gives me crap to this day. I think it's extra hard for you because you're doing it over there by yourself."

This makes me cry even more.

"Oh no! Don't be upset. It does get easier. She'll be a big girl before you know it. In the blink of an eye. The nights are long, but the years are short. You'll only get about 18 summers with her and then you'll be crying because she's left home. Also... hold on..."

"What?" I'm hoping for some more words of wisdom.

Middle sis pauses for effect. "Erm... when you have a child, you lose your mind, but you find yourself."

"Are you reading parenting quotes from the internet?"

"Are they helping?"

I sniff. "A little."

28th June, Pretending

My mother-in-law is calling, again. It's the second time this morning. Can't she tell I'm busy? Actually, that's not fair. I'm just tired and not really in the mood to speak to anyone right now.

I answer with a salaam, then she gets to the most important question of all: "What did you cook today?"

I look over to the kitchen counter, which plays host to a sad, crushed cardboard box which once housed chicken and chips.

"Chicken curry," I decide is the best answer.

"And what is he doing?" M's mum asks, referring to her son.

M is currently changing H2's nappy in the bedroom. I better not tell my mother-in-law that. I'm sure she'll take it to mean that he does all the nappy changes and night feeds, even though I breastfeed. I know what Bengali mother-in-laws are like.

"He's just come out of the... er... bathroom. Would you like to speak to him?"

I go over to the bedroom and toss the phone to my husband before my mother-in-law has a chance to ask any more questions. Fortunately, he's done changing H2's smelly nappy and is free to speak.

I take my daughter in exchange and hover near the door so I can eavesdrop and make sure my name isn't taken in vain.

"Nothing much. We've just eaten," M says.

I poke my head round the door and plead to M with my eyes: *Don't say we've had takeaway. Don't see we've had take-away for the third time this week. Your mum won't accept the excuse that we have a restless, cranky baby. Nor that I'm chronically tired. So, please, let's pretend.*

"Yeah, we had chicken curry," M says.

I trained him well.

30th June, To wake or not to wake?

I have a huge dilemma. H2 is, on this rare occasion, fast asleep. It's 4am, and I really ought to get some rest myself, however, there is a suspicious smell coming from her bottom.

M, of course, is worse than useless right now as he's fast asleep. He does have work in the morning, so I shouldn't really disturb him. I'll give him a gentle elbow instead.

How bad would it be if I let her sleep with a poo in her nappy? After all, she'll probably be up in about an hour or two. Would it be that problematic if she slept in her own faeces for a short while? Then again, she is a new baby with delicate skin.

I know, I'll check the mums' WhatsApp group to see if anyone's awake.

Damn them, they must all be asleep as the last message was sent hours ago. It was Genevieve saying how she is struggling to breastfeed through the night as she keeps nodding off while sat up. I must tell her about the lying down feeding method.

For now, I've got bigger problems.

I guess, if H2 had farted, the odour would have dissipated by now. I put my face towards her tiny bum. Honestly, the things you do as a mum. Sniffing bottoms comes so naturally to me now. She still smells.

I go onto a mum forum, which is proving to be a fountain of knowledge throughout this new mum phase. I type in: Should you change your baby in the night if they've pooed?

This throws up a number of threads, suggesting that this is a question that keeps many mums awake at night.

BossLady1234, says: *The best thing to do is carefully change their nappy, so you don't disturb them. Watch out for those pesky velcro fasteners because they can be noisy.*

Forget that. H2 wakes up if I dare move an inch away from her. I doubt she'd sleep through a full outfit change.

I need another opinion. I elbow M again.

He cranks his head up, eyes wide. "Huh, what?"

"H2 has done a poo. Or it might be a fart. Should I change her?"

M rests his head back on the pillow. "Leave it. If she's asleep, don't disturb her." He checks the time on his phone. "She'll be awake in a bit, anyway. So will I, as I need to get in early for a meeting."

"Should I not check her bum at least?"

M starts snoring again.

I go back on the mum forum.

Beckymumoffour says: *Honestly, I wouldn't bother. If they're asleep, they're asleep. It shows they're not too bothered by it, so why change them and risk waking them?*

That is very sensible advice from Becky with the four kids.

There are some replies to Becky's comment...

Mumontour says: *That is absolutely disgusting. If a baby poos, you change them straight away. You don't let them sleep for hours. It's cruel.*

Cheeselover91 says: *Their tiny bum is so delicate at this stage that leaving them in a soiled nappy for too long will give them a rash :(*

Girlnextdoor says: *How would you feel to be sat in your faeces the entire night and unable to change yourself? I feel sorry for your kids.*

While Glammama74 says: *Honestly, I don't see why some people have babies if they don't want to look after them properly. Leaving them to sit in their poo, just so you can get a good night's sleep! Someone call social services!*

Given the general consensus online, I decide I better change H2.

Now to be stealthy.

I delicately undo two of the popper buttons on her baby grow. She jolts, then goes back to sleep again. I carefully lift one tiny limb out of the leg hole. Damn! Her big toe gets stuck en route. She blinks again, then goes back to sleep. My God, this might be the first time in the history of H2 that she sleeps through anything.

I slide the leg out and gently lower it onto the bed. I repeat with the second leg. I bend it at the knee, then she kicks up in some strange reflex.

That's it, she's awake.

Better get this show on the road. I peer through the gap in her nappy. I can't see anything, so use my phone light, much to her annoyance. H2 is now pissed off and crying. Oh well, better to have a crying baby than a sore one.

I shine the light around the nappy to conclude that she did indeed fart.

H2 wriggles around, screaming to be held.

M's head jerks up again. "I told you to leave it!" He turns the other way and flops back onto the pillow, though he's unlikely to sleep through this symphony of crying.

I guess that's us up for the day.

1st July, Are you feeling depressed?

"We finally have a wedding date!" Julia shrieks down the phone.

"Oh, great! When's the big day?" I ask.

Julia pauses as if she wants to drum up some suspense.

"The 10th March. It'll be an early spring wedding."

I mentally work out how old H2 will be and if I'll be done with breastfeeding by then, as the latter will dictate my outfit choice.

"Miles' father is being incredibly stingy with the guest list and initially wanted no small children..."

Wait, what? How will I attend her wedding without H2? Where would I leave her? I hold my breath and wait for Julia to say more.

"Don't worry, I rubbished that idea before it had a chance to form. I know it will be difficult for you to get childcare and there's absolutely no way I wouldn't have you at my wedding. Also, my future father-in-law has clearly forgotten that my own sister will have a baby, too. I said the more children, the better!"

I exhale. "You'll be glad to know I've only got the one kid to bring with me. That's plenty enough."

"And I'd love to see her there. How is baby H2 doing? I'm missing her cuddles."

"She's missing you too. You need to come round and see her."

Julia sighs. "I will but it's been crazy here with work. God, I sound like a broken record but it seems like people are never not getting divorced. However, I will try and fit in time to come and visit before all our weekends are tied up with the fun and games of wedding planning. Honestly, I don't know how you did it in such a short space of time. Not to mention pulling it off so spectacularly with all those guests. We're aiming for under 150 people and even then, we're struggling to find a venue to accommodate that many.

"See, that's where you guys go wrong," I say. "You should be like us Bengalis who hire the wedding hall that throws in the food at £15 per head."

"I wouldn't mind, though my prospective in-laws will probably have something to say about it."

"And there was me thinking it's just us Bengali girls who don't have a say when planning our weddings."

Julia and I both laugh.

"ARE YOU FEELING DEPRESSED, like you can't go on?"

That's a bit of a blunt question. I wish the health visitor had at least added some preamble to soften the blow.

I gaze out of the window. There's a group of students heading into a bougie café. That'll be the best time of their life. Being a student. Completely carefree, with the only worry being where to go out. They have no idea how good they've got it.

I think back to the time in hospital, my second time round, when I was losing my mind because H2 would not stop crying and I was casually advised to figure it out, otherwise people may be concerned. I took the midwife's advice and decided I shouldn't make a fuss or draw attention to the situation. I shouldn't highlight the fact that I was struggling.

Now, I'm on my bed, opposite the health visitor, who is sitting uncomfortably on the office chair I had to wheel through from the second room. What was once a spacious bedroom, is now claustrophobic thanks to H2's gigantic cot. At the time, it made financial sense to get one that will convert to a toddler bed. Now, given that H2 has spent a grand total of one hour in that cot and practically lives in our bed, it might just be our worst investment ever.

The health visitor is making notes of everything I say. It all looks very official.

"No, I'm fine," I reply.

H2 is in my arms, looking at the health visitor in judgement. In recent days, she has developed a very grown-up face. It's like she's an old soul, judging all the time. I can't say I hate it.

"And have you got her into a routine, mum? Is she sleeping well and feeding well?"

"Hmm... we're working on it. I'm going to take her to a breastfeeding support group. There's one next week. As for the sleep front, we're not going great."

"That's perfectly normal at this stage. But what you can start to do is get her into a little routine. For example, give her a bath before bed, settle her down, get her nice and cosy. That should help. Hopefully, by the next couple of weeks she'll be sleeping through."

She makes it sound so easy. Is it? Am I missing something?

"She doesn't seem to settle unless she's on me. Is it because she doesn't have a dummy?"

"No, no. Dummies are terrible for babies. They're bad for the teeth. Bad for facial muscles. It also interferes with the jaw development."

I raise a hand to my chin. I was given the dummy as a baby. Has it had a negative effect on my mouth?

While I'm fretting over my bone structure, the health visitor weighs H2 on a mobile scale. I whisper a prayer under my breath. It is answered, as I am told she's gaining weight nicely.

"There is one thing. She has periods when she just cries for ages. One day was particularly bad. I think it went on for hours."

"Do you think she was hungry?" the health visitor asks.

"No, I don't think so."

"What about tired?"

"I don't know. I tried to get her to nap but she wasn't having it. She would temporarily fall asleep on me and then scream as soon as I put her down."

The health visitor smiles. "Then, I only have one thing to conclude, it looks like you have a baby on your hands."

THE NCT MUMS WHATSAPP group is alive and kicking this afternoon.

Melanie: *I've just had my first baby-free outing. I managed to go swimming while my parents looked after Jasper. It was so hard being away from him. I thought there was an invisible string that connects us.*

Genevieve: *You're so lucky! We don't have any family near us, so Oliver has been attached to me!*

Me: *Same here. I fantasise about the days I can go to the toilet uninterrupted.*

Genevieve: *Lol. I know the feeling. We are looking into getting a nanny as I'll be going back to work soon. I'm counting down the days if I'm honest.*

Melanie: *I'm quite the opposite. I'm dreading going back to work and I've got nine months left!*

Claudia: *Sorry, guys, I've been dipping in and out of these messages. We are in Hong Kong. I think the little man is enjoying the climate here.*

Me: *It's so impressive that you've travelled so far with a baby.*

Claudia: *It's actually not that bad. I was nervous but he slept the entire flight and so far has been pretty happy just being pushed around in the pram. I'm so relieved, as Jean Patrice and I are frequent flyers and didn't want that to change because we've had a baby.*

And there's me suffering a bout of anxiety when I go to the supermarket with H2.

6th July, Jam and Jam

I think I could get used to this. I've barely sat down at the breastfeeding support group when the lactation consultant, Angela, takes a shine to H2 and asks if she could hold her. I practically shot her over like a basketball.

I feel light and hands-free. If only I brought a packed lunch with me. Or crisps.

"Let me know if I'm hogging her," Angela says, while H2 dozes off on her shoulder.

"Oh, there is no danger of that."

I was initially going to ditch the idea of attending the breastfeeding support group, now that I'm confident H2 is gaining weight and we've all but ditched the bottles. However, as I've realised with the playgroups, 90% of the reason to be there is for mum and 10% is for baby. Given that every other aspect of parenthood is so heavily skewed towards the child, I think it helps create some balance.

"I don't know why she won't latch on," says another mum, who looks as though she's about to cry. So far, she's excused herself twice to settle the baby outside.

"She will, Ingrid. You just have to persevere. I think you being relaxed also helps. You know what it's like when you're all flustered and they've done a poo and you're trying to change the nappy. Suddenly, you can't get their legs out of the baby grow, or you can't find the sticky bits in the nappy.

Or you can't get those bloody buttons on. Trust me, I've been there. However, when you relax and take a deep breath, it's all okay. The baby will relax with you. Otherwise, they'll pick up on your anxiety."

Though it's easier said than done, everything Angela says makes sense. I wish I'd heard her pearls of wisdom when I first had H2. When I was being told that breastfeeding should hurt. That I'm a mum now. This is how it's going to be. I wish I knew it was normal to be in a constant state of panic.

"How about you, mum? What's your story?" Angela asks another lady with dark, wavy hair and tired eyes.

"I'm Dahlia. And I don't have much of a story, really. I tried not to mix feed but I have to. I didn't want to give Jonah bottles at all but we had quite a traumatic birth and he was in Neonatal Intensive Care for the first two weeks. My supply's been low since and I worry he's not getting enough."

"Rubbish!" Angela frowns. "They tell you stuff like that but the more you feed, the more your supply increases. Don't listen to people saying you can't do it. And about your supply being low... who told you that, and how do they know? Did they use a measuring jug?" Angela laughs but Dahlia just looks at her son with the same look of guilt that I've been wearing for a long time.

This room is covered in posters extolling the virtues of breastfeeding. Posters warning that should you dare bottle feed, your baby will suffer with bad teeth, an under-developed jaw and bad skin. They might as well go the whole hog and say your baby will end up ugly without breast milk. That seems to be the implication.

Despite Angela's earlier warmth, I find her advice to Dahlia unhelpful. After all, how you feed your baby is such a personal choice with so many factors that come into play. Whichever way you go about it, you'll always feel like you're doing something wrong, so the last thing you want to hear is *try harder.*

"YOU'RE A RIGHT ONE, aren't you?" says Jam, holding H2 by the armpits. I'm scared her neck will jerk back.

"She properly is," says M. "The other night, she wouldn't sleep for ages. I had to stand outside with her near the fire exit. It was chucking it down and, after standing around for ages, she fell asleep on me."

"You don't want her to get used to that, man." Jam strokes her bristly, spiky head. "All you need to do is put her down so she gets used to her surroundings. You could put toys in her cot or her favourite blanket so it's all cosy. That'll help her sleep. She'll cry for an hour or so, then she'll get used to it. She needs to know who's boss."

Jam's advice is based on no experience whatsoever. God, I hate that everyone has an opinion on raising my baby.

"Anyway, how's things with you and your lady?" I ask in the hope of a change of subject.

"She's alright." Jam's cheeks turn crimson. "In fact, she's met my parents. I've met her parents, too."

"Blimey man," says M. "That's come on a bit, hasn't it?"

"Yeah, a bit. I'll update you as things go on. I don't want to say too much now, except that it went well. I think your family is pretty similar to mine, in that they're getting excited from the get-go. Her mum is talking about wedding dates and stuff."

"That's Bengali mums for you," I say. "Do we have a name for this special friend?"

Jam grins. "Jammana."

M and I smirk at each other.

"You serious?" I ask. "Jamshed and Jammana? Jam and Jam!"

Jam squints. "Oh yeah, I hadn't thought of that."

I leave the boys to it while they watch TV. M insists on keeping H2 with them so I can nap. I can hear the TV blaring and it sounds like it's not a child friendly programme. Shots firing. The F word being thrown around loosely. I'm not sure if this is bad parenting on my part but the opportunity to lie down without a small person nuzzled into my chest is hard to resist.

I check in on the mums WhatsApp group.

Of course, there's new material.

Melanie: *Ladies, if you've not already got one, I can't stress how much the baby carrier is an absolute game changer! I've had Jasper in the sling while I managed to clean the kitchen, hoover up and I even did a little wee while he was sat on me. All the while, he slept!*

It looks like M and I might need a shopping trip soon.

12th July, Logistics

"**E**ven the most basic things are a mission," I tell M before he heads out. There's about 20 minutes before H2 wakes up from her micro nap so I might as well get my rant in while I can.

"What's the mission?" asks M, tying up his shoelaces.

"The dentist keeps bothering me to book my check-up. I'm well overdue."

"Why don't you book it?" M has momentarily forgotten that we have a hyper-alert baby that may not appreciate the sound of her mother's teeth being scraped clean. Then he remembers. "I can take the afternoon off. I'm sure work won't mind, as I've been there a few months now."

"Yeah… but the other thing is…" Oh, God, I feel so feeble even saying it. "My dentist isn't nearby. I registered in Blackfriars because it was the one nearest to my work, before I got made redundant, that is. So now I'd have to get the Tube and all that and-"

"Babe…" M comes and sits next to me. He places his hand on mine. "You're going to have to do this sort of thing. Unless you want to never leave Aldgate in the next few years, you'll have to take the Tube with the baby from time to time. You'll be fine. I've seen loads of mums do it."

M adjusts his shirt collar in the mirror. He looks so smart these days. It's hard to believe that just six months ago, he lost his contracting gig and his confidence. He let his greying stubble grow long. He didn't shower everyday. He wore well used, holey t-shirts. Now, he's got himself a good job and pulled himself together. With a small baby to support, I'm grateful for that. I just wish I could find my confidence, too.

I open my phone and dial the number for the dentist. It rings twice before I decide to hang up. I'll book an appointment later, when I feel more able to conquer the London Underground. I'm already overdue a check-up. What's another six months?

22nd July, Too much information

The upside of being at mum's? Some respite during the day as my mother helps with the mothering. The downside? Nosey guests popping round, unannounced.

Auntie Jusna has come over because, in her own words, she was dying to meet H2. She was so eager that she didn't even have time to call ahead. A bit of warning would have been nice. That way, I could have at least changed the top I've been wearing since yesterday. By that I mean I literally wore it through the night. My daywear and nightwear have officially become one.

Auntie Jusna has brought my cousin, Hassna, who has her own baby in tow. Well, Habib's grown into a toddler since I last saw him.

"I couldn't stop thinking about you. How have you been, all alone over there?" asks auntie Jusna, forehead creased up with concern.

"It's okay. I'm okay now. The birth was difficult because I lost a lot of blood and had a bad tear."

Auntie Jusna laughs nervously, mum shakes her head at me and Hassna looks sympathetic.

"That be shame. How long you stay for?"

I look to mum as she is the one hosting me. "As long as she needs," mum replies.

"Good! Stay for rest of month and recover!" says Auntie Jusna as though it's her house. "Your body need time to recover. Also, your mum and dad not able to go over much. You living so far away, alone by yourself. I was so sad for you when your mum told me they only stayed for a few days after baby was born."

Do not let auntie Jusna make you cry, I tell myself. *You're better than that.*

Auntie Jusna attempts to hold H2 but my baby starts screaming. She's got good instincts.

"Oh! She be naughty one. Hassna's boy go to everyone. Look at him, he's always smiling and happy and friendly."

Habib has taken over H2's play gym and is tugging away at the plush animals dangling from the bar.

"How much did your baby weigh?" asks auntie Jusna.

"Erm... 7lbs, I think."

Auntie Jusna nods. "*Acha acha,* quite healthy weight. Not as heavy as Habib but still okay. Did your in-laws come over to see you?"

"My mother-in-law came for a couple of days."

"Good, good. Did she cook for you? Hassna's in-laws gave so much curry when she had baby. I say, why give so much?"

I smile.

"And what did your in-laws gift baby?"

I turn to mum, who looks as uncomfortable with Auntie Jusna's quick-fire questions as I am.

Thankfully, baby H2 rescues the situation with a loud, wet fart. That's my girl.

"I better change her," I say.

Mum and auntie Jusna go to the kitchen to make tea and Hassna sits closer to me, unperturbed by the smell of H2's soiled nappy. "It's not such a bad thing being away from family."

"Really?"

"Yes," she replies. "You can raise your baby how you want. No one meddling. No one telling you how you should feed them or what you should dress them in. No opinion on how often to nap them and hold them and raise them."

She goes over to Habib, who is threatening to disembowel the fabric owl from H2's play gym. After a tug-of-war between mother and child, Hassna pulls Habib away, as he screams in protest.

"Enjoy this baby stage, when they don't fight back," Hassna says over her shoulder before she leaves with her screaming toddler. "Once they get a mind of their own and discover they can kick and fight, it's a whole new ballgame."

I ponder her point but, honestly, could it get any harder than this? Surely not?

"YOU SHOULD NO TELL everyone about your private business," says mum as soon as auntie Jusna and Hassna have left our house.

"What do you mean? What did I say?"

Mum giggles coyly. "You know, about your tear and things. That's your private part. You don't need to tell everyone how many stitches you had."

"Okay." I sigh. I hadn't even thought about that before. Since having H2, I've told anyone who cares to listen about the ordeal I went through. It's quite the dinner party conver-sation.

"These other ladies, they never tell about their business. We no know if Hassna ripped bottom or not. Some things are kept private. They no tell you, so you no need to tell them."

Mum goes into the kitchen with the empty cups and crumb-coated saucers. I cuddle H2 closer. Therein lies the problem. They don't tell us so we don't tell them. Us women keep these things quiet, buried, like some shameful secret. That is what hinders our healing.

I CALL MY MOTHER-IN-law with trepidation. I say this because, given that I'm only a 25-minute drive away from her, I feel like she's going to ask the inevitable.

"Will you come see us?"

Yep, she's asked the inevitable.

"I'm not sure, mum," I reply. "I just don't feel confident driving as I hardly drive in London and I've never been in my car with the baby in the back. Plus, it's quite hilly where you are."

My mother-in-law sounds like she's sipping something. I imagine it's tea. "Yes, yes. And no, no don't drive, if you no confident. It is hilly here. Don't want to be all bumpy with baby. Is my granddaughter okay?"

I check on H2 to see that she's managed to roll all the way from the ottoman, where I'm sitting, past the coffee table, to the opposite sofa. Bloody hell! That's a new skill.

Isn't she too young to master rolling? I don't know whether to be proud or scared.

"She is fine," I decide is the safest reply.

"Is she feeding well? Putting on weight?"

I don't know if M's mum is asking as a typical Bengali matriarch, or I will forever be answering these questions because I am the woman who couldn't feed my baby and had to take her to A&E just a few days after she was born.

"She's doing good. Her thighs are all chubby now."

My mother-in-law laughs. "Good, good! She should be a chunky monkey. Children should keep on gaining weight and stay chubby. Even when they start school."

"Erm... I'm not sure if they should when they're school age-"

"Don't talk silly! It annoy me when they keep talking about all this obesity, *mee-sity*. All my children were plump when they were in school. Nobody could say they didn't eat."

I don't know if that's a good thing or a bad thing. "Is dad well?" I ask.

"Alhamdullilah, he well. Just watching Bangla news."

"Who that?" I hear my father-in-law ask.

My mother-in-law responds to him, saying it's H2's mum. I better get used to that now. They say after children you lose your identity and start being referred to as the mother of your child. I hope that beneath this new label, there is a bit of me still left.

After we say our goodbyes, my phone pings.

It's Bushra:

Hey, I saw on your Instagram that you're back at your mum's. Well, I saw a picture of your baby's foot, anyway. When you gonna start showing her face? Or are you doing that preten-tious incognito thing that some celebrities do? Anyway, do you fancy meeting up? We can go Didsbury and find a nice cafe. I could do with speaking to you about Ahmed. Don't be annoyed with me, but I'm still not sure (embarrassed face emoji)

Normally, I'd admonish Bushra, asking her, what is there not to be sure about after all this time? I'd be having a word with her about stringing him along, while also extolling the virtues of the good guy versus the hot guy. However, the Ahmed factor is overridden by another issue.

How would I meet Bushra in Didsbury? Would it be fair to leave H2 with mum and dad? Will they be able to handle her? How would it work with all this sporadic breastfeed-ing? I still don't have a routine. As for taking her in the car... I technically could. I do have her car seat as that's what she came in.

Then again... I don't really know the roads there very well. What if I get flustered? Or my phone map decides to play up? There are too many questions and not enough an-swers. I know, deep down, I'm giving myself excuses to not do things. Shame on me, I was always proud of myself, the Asian girl that defies stereotypes. That built a career, that has her own money, that looks to a man for nothing. I used to revel in showing my white friends and colleagues how I was their equal. *Look! I can do all the things you can do.*

Now, such a simple task seems insurmountable.

I reply to Bushra:

I've got quite a busy couple of days before I go back to Lon-don. Perhaps another time?

"PUT HER DOWN," SAYS mum as she spies me holding baby H2's cheek against mine.

I can't help it. She's so squishy and adorable.

Honestly, motherhood is so messed up. In the day, I'm like a zombie, yet at night, I'm buzzing and I can't go to sleep. I don't know if it's the anticipation of a feed, or the worry that I'll squash her as we are bed-sharing, or just love hormones that come with being a mum but I find myself awake, embracing H2 long after she's fallen asleep, milk-drunk.

"You need sleep, too. You never know when she's going to get up next. Knowing this one, it will be very soon." Mum turns over and goes to sleep.

Having me stay over is hard for mum. Well, hard for the entire household, in fact. Dad has been carted out of the main bedroom, which houses a single and double bed (mum has always kept an extra bed just in case guests come, or my sisters stay over in the school holidays. I'm not sure if that's a Bengali thing, but hey). H2 and I have taken up the double bed, while mum is next to us on the single. So I've not been the only one getting broken sleep.

I reckon one person has been sleeping like a baby, and it's not H2. M is blissfully snoozing away in London, while I am here, up all hours with my baby. It's not fair, but this is my life now.

29th July, The cold shoulder

There she is. This is my chance to speak to Taslima. It'll be nice to have her round. It'd be nice to see more of her, especially as she lives on the same floor.

She's talking to Fabrizio at the front desk. As I get out of the lift, I make a beeline towards her. Actually, it's not towards her. I'm heading out of the door to a stay and play session. Though I wish it was a leave-your-kid-and-go-get-some-sleep-whilst-they-play session.

Taslima stops mid-giggle as she sees me in the corner of her eye, then she says to Fabrizio: "Right, I'll leave you to it."

"Yeah, and good luck with the private tuition. I didn't do that back in the day with my kids."

"It's all changed now," she says, stepping away from Fabrizio's desk. Is she trying to get away from him, or me?

"Hey, how are you?" I ask, trying to disguise any eagerness in my voice.

"I'm good. I'm just on my way to the Arabic class to collect my girls. I'll see you around."

See you around? Have I been reduced to an anonymous, faceless, nameless neighbour? What happened? What went wrong? Did mum put Taslima off when she popped round just after I gave birth? Was mum too strong, too forthcoming, in asking her to keep an eye out for me? Did Taslima feel burdened with responsibility? I can't see what else it could be. I thought we were friends. Or at least I thought we were becoming friends. *Why is she ignoring me when I need friends the most?*

I try to shrug off these feelings as I make my way towards the playgroup but it's hard. I can't help feeling like I've done something to annoy Taslima. Also, I can't help feeling annoyed at her, even though I don't have any right to be. She doesn't owe me anything.

Taslima is walking in the same direction as me, though she has paced ahead. I don't even bother trying to keep up with my bulky pram.

IT'S NICE TO SEE A familiar face at the stay and play group. Chandni is there with baby Rohan.

"His new favourite thing is biting everything. When he's not chewing on his fist, he's attacking the toys," says Chandni. As if to prove her point, baby Rohan gnaws on a plastic block. "And for that, I'm grateful I'm not breastfeeding."

"Oh yes, you get to escape the biting," I say. "I have been victim to my one clamping down when she's hungry. And I thought labour was the hard bit."

Chandni takes the block from Rohan. He replaces it with a furry caterpillar toy. "God knows how sanitised these things are." She rolls her eyes. "Good for the immune system, I guess."

"Oh, don't worry, mum," Liz, the playgroup lead, says. "We sterilise all the toys after each session."

Chandni stretches out her bottom lip as though she's been scolded. I giggle with her. It's like we're naughty school-girls.

"It's mad, isn't it?" says Chandni. "The labour pains, there's nothing quite like it. I ended up having an epidural and C-section but it wasn't for lack of trying. The things I went through. If I'd have known. I mean, really known what it's like, who knows what I would've done." She looks loving-ly at her son. "I wouldn't change a thing, obviously, but it's not to be underestimated how much we go through to get here."

Chandni makes me think back to my labour, which I still haven't quite gotten over. I stopped journalling about it but occasionally at night I find myself wincing, reliving the expe-rience. I have moments when I feel really sad, having enjoyed an intervention-free birth, only to end up having an epidural after H2 was born. I wonder whether I'll be scarred for life by my tear. I wonder whether time will heal all of this. Phys-ically and mentally. Everything still feels so raw.

"It's like an unspoken thing," I say. "My mum never told me how hard childbirth was. My sister did kind of warn me that you feel like you're dying but, as you say, you don't tru-ly understand that until you've gone through it. The weirdest thing is, people keep telling me that time will make me for-get and then I'll want another before I know it. I just can't imagine that. I remember saying to my husband when H2 was born, whether it would be selfish if we didn't have any-more and she was an only child. And there was me thinking I'd have three before I became a mum."

"I'm the same. I can't bear the thought of having another just yet. I'm still getting over this one."

Another mum sits next to us on the play mat. She has the longest black hair I have ever seen. I don't mean in a Rapunzel way. It's bedraggled and slung into a defeatist, low ponytail, one that is reserved for mums who don't have time to do anything else with their hair. And yes, since H2's been born, I'm sporting the exact same style. I wonder if she's Bengali.

Then, Liz welcomes her by saying: "Nice to see you again, Ruhela," and I feel fairly confident that she is.

I notice that we three are the only ethnic minorities in this group and we're all sat together. I hope the other mums don't think it's deliberate, because it's not.

Ruhela's son is older, he looks nearer to one. He nestles himself between his mum's folded legs.

Maybe I can make myself a little mum clique.

"How old is your little one?" I ask, confident the usual etiquette around talking to strangers in London doesn't apply in baby groups. Frankly, everyone attending is desperate for some adult company.

"Aadam is 11 months," she says, as her son loses his initial coyness and starts stomping around on the spongy play mat, dangerously close to H2's head, as she lies on her front, taking it all in.

"Congratulations, you've almost made it to a year and kept your baby alive!" I say. She looks at me funnily. I better ask something else. "How are you doing with the sleep? Does it get easier?"

Ruhela reacts as if I've asked her if the sky is blue. "Mine is fine. He never gave me any trouble and started sleeping through from the first 10 weeks. He loves his sleep, this one."

I sigh. "I can't get mine out of my bed."

This is greeted with a frown. "You want to get her out of that habit. I never had mine in my bed. I was too scared of squashing them, plus I didn't want them to get used to me. It's quite an Asian thing to do, isn't it? Bed sharing?"

I want to tell Ruhela that, though it may be an Asian thing, my mum never bed shared. She had me in a cot. So did big sis with her kids. Though this aside has made me think I should keep my bed-sharing ways to myself and not mention it to the NCT mums on the WhatsApp group. After all, I'm the only brown one there. I don't want to make myself stand out even more than necessary.

"How's the feeding going?" asks Chandni. "My Rohan was feeding well at first, now I can't get him to eat much beyond baby rice and pureed pear."

Ruhela furrows her over-plucked eyebrows as though our parenting struggles are alien to her. "My boy eats really well. He'll have anything. This morning he had two Weetabix and a banana."

I eat two Weetabix and I'm a full-size adult. How is her son eating that much?

She's about to let us know. "Because you're giving him purees, he's not eating much. The best thing is to do baby-led weaning, when you offer them chunks of food. I started with sticks of cucumber and he absolutely loved it. Purée is the old-school way. It makes kids fussy eaters later on, as they don't know about textures and flavours. You should definitely try baby-led. You might have more luck that way."

She goes over to Aadam who has knocked over another baby's wooden tower block.

Chandni and I, already questioning our parenting, are left feeling even worse. Perhaps I won't create a mum clique with this lady.

I REALLY SHOULD GO to sleep. It's 1am, and H2 has just finished her, I would guess, third feed of the night? Or was it her second? I don't know, it's all one big blur.

Anyway, instead of sleeping, I'm scrolling on my phone. It's pointless stuff about absolutely nothing that needs urgent attention. My work email barely pings these days. Vanessa has got it covered so well, I hardly need to check in. I just have to pay her invoice every month.

Social media is full of heartbreaking images. Grown men are crying at the sight of a food parcel. Children are cheering after being given a ladleful of watery soup. These scenes are punctuated with posts from fashion influencers dining at decadent restaurants, where the food is so plentiful that you know most of it will be thrown away at the end of the night. What a dystopian existence we are living.

Naila has a big bump now. She's posted a picture with her toddler son sitting atop her huge belly. Is that even safe? Her hubby, Darren, is stood behind her, looking lovingly down towards her bump while holding her at her hips. I could never get M to do a pose like that with me. Not for all the money in the world. He'd feel so awkward about holding my hips for public consumption. How does Naila get Darren to play along with this social media charade? I need tips.

Her caption reads: *My world,* except she couldn't be bothered spelling 'world' so she's used a globe emoji instead.

I see Bushra has posted an update. She is rarely on social media and has a private account that only friends can follow. However, she is happily posing with a new piece of jewellery. Is that a gold pendant? Is it a gift from a certain someone? A certain someone that used to work with us and that she was mortified about being set up with? I must check in on her and Ahmed and see if she's still having doubts.

My uni friends, Reena and Sonali, who both got married when I was heavily pregnant with H2, are posting on Instagram more frequently now. Reena has shared a picture from a date night at a sushi restaurant. Sonali is on holiday in Cancun. I shouldn't be jealous. It's their time to be loved-up and child-free and living their best life. I was the same once.

My phone pings. It's an update from the NCT mums.

Melanie: *How is everyone doing? I'll be honest, I'm really struggling tbh. Jasper's got his first cold. I felt so sorry for him constantly being snotty and crying that I ended up putting him in my bed. Something I thought I would never do! I'm tempted to sleep on the floor! Thankfully, it's Rory's shift in an hour.*

I look over to M, snoring away. I nudge him slightly.

Genevieve: *Do you guys take turns at night? That's so good! Because I'm breastfeeding, it doesn't really work for us.*

Me: *Me neither. I thought we would be over the sleepless nights by now.*

Melanie: *To be fair, my one is usually a deep sleeper. I think the dummy helps. But this cold has knocked us for six. How is everyone otherwise?*

Me: *All good here. I took H2 to a playgroup today. To be honest, it's more for me to get out as she doesn't play much.*

Melanie: *Good for you! And you should go out. She'll be getting something from it, believe it or not. They absorb everything at this early stage.*

Genevieve: *That is good. I've not been doing enough of that. Everything here is okay. It just gets a bit lonely sometimes.*

Lonely. *Lonely.* That's the feeling I've had since H2 has been born, though it's something I couldn't admit to.

Where does it stem from? That pride? That feeling that I can't admit my true feelings? I don't know if it's from childhood, when it wasn't cool to admit you're friendless. I applaud Genevieve for saying it. We need to have these conversations more. We need to hear that motherhood is lonely. Not just that it's amazing and magical and that we should cherish every moment because they'll be grown in the blink of an eye. That's what we always hear. We need more than that. We need to acknowledge the ugly truth. That most of the time, motherhood is really, really hard and almost all the time, it's achingly, bone-crushingly lonely. When I'm lucky enough to get a visit from Julia or see an old acquaintance, I feel like I'm only half there. My mind is concerned with H2. Is she okay? Is she about to cry? Does she need a feed? It's only when I go to playgroups that I talk to other mums who tell me that, yes, it's shit and they don't know when it will get easier. That's when I feel like I have some solace. And even then, all of it revolves around the baby.

It's such a weird concept, being lonely, when you are literally never alone. There's always a small person attached to you. However, why did I struggle to admit that, when it was so easy for Genevieve?

Perhaps due to fatigue, my mind spins me back to when I was younger. Primary school, in fact. I was the only brown kid in the class and I don't know if racism is learnt or innate but I felt different. The other kids knew I was different, as well. Most of them played together without me. Apart from Julia, of course. The only problem was, Julia would go on holiday twice a year, in term time. Those were the good old days when you wouldn't get fined for taking your kids out of school.

I remember walking around the playground, aimlessly, during the three weeks that she was away. It's not like we only played with each other, we had other friends. We played tag. But it was a very selective game. And without Julia as my ally, I didn't have the confidence to invite myself into other circles. They didn't ask me, either.

Mum spotted this early on, when she'd see me through the school fence at playtime. Or at hometime, when all the kids would race ahead of their parents, skipping and linking arms with each other. I didn't do that.

Mum started giving me extra pocket money, with a strict instruction that I can buy some sweets for my friends from the tuck shop. This was a novelty. Mum was generally quite tight with the purse strings. She had to be. There wasn't a lot to go around. For her to be so generous meant that she really knew I had to buy myself some friends.

I remember one day getting some strawberry laces. Amanda came over and asked if she could have one. Her parents are more strict with sugar, she said. Of course, I said yes. I wanted to be the generous and, hopefully by default, popular one. Like a less sinister version of the Pied Piper of Hamlin. Amanda pulled out a strawberry lace, only to find two more stuck to it.

"There's loads of sweets here!" she called over to her group, which comprised of Vicky, Jane, Kate, Ian and Jim. I think Jim was racist. Years later, he called me a Paki, then dismissed it as a joke.

They all gleefully took a lace out of the paper bag.

"Awww, is there no more left?" asked Vicky, as she was the only one without a lace.

I crumpled the bag and said no, hiding the last one. I hadn't had one yet and they were my laces.

She leaned closer. "Oh, there's one!" She spotted the last one peeping from the bag and pulled it before I had a chance to say anything.

Without so much as a thank you, they all ran away and played. So not only was I still friendless, I didn't even have any strawberry laces as a consolation.

Why do I recall that so vividly? Is it a core memory? I felt lonely then and I feel lonely now. Yet, nearly 30 years on, I still haven't figured out how to own it.

6th August, Daddy-daughter time

"**C**oochie coochie coo!"
Through the gap in the doorway, I bear witness to the most unusual sounds and sight from M. He's lying down on the sofa, holding H2 under her arms and gently bringing her back and forth towards him, so their noses touch. She's more animated these days and can bend her legs up and giggle back at him.

They are besties.

M has given me my usual Saturday morning lie-in, on account of me being up through the night with her every night. Usually I lay in bed, attempting to get some sleep but it never works. Once I'm awake, I'm awake. So instead of forcing a nap, I decide to see what the commotion is.

He is so playful with H2. He marvels at her round cheeks, little nose and chubby hands. Don't get me wrong, I love all those things. Her feet in particular, so squishy and small, are my personal favourite. However, my moments of adoration are fewer because most of the time I'm dealing with... all of it. And it is a lot. I think because I have H2 all of the time and M has her some of the time, he is able to enjoy her more.

He gets to drink hot tea at work. Pee with the door closed. He gets eight hours of what I now feel is absolute bliss. Staring at a screen and talking to grown-ups. He gets to wear fresh day clothes and proper PJs at night. He doesn't have the repetitive schedule of feed, change, nap unsuccess-fully, feed, change, nap unsuccessfully. Even so, despite all of this, my heart is happy that M and H2 have such a great bond. She really is daddy's special little girl.

I'm tempted to join them but as I see my baby go in for another nose bump, I decide to leave them to have their time. I can at least lie on the bed and scroll on my phone, attempting to fall asleep.

It turns out the phone isn't much solace. My Instagram feed must be reading my thoughts as it's now full of mums, looking blissful. One influencer captions her photo: *Two weeks postpartum and first dinner out.* She is standing in front of a grand building, which looks like it is in London. She's wearing a hot pink mini dress, which suggests she hasn't even given birth as there isn't an inch to pinch on her body. Who took the photo? Who is she out with? She sure as shit doesn't have a baby hanging off her.

Naila's feed is equally aspirational. She has violet contact lenses now. I guess she's working her way through the rain-bow. She's cuddled up on Darren's lap, as they look into each other's eyes. I wonder what uncle Tariq and auntie Rukhsana think of such public displays of affection for all the world to see? Then again, they're as technologically unsavvy as my parents, so probably haven't seen her social media posts. Per-haps I might have to accidentally show them when I'm at their house next. Yeah, I'm spiteful. What of it?

Every photo of hers is so carefully put together. Her clothes are always freshly ironed, or new. Her hair is nicely done up and she has a full face of makeup. Where does she find the time? Where does anybody find the time to do anything when they've had kids?

I flip over to my WhatsApp group. Let's see if the NCT mums are more supportive.

Oh, it looks like Genevieve has found a nanny. She said she is nervous about leaving her baby at such a young age but she's also looking forward to going back to work. Her husband will work part time from home, so there'll be someone in the house. I'm guessing Genevieve is the breadwinner.

Melanie says she's got her parents round, again. They forced her to go and grab lunch by herself. I can't remember what it's like eating food without having a bout of anxiety about a small person waking from her nap to interrupt me. And, honestly, my parents wouldn't need to force me to go for lunch. I would happily toss my baby over to them in exchange for a leisurely Caesar salad.

Claudia says she's got her baby sleeping through now. Blimey. How did she manage that? I have to find out more. I ask her what's their secret.

She replies: *We have a little routine where we give him a bath, then a baby massage. Then we take him into his cot and start singing lullabies to him. We stay near the cot but don't pick him up. He cried a little bit at first. It wasn't very nice but then he settled. Now he sleeps through. Thank God!*

Why do I struggle to leave H2 to cry? Is that the only way to get her sleeping better? Speaking of sleeping, I've been scrolling my phone for 15 minutes now. I really ought to either get up and start the weekend or attempt some shut eye. Though I doubt the latter is going to happen. I guess that's where H2 gets it from.

19th August, Casual colourism

"**C**an I hold her?" asks my oldest nephew.

I remember holding *him*. He was the chubbiest baby with the rosiest cheeks and the fairest complexion. Then he grew into a cranky toddler and now he's a monosyllabic teenager, with the hormonal acne to match. These are the most words I've heard from him in a while.

"Of course you can," I reply.

H2 is the star of the show during this trip to mum and dad's. So far, everybody has been scrapping over who gets to cuddle her. I don't blame them. Objectively speaking, she's adorable. Subjectively speaking, she's a sleep thief but also beautiful.

Seeing her surrounded by my nephews and niece, craning her little neck round as though she's surveying her subjects, my heart swells. I've always been the auntie. Now I'm like my sisters. I have one of my own. It's my turn.

"I couldn't imagine you with a baby, auntie," my niece says, letting H2 wrap her hand around her index finger.

"Neither could I. I was always the cool auntie. I still am now though, aren't I?" I say, very aware that my oversized check maternity dress won't give me any street cred.

The older two giggle and don't say a word. I guess I'm not down with the kids anymore.

"Auntie," big sis' youngest son bats his feathery eyelashes at me. "You know there's a new Kung Fu Panda movie out now, don't you?"

"There is a new one?" I ask. "The last one was out years ago."

"That's true." My nephew nods. "Do you think we could go and see it?"

I stroke his cheek, which is leaner than it used to be. "Oh, I'd love to but what would I do with the baby?"

He thinks for a minute. "Oh yeah, I guess you couldn't leave her, or could you? Could *nani* look after her?"

"I think it might be a bit too much for your grandma."

He looks down at his stripey socks. "That's a shame. The last one was so funny."

I think back to the time I took my all nephews and nieces, including middle sis' kids. I'd always take them to the cinema when they stayed over. It was my special treat. That movie turned out to be fun for me, too. "I remember laughing more than you guys. It was so funny."

My niece, who has now taken her turn to hold H2, asks me: "Auntie, would you ever be able to do the things you used to do? Like going to the cinema or taking us bowling?"

"I think I will, eventually," I reply, though I'm not sure when eventually will be.

"Are you kids bothering your auntie about Kung Fu Panda?" Big sis walks in, shaking her head. "I told you, she won't be able to do things like she used to before. We'll go and see it when we get back to Bristol."

"But we never go to the cinema. Dad is always busy working at the restaurant," says her eldest son.

Big sis ignores the gripes of her son and turns to me. "How is the little lady treating you? Is she sleeping through the night now?"

I wish people would stop bloody asking me that. Is it realistic that she should be sleeping through the night at this age?

"No, not yet," I say.

"Blimey, lady," big sis gasps unnecessarily dramatically. "She's still keeping you awake! I think all mine were settled by that age. After all, she's not a newborn anymore."

I glare at her. "Yes, but you knocked all yours out with formula and dummies."

Big sis' kids exchange nervous glances. I shouldn't have said that. It was unnecessary. I just take everything so personally these days. It feels like H2's lack of sleep is a blight on my parenting.

Then they come. The tears. Oh no! Not in front of big sis.

"Um... are you?" Big sis comes closer for a better look. "Are you crying?"

H2 even turns to gawp at me, while my nephews and niece look like they're mentally deciding who should leave the room first to escape the awkwardness.

"It's just... it's just really hard. I don't know why I keep feeling the way I do. Should I always be crying like this?"

Big sis pats my back. "Don't worry, lady. You're tired because kids are hard work. I think it's even harder for you because you're completely by yourself over there, without any family round."

This makes me cry even more.

"Oh lady, it's okay. You're not going doo-lally or anything. You just need to get on with it. Don't dwell on these feelings and don't overthink it. It's best to keep yourself busy and get on with it. Over time, it will get easier and she'll get older. And the cheeky blighter might sleep through."

"You think I'll be okay?" I ask.

"Well, you'll have to be, lady. What's the alternative? Getting all depressed by yourself over there? That won't help anyone."

Dad comes into the room to grace us with his presence. Oblivious to my tear-stained face, he goes in front of H2 and claps slowly to get her attention. She takes the bait, seemingly trying to copy his motion.

"*Eh yah! Eh yah!*" Dad makes the same nonsensical sounds that he made for all the grandchildren. Both he and H2 laugh together.

"Do you want to hold her, *nana*?" asks my niece, passing H2 over.

Dad takes H2 and holds her tight against his chest. He looks unsteady, which makes me terribly nervous. His legs buckle slightly. Dad's not as strong as he used to be when he would carry my eldest nephew on his shoulders. I tell him to have a seat on the sofa bed.

H2's spine seems to get stronger by the day. She lifts her head back to get a better look at dad, who smiles back at her.

I love their bond.

"She's not a fair one, is she? Not like all the other grandchildren," he says.

"Oh, dad." Big sis huffs. "That doesn't matter," she says, knowing full well that in the Bengali community, that shit still does matter. It even matters to her.

My nephews and niece, who are of various shades of beige, don't notice dad's colourism. They've heard it before. They're desensitised. I've heard it before too, plenty of times. When dad's previously said it about H2, I've pretended not to notice. However, this time, I'm wounded. Why? Because he did it in front of them. The lighter-skinned kids. Just like when I've been called dark in front of my siblings, the embarrassment, the pity and shame is magnified.

I wanted colourism to end with me. Being the only dark-skinned girl in my family, I felt it all my life. I figured after being married and M not caring about what shade of brown I am, I thought I was over all that. However, dad tossing that out so openly has brought me back to reality with a stark reminder that fair is indeed still considered beautiful.

I know dad doesn't mean it. I can see the way he's holding H2 that he loves her as much as all the grandchildren. It's just something he says. It's something all the older people say. It's just an observation. They don't know they've been colourist. They don't think anything at all. They just fail to realise that something they put out so casually is so loaded for me. Especially now, when pretty much everything triggers me.

"She's such a cutie, though," my niece offers in consolation.

20th August, Most unwelcome guests

I don't want to sound like an unsociable cow but does auntie Jusna deliberately coordinate her visits to my parents when I'm staying over? If so, I wish she wouldn't.

It's not like she's ever been a doting, loving auntie. Though you wouldn't know from the sweet honey that drips from her mouth.

"Oh, how are you doing? Your life has changed so much," she says, rubbing my arm while simultaneously rubbing it in that I'm a new mum with no life.

"Come on, mum, it's not like she's the first woman in the world to give birth," says auntie Jusna's eldest, my cousin Rashda. "You've got your own child at home, struggling with motherhood. I don't know why you act like it's such a surprise." She turns to me. "Honestly, I've seen Hassna more since she's had the baby, than when she lived at home."

Mum looks up from her cup of tea. "How long has Hassna been back?"

Auntie Jusna avoids eye contact. "Maybe few weeks. Not sure."

"Hmm." I can tell from that sound what mum is thinking.

Auntie Jusna looks out of the window. "Your bay tree is getting too big. Get my brother to trim it. Look, he's here now! Why you no trim the bay tree and kill weeds? You let them grow too much, they grow cracks in paving. Already got big gaps between slabs."

Dad, who only came in to exchange pleasantries before going back upstairs, looks wide-eyed. "*Eh-heh*. How I do this? My back hurt. Anyway, stay good. I go pray."

I'm pretty sure the next prayer time is not for another hour, but I don't blame dad for wanting to escape this group of women.

Then dad notices Rashda, who hasn't visited our house in years. "Are you well, Rashda?"

"Yes, uncle," she replies.

"And your husband? He well?"

Big sis and mum stare at each other. Auntie Jusna frowns while Rashda sips her tea. "As far as I know," she replies.

Having made things awkward, dad takes his leave.

Rashda changes the subject. "Did you drive here yourself?" she asks big sis.

"Oh no!" Big sis chuckles. "My husband dropped me off. I couldn't imagine driving this far by myself. That's what he's there for."

Rashda offers a wry smile. "I used to be that woman. Getting driven around. I couldn't imagine having to do it by myself, until I had to. Until my life as I knew it completely changed and I found myself divorced with three kids."

Everyone sips their tea in silence.

"Is he in touch with the kids?" big sis asks.

Auntie Jusna looks uncomfortable. The carefully curated vision of her family did not feature divorce.

"Yeah, he has them for the weekends and we alternate during the holidays. He does his best to shower them with gifts, while I have to be the mum and make the unpopular decisions, like telling them to do their homework or finish their dinner."

"How do the kids find it?" Big sis isn't done being nosey. "It's a big adjustment, after all."

Rashda looks down at her gold bangles. I'm not sure if they were part of her wedding jewellery. She twists them around her delicate wrist. She's still beautiful after all this time. Thinner, but still beautiful. She had scores of proposals back in the day. Not for a second did anyone think she'd be the one that ends up single.

"*Acha*, we must get going," says auntie Jusna. "We left Hassna alone with baby. Must go help her."

Once they leave, mum and big sis congregate around the table over tea, leftover biscuits and gossip.

Mum says: "Hassna been at her mum's for very long time. I wonder if she having trouble with husband? Every time I call there, she seem to be staying over."

"That is strange," big sis agrees. "Obviously, you won't get anything out of auntie Jusna. Did you see how quickly she got going when I asked Rashda about her marriage?"

"True." Mum looks smug. "She less nosey, now she got her own problems."

"You don't have to be so happy about it," I say. Big sis and mum look up at me, in shock. "The pair of you. Poking your nose in their stuff. Just because auntie Jusna's like that, it doesn't mean you have to be. I thought we were better than that. Rashda looked really uncomfortable when you kept asking about her marriage."

Mum nods. "Yes, yes. It bad to talk about other people. Say bad about them, same thing may happen to you."

I'm impressed at her back-pedalling.

"Blimey, lady, I didn't ask anything unusual! They're the general questions you'd expect to ask your cousin. It'd be weird if I didn't show any interest in Rashda's life. And you are just as bad, mum," says big sis.

"Eh? What I say?" Mum assumes her usual innocence.

Big sis carries on: "What is the consequence of me asking a few questions? They won't be as big as the consequences I faced growing up. Auntie Jusna used to say what she wanted, stir all the crap and get away with it. If it wasn't for her, I wouldn't have been packed off to Bangladesh to get married. If it wasn't for her, I would've been able to continue with my studies. If it wasn't for her, whispering poison in dad's ear, always saying things, I would've had a proper childhood. She literally had a bone to pick with everything. The time I permed my hair. The time I dyed it brown. I couldn't even be seen talking to a male classmate without being worried what people would say. It's always instilled in us to be ashamed and most of it came from her. And now her life isn't rosy and her daughter isn't having the perfect life, I'm supposed to sit quietly?"

"But her daughter shouldn't pay the price for her shit-stirring ways," I say.

Big sis huffs. "I shouldn't have paid the price for her stirring ways, either." She takes the last chocolate biscuit.

That was more than I expected but, right on cue, H2 starts crying. I guess she's had enough of being held by pre-teens in the front room.

As I reclaim my baby, I look at my niece and nephews. Big sis has made an amazing life for herself and created beautiful children but she still harbours feelings of resentment. Trauma and hurt from decades ago that haven't properly been addressed. That's the problem with my family. We don't talk things through. We don't hash it out. We don't expose our feelings. Our deep, dark feelings.

Mum has stuff, too. She's been wronged by dad's sister, so there is pleasure in the karma of seeing auntie Jusna's kids live not so perfect lives. And that is how the cycle of resentment-bitterness-stirring continues.

I think my entire family need to attend therapy. Myself included.

IT'S 11.30PM. H2 IS having what I'd call a nap, and she'll likely be up in about 90 minutes. I should really sleep too but instead I respond to the messages M sent hours ago.

M: *And how are my two favourite people?*

Me: *All good. We had some visitors today, auntie Jusna and my cousin, Rashda.*

M: *Is she the nice auntie or the stirring one?*

Me: *The stirring one. The nice one is auntie Rukhsana. Even though she's been a bit rubbish recently.*

M: *I know. I'm missing the curries. How is everyone else? Is H2 giving you some rest?*

Me: *No chance. She seems to be even worse here. Maybe it's a change of scene and change of bed. Plus, I don't have you to take H2 in the mornings.*

I wish I hadn't said that. I wish I hadn't said anything that might give M the opportunity to ask, or wonder, why mum doesn't take baby H2 off my hands. Even for an hour. Truthfully, I'm not sure why she doesn't. Though I have a feeling she's just tired. I've seen mum practically raise my oldest nephew. I can't blame her for wanting a break from grandmothering, though I wish the timing was different. Sometimes I wish I was the eldest and mum was young and fit and able to be hands on. I wish motherhood didn't come for me when mine and M's parents are old and it feels like I'm doing it by myself most of the time.

M: *Awww, you'll be home soon. I'm looking forward to collecting you guys on Sunday.*

Me: *Have you missed us? I thought you'd be enjoying the sleep.*

M: *The sleep has been good, to be honest with ya. I feel like it's the first time in ages I've had a full night's rest.*

Me: *You're not the one up in the night!*

M: *I'm not up in the night but I am being woken up as I'm in the same room and I hear her crying.*

I don't reply.

M: *There's some other news...*

Me: *What is it?*

M: *It's only Jam, finally sorting himself out.*

Me: *What do you mean? Is he getting married? To Jammana?*

M: *Yep.*

Me: *Blimey, I knew he was getting serious but I didn't expect that much progress.*

M: *Have you forgotten our wedding? Or every other Bengali marriage that is organised very quickly after the parents meet?*

Me: *True. When's the big day?*

M: *It's going to be early next year, I think. Which is a pretty long engagement for our lot.*

Me: *It is.*

There is a bit of stirring from H2, so I quickly plug in the pacifier, A.K.A me, and she settles back to sleep. Unfortunately, I need a wee but I can't move. Mum, on the next bed, is fast asleep and H2 is superglued to me. I'm stuck.

M: *Also, are you going to your parents' for the Christmas holidays?*

Me: *I don't usually plan that far ahead. But aren't we both coming up for the holidays?*

M: *Yeah, of course we'll go together. I thought I'd check if you want to have a longer stay at your mum's, that's all.*

Me: *I probably would stay a few extra days.*

M: *Cool.*

Me: *Is there a reason you ask?*

M: *There is (sheepish face emoji)*

Me: *Well, go on.*

M: *It's just, Jam was asking if I wanted to go away in December. Just for a couple of days to Germany. Not like a proper stag do or anything but it would be nice to get away. It'll be my first trip abroad since H2 was born. I figured you could stay at your mum's so you're not on your own.*

I don't reply.

M: *What do you think? Would that be okay?*

My initial thoughts are: *You've got a bloody nerve. You've not had a holiday? You've not had a holiday?! You're complaining of lack of sleep and lack of holiday and the lack of a break but I'm the one that's been dealing with this baby 24/7 and I've not had a single day away from her. Are you having a laugh? If anyone needs a holiday, it's me! I'm the one that's been breast-feeding round the clock and slowly losing my mind. So, no, you bloody well can't palm me off to my mum and dad's while you go on a jolly.*

Then I reply...

Me: *Yeah, that's fine.*

28th August, A jaunt through the city

I'm going to say it. Sometimes, just sometimes, I wish I was ill. Not seriously life-threateningly ill but poorly enough to justify being hospitalised. Maybe for a couple of days or so. That way, I could get complete, unadulterated sleep and a break from mothering.

Is that a bit messed up? It probably is. Anyway, enough about that. I'm going to take H2 on a jaunt. We'll walk towards Cheapside and I can show her my old workplace. I haven't told anyone I'm coming. To be honest, I'm not sure who will be in, given that I work in a co-working space filled with other small business owners. Though there won't be regular colleagues there, I am hoping to catch some familiar faces, like Benedict, the logistics guy who was going to buy my PR course (must chase him on that) and Neetu, who is probably back from maternity leave herself. She was due after me but I remember her saying that her mum will come over to help her look after the baby while she gets back to the business of selling curries. It must be nice having that support, not that I'm jealous or anything.

Speaking of not being jealous, the inspiration for this trip came from the mums' WhatsApp group. Melanie has started going back into her office for 'keeping in touch' days. She posted about peeing with the door closed and drinking coffee while it's still hot. While I will have no such luxury at my office, as I still have my baby very much with me, it will give me some sense of normality to see faces beyond mums, and M.

We walk down Fenchurch Street. It's a beautiful day. The sun is shining. The birds aren't singing, because there are no birds nearby as there aren't enough trees and it's far too polluted here. But still, the sun is shining.

H2 is now out of her bassinet and in a more open pushchair, so she can see more of the world. I've currently got her facing me, though she keeps tilting her head round the back of her seat to have a better view of her surroundings.

As we get to the traffic lights, a motorbike roars past, with its engine doing that juddering, farting sound. H2 jumps, her lips quivering.

"It's okay, it's okay, it's okay," I say, stroking her cheek.

What an absolute dickhead. Did he not see me with a pram? Did he not care?

I calm myself by taking a deep breath. Any tension I feel will be passed on to her. I need to be a calm mum, so H2 can be calm, too. It's hard as this goes against my very nature.

Okay, the next part of this jaunt is a bit tricky. The road towards Saint Mary's Axe has a steep, narrow, bumpy pavement. I never realised that before. I've walked across here countless times. Even in heels. H2's sturdy but chunky pram is more suited to the rugged open countryside, not narrow city streets. It's a struggle pushing it along, with the right side wheels half coming off the pavement. I heft the pram back up and level myself. God, it's hot. Why did I wear a thick top in August? Oh yeah, none of my summer dresses are nursing friendly.

I look at H2. She's scratching the back of her head. She does that a lot. Her skin has been quite dry lately. I've been doubling up on the coconut oil but it doesn't make much difference. Why are other babies silky soft, like the ones I saw in playgroups and the breastfeeding support group?

Oh God, I think H2's cut the skin on the back of her ear. She's bleeding. Are her nails really that sharp? Pushing the pram with one hand, I reach into my bottomless pit of a bag to find a wipe to blot the blood and emerge to find some men in suits in front of me. They're standing outside a pub. Shouldn't they be working? Then again, it's lunchtime. I've forgotten what the timetable is for the rest of the world since I've been in this mum bubble.

Pints in hand, not a single man moves out of the way for me. The tossers. I'm not getting onto the road. Not with a pram. I'm even hotter now. Damn this weather. Defiantly, I charge towards them like a bull. A couple of guys lean against the wall, looking rather put out by this brown lady pushing a pram. They look at me as though I don't belong, in every sense of the word.

"Don't worry, you're not in the way or anything," I say as I go past. Wow, that was bolshy of me! Would the pre-mum me have dared say that, especially when outnumbered? That's one plus of being a mum. When you've endured the ultimate pain of childbirth, a few lanky men in suits don't seem that intimidating.

We get towards the busy thoroughfare near Monument. Red buses are blaring past. Taxis are beeping away, annoyed with the cyclists in their way. Everything suddenly feels smoggier. I glance at H2, searching for signs of tears. She's looking around, wide-eyed and I can't tell if she's going to cry or smile. That reminds me, is there anywhere I could breast-feed if she needed it? When was the last time I fed her? Did she have enough?

A bout of panic rushes over me. I can't do this. It's not worth it. It's not worth going to see my old workplace. It's not worth going to see my old colleagues. Sod all that. I need to get back. This is a big enough step for me. I ventured out further into the city than I have in the last five months. This is progress. That's plenty enough. I've got nothing else to prove.

As I turn away, I feel a small sense of achievement but a bigger sense of disappointment in myself that this seemingly normal task other mothers are able to do, is so difficult for me.

7th September, Waiting on M

"**S**he is lovely!" says Marianne, the latest health visitor.

I like Marianne. Straight away, she wanted to cuddle H2, which gave me a much-needed break. Plus, she hasn't mentioned anything about sleep training yet.

H2 seems enamoured with Marianne's fire engine red hair, a shade you can only get from a bottle. I'm not sure if Marianne's got kids. I'm not sure if she's my age or younger but one thing I can tell is that she's a natural with my baby.

"I have to ask some questions and I know they're not very nice but we just need to go through them, is that okay?"

I know what's coming. "Yeah, sure."

"Right, so... how are you feeling?"

"I'm okay. Tired but okay. She doesn't really sleep much." I stifle a yawn.

As if on cue, H2 slides off Marianne and rolls onto the floor.

"I see what you mean about her being active. She won't need to go to Tumble Tots. She could teach the class!"

I smile. It's hard to offer much more in the way of small talk these days.

"She'll be sitting up soon, and then it'll be time to start weaning," says Marianne.

"Yeah, she'll be six months in a few days. I think I'll wait until the weekend to start weaning, when my husband is home to help me."

Marianne nods. "That makes sense. The weaning stage can be quite daunting but also fun. I can talk you through that if you like but first, I'll just go through this..." She looks down at her questionnaire. "This one isn't very nice but I have to ask... have there been any times when you felt down or depressed?"

I look out of the window. There's a new building going up across the road. Not a second goes by without the sound of drilling and buzzing. Our white windowsills are black with dust. I must have Ana, the cleaner, round again. There's plenty to clean, even though there's not much square footage to cover. My pokey flat has never felt this small. Since I became a mum, the pram has to live in the kitchen. There's nowhere else to put it. The bedroom is monopolised by the giant cotbed which H2 is yet to sleep in. Layers of clothes grace the heaters as we don't have a dryer or any outdoor space to hang the clothes. Who wouldn't be depressed in this environment?

Do I share all this with Marianne? Is it worth it? She's looking for an answer.

"It is hard," she says. "But if you are struggling, just know that it's very common. You'll have days when you can't even look at your baby, as gorgeous as she is. And it's okay. It's okay if you need five minutes when your partner gets home to go to the bathroom and lock yourself away. Because it can be quite intense when you've got her all the time."

I blink away what seems to be the formation of a tear. Please don't cry in front of the health visitor. Please don't. I managed to keep the tears at bay of late. I've had a good run. Let's not break it now.

I reply: "Sorry, hayfever. I am quite tired. And... if I'm completely honest, and I don't know how much this is normal... though it probably is, so I don't want to make a big thing out of it, it's just... I do find myself a bit anxious some of the time."

H2 plays *Wind the Bobbin Up* for the health visitor's amusement. Marianne smiles back at her, enchanted. How could I have any negative feelings towards someone so adorable? Everyone who encounters H2 falls in love with her. What is my problem?

I look at my daughter as she winds her hands together. Her tiny fingers look dry. I wish I'd slathered her in coconut oil before Marianne's arrival. I turn my attention to my own hands. I need to cut my nails.

"How often would you say you feel anxious?" asks Marianne.

All the fucking time, I want to reply.

"More often than not," I say, instead. "I'm guessing everyone feels like that when they've had babies, right?"

Marianne tucks her long fringe behind her ear. "If you want, I can visit you again in a couple of weeks, with a more detailed questionnaire. Again, it won't be very nice but it will help us determine whether your anxiety is normal worrying, or a bit more than that."

"And if it is more than normal?" I'm scared of the answer.

"Then we can look into options. You could do talking therapy, which is over the phone. That would be at a time that suits you and with a trained professional. You'd get to talk about your feelings. It's quite nice because it's somebody who isn't a friend or family member, so you'll feel less, perhaps, judged. But we can look at that if you need it. First, we should get the questionnaire out of the way. What do you think?"

Talking therapy? I always thought that was for people who are truly unhappy. I'm not sure about it but it's probably worth exploring what all these muddled feelings are.

"SORRY, BABE. I WAS going to get home earlier. I was ready to leave work and then Jam called."

Here we go.

"He said he was in London for one night only and asked if we could meet for some food."

"Have you eaten, then?" I ask.

"Not really. He wanted to go to the chip shop, so I had a couple of his chips, but I figured I'd eat with you at home." M looks towards the kitchen. "What's for dinner?"

I turn away from M. "I haven't had a chance to make anything. Every time I attempted to go to the kitchen to do something, she started crying. Your daughter wants me to be no more than one foot away from her at all times, even when she doesn't want holding. You would've been better off eating with Jam."

"It's alright," says M. "I can go out and grab something for both of us."

H2 has rolled near the radiator and is playing with a hairball. I take it off her before she puts it in her mouth.

"How is Jam?" I ask, despite not being bothered for the answer.

"He's a bit stressed, to be honest with ya. They're at that stage of wedding planning where they talk about how much money he should give her. Apparently, her dad is demanding 15K."

"Blimey, that's a bit steep. Or is it? I remember when we got married, I wasn't even bothered about how much you gave, as I've got my own money. Maybe I was being naive and selling myself short."

"Nah, I knew you were a keeper from that moment. Jam's dad is panicking over it as he'll be the one paying for it, even though Jam's offered. He's paid for all his other kids and, out of pride, he won't want Jam to pay for himself."

"Does Jam's dad have £15,000 lying about?"

M huffs. "I doubt it. But you know what it's like with Bengalis. Gotta save face."

"What will they do?"

"Jam being Jam, he'll stress about it for a bit but then he'll agree. He's waited long enough to get married so he won't call things off over money."

"And there was me thinking men held all the cards."

M picks up H2 and blows raspberries at her neck. "When this one's grown up, it'll be completely different. Most of these traditions will be gone." M looks to me. "Are you okay?"

I sigh. "I'm just tired. When you get home after 8 o'clock, it's hard because it doesn't leave much time for me to get a break."

M sits next to me with H2. "I know, babe. Has she slept much today?"

"Not really."

M looks stern, which isn't his default mode. "Do you not think we should try and get her used to sleeping longer, without you needing to feed her all the time?"

"You don't think I've tried?"

"I mean, more than that. Like leaving her to cry for a bit. She is nearly six months old now. How long can you walk around like a zombie? It's not good for you or her."

I don't respond and instead peel the end of a nail that has come loose on my index finger.

M puts an arm around me. "Just think about it. Anyway, I'm here now so why don't I help you with the bedtime routine? Or at least pretend like we've got one."

I nod.

"Cool, and I'm sorry babe, but I need to-"

"Go to the toilet?" I interrupt. "I could've guessed."

"I'll be as quick as I can," M says, taking his phone with him.

24th September, A sleepless night

"Hello... what you doing?" asks mum.

"Erm... you called me 10 minutes ago. Have you forgotten?"

Mum gasps. "Did I? I didn't realise." She giggles. "Anyway, what you doing?"

"The little minx is napping, so I'm lying down with her, even if I won't fall asleep. I spent the morning trying to encourage her to sit up."

"Sit up? Is she ready? Don't make her do anything unless it be safe," mum warns.

"Obviously, mum. She is nearly six months old now so she's ready to sit up. I put plenty of cushions around her, don't worry. It'd be nice to not have her on me, or rolling around into dangerous places all the time."

"That be true but just make sure you support her with lot of pillows."

"I know, mum. I just said that."

"Okay, no worries. What she doing now?"

"Mum! I just told you she's napping!"

"Okay, okay. I no disturb you. You go get some rest, okay?"

"Alright, mum. I'll speak to you later."

I know I should get a nap with H2. Even if it's just for 10 minutes. However, I'll quickly check my group WhatsApp to see if there's anything new...

I SHOULD'VE KNOWN. Of course, the nighttime would be horrific. When exactly does it start to get better?

H2 has decided she wants to be fully awake. Now, I wouldn't mind if she'd be content with playing with her feet, lying down or practicing sitting up without me. However, she wants me to cradle her and walk around the flat. Any attempts to even sit on the bed have her crying and bobbing her head up and down in a bid to get me moving again.

This is madness. Is she teething?

Worse still, there is the constant white noise of M snoring in the background.

"This is ridiculous!" I shout, in the hope that my sleepy husband will wake up.

He's still snoring. God, I hate him sometimes.

I hover near his head. H2 is gargling and making weird baby noises. Some drool drops from her mouth and lands on M's neck. That ought to wake him.

Nope, he's still asleep.

"Can you believe this?" I say.

He wrenches his head up, startled. "Huh? What?"

"She's been awake for the last hour. I don't even know how you sleep through it?"

"Just put her down!" M turns his head the other way.

"Every time I put her down, she cries."

M, face muffled by the pillow, says: "Then let her cry. She needs to learn to settle herself now. It's been going on for ages. Every other baby seems to sleep through. Why is it so hard for her?"

I don't have a response. Does every other baby really sleep through? Is this not normal behaviour?

"Let me try and feed her." I place H2's head near my chest. She pulls away and cries some more.

M gets up out of bed. This is a first. "Give her to me."

"No, it's fine. I'll settle her."

Despite my plea, M takes H2 out of my hands. He goes into the living room, slamming the door. I hear crying. Excessive crying. Wounded, tears of trauma. I can't take this. It's like an alarm. An emergency siren I must respond to. Why doesn't M feel the same way about H2's crying? How is he okay with it? How does he sleep through it?

I can't leave H2 with him. God, why did I say anything? Why did I wake him up? He's got work tomorrow.

I try to ignore the cries and check my phone. I send a message to the group.

Me: *A bit of a rough night here. H2 has been awake for the last hour with no sign of going down. Please tell me it's not just my baby that's on one tonight?*

It doesn't take long before someone starts typing.

Genevieve: *I feel your pain. Not quite sure how I'm going to survive the night. I had to hand my baby over to my husband as I couldn't take it anymore. I can hear her crying but I just need to sleep. I've got my back-to-work day tomorrow morning.*

Genevieve has entrusted her little one to her husband. I need to do the same. I need to relinquish control. I need to block out the noise.

She's still crying. There's no way I can listen to this and go to sleep.

Please just stop crying. Please just settle to sleep, I whisper to myself and say a prayer.

Still more crying. I can hear M shushing her loudly. That will make her cry even more. Shushing doesn't work for adults. It's certainly not going to do anything for a baby.

I can't take this anymore. I go into the living room to see H2 nestled on M's shoulder, crying her eyes out. At least she's being held, even if she's not being carried around, as she would like.

"What are you doing? Go back to bed!" says M, with more anger in his tone than I am accustomed to.

"I'll take care of her. You've got work in the morning."

"No, leave her. She'll eventually fall sleep, crying. Then she'll realise she can't always have her way."

"Have her way? She's a baby! She's not trying to manipulate you."

I scoop H2 into my arms and she momentarily stops crying, because I'm stood up. Little cow.

"See! Are you going to walk with her the entire night? You're making a rod for your own back. If you keep getting up every single time she cries, she'll never learn to settle."

I walk out of the room, uneasy about M's angry voice. As I leave, I hear M slam the living room door shut. I lay down with H2 in bed. I nurse her back to sleep. She sounds like she's shaking, distraught.

M walks into the room. "If you keep doing that, that's all she's going to want all the time. And you're never gonna get a break. You're always gonna be moaning."

I say nothing, while M grabs a pillow and takes it into the living room. A stray tear falls from my eyes and lands on baby H2's cheek.

25th September, Aftermath

My mother-in-law calls. "What you make today?"

That's all she cares about. No questions about me, the state of my mental health or my daughter. She wants to know if I've made a curry for her precious son to eat.

"I haven't had a chance to make anything today," I say truthfully, for a change.

"You all have to eat! Make something when she naps."

"She barely naps."

"That be because you breastfeed! She never be full. She always hungry."

I say nothing.

My mother-in-law mutters something, likely to my father-in-law, then says: "You young people. One baby and whole home fall apart. I had four kids and managed to cook and clean and my babies all slept."

And just for that, once this call is over, I will buy myself a portion of chips and eat most of it before M gets home. Yeah, I'm petty like that.

H2 IS DEFINITELY READY for solids. She is sniffing around my chips like a hound. She can think again if she expects me to give her a greasy, deep-fried potato. Her first meal will be something more age-appropriate, thank you very much.

I hear the door lock twist open and my stomach lurches. I know it's M. My M. Except it's not the same. Things are different. We haven't spoken since he stayed on the sofa last night. He left with a grunt this morning. I'm hoping he's not moody. I could do without it.

He comes into the living room. "You alright?" he asks me without making eye contact.

"Yeah, I'm fine. Do you want some chips?"

"In a minute. I just need to poop and shower first. It was boiling on the Tube."

Damn M. That'll be another half an hour. The tension is killing me. We need to sort this out.

H2 is still sniffing around my food. I'm tempted to give her one, but the heady concoction of salt, vinegar, and overused cooking oil will probably be too much for her underdeveloped pallet.

M comes out of the bathroom quicker than usual. Maybe he's ready to talk, too.

He takes H2 out of my arms and sits with her on the adjacent sofa. He kisses her on the head and asks her about her day. Wouldn't it make more sense to ask me, given that I'm the one that can verbalise? Oh well, I shall save my internal snark for later.

"So last night..." I begin.

"Yeah..." M still doesn't look at me.

"You really went for me."

M looks up. Usually, he is full of apologies when we have disagreements. This time, he says: "It's because you make things more difficult than they need to be. H2 isn't sleeping properly because she's used to sleeping on you. That's why everything is more difficult. You've made things harder. You didn't want to give her the bottle, even though she was ill from not being fed properly. You didn't want to give her a dummy. You struggle to put her down. How is she going to get used to sleeping through, or sleeping better, at least, if you don't give her a chance to settle herself?"

Settle herself? That sounds like a learned term. Has he been speaking to some dad at work about this? Or his friends who have kids?

"I do try to settle her. I've tried different things, like putting her down and then picking her up when she cries."

"You need to stop picking her up, then! I have to go to work in the morning. It's a new job. I still have to prove myself because with you barely working, I can't risk being made redundant again. You made that pretty clear before she was born, if you remember."

I think back to that fateful argument on the bus home from the NCT class, when I was 38 weeks pregnant. So much was said. So much resentment spilled over. M was out of work. I was stressed about the future. Now, I feel like he's throwing all of it back in my face.

Usually I'm the one filling the gaps. Usually I'm the one not short of a word or two. This time, with my depleted mental and emotional resources, I'm speechless.

Instead, the words are left to M: "You can't have it all. You can't get annoyed with the way I do things. You're not the only parent here. There's two of us. And you can't get annoyed at me for not being able to get up in the night with her. I'm the one going into work. It's not easy."

"It's not easy for me, either. Doing all this. It's not easy."

M shrugs. "It's kind of your job now. Isn't it?"

His words wound me. M, my M, how could he say that? Is that fair?

His job is paying for the roof over our heads. My job is keeping our baby alive. His job is 9 to 5. Mine is 24/7. He can close the door on his job at the end of the day, my door is always open. He has a distinct line between his work and personal life. My whole entire life is consumed by this little one. I have no boundaries. So what kind of job is that? Where is my respite? Where is my lunch break? Tea break? Where are my workers' rights?

Of course, my brain doesn't work like that. I can't articulate these mushy thoughts, so I do what I've been doing ever since H2 was born. The only thing I can do in this situation. I cry. I cry like a baby.

H2, sensing the tension, starts crying, too.

M comes over, with H2 in one arm. "I know you're tired and stuff. And I didn't mean to be a dick. It's just that you can't go on like this. I know it's hard, but we have to try and find a way to make it work."

He put his arm around me. I don't resist. Even though in my mind, all I can think is... bastard.

6th October, Weaning

Even though we're sort of not friends, M and I have joined forces on one thing. Weaning baby H2.

Today is the day where she gets to try her first solid food.

I know baby-led weaning is all the rage. The health visitor told me we should start giving her things that she can grab with her own hand and feed herself. However, I have decided that is the way to anxiety for my already-fraught self. Therefore, I'm going to do what parents did since time began... I'm going to start with purée.

My mush of choice is porridge. It's wholesome, filling and doesn't require any blending. Winner.

I say, *Bismillah*, as I put the soft plastic spoon towards H2's lips. She gets fed up with my dithering and grabs the spoon with her chubby fist and clamps it in her mouth. That's my girl.

"Okay, so can we call porridge a success?" I ask.

"I think so," says M as he strokes H2's chubby cheek. "My little food hoover. Can I have a go?"

"Be my guest," I reply.

M tries to wrestle the spoon from H2's hand but she's gripping it tightly. She then rubs the remnants of porridge around her cheeks.

"I'll get another spoon." M heads to the kitchen.

I grab a wet wipe to clean her cheek, then I notice something.

"Have a look at this," I tell M. He comes back with an orange spoon that matches H2's tiger-emblazoned feeding bib. "The side of her mouth is all bumpy."

M lifts H2's chin for a better look. She is itching the area. What could that be?

"Do you think it's because she wiped the porridge on her face?" asks M.

"Maybe but why would porridge cause her to react like that?" The raised little red bumps around her mouth have spread across her cheek. I don't like this. I don't like this at all.

M unclips H2 from her feeding chair and takes her near the window. I'm not exactly sure what that's going to do. I can't imagine the London smog is going to help. He then takes her to the kitchen and pats her face with cold water. The redness doesn't fade but it doesn't seem to be getting worse, either.

"Do you think it was an allergic reaction?" I ask.

"I doubt it. It's probably just her body adapting to something new. Let's try with something different, maybe tomorrow."

I hesitate. "When you're in work?"

M scratches his head. "Maybe not tomorrow, then. There's not a timeline on these things, is there? We'll do it next weekend."

The bumpy redness on her cheek slowly subsides. I rinse the porridge bowl and try to wash away any worries about whether feeding her so infrequently would be detrimental to her development. According to the mums on the WhatsApp group, they started feeding their kids a variety of things every single day. Blooming Claudia's baby is on three square meals, pretty much.

As I sit next to M on the sofa, he rubs my hand. "Don't worry. We'll try again."

I smile at him. Though, deep down, I'm very worried and also not his friend yet.

18th October, A trip to uncle Tariq's

Gosh, I've never felt so popular in my life. H2 has, so far, given me 30 minutes respite by napping (is that a record?) and while I spend it wisely having a much-needed shower, my phone keeps buzzing away with correspondence.

I hurriedly check my messages before she wakes up:

Julia: *Hey I know you've got your hands full with H2, but when you get a second, I'd love to get your thoughts on a wedding venue. I'm in love but Miles isn't totally convinced yet.*

Bushra: *Oi, stranger, what you doing? I never hear from you these days. I wanted to speak to you about Ahmed. Honestly, it's so confusing and I'm still not sure how I feel about him. I know you're mad busy these days but I'd appreciate a chat.*

Sophia: *Hi hon, how are you? Just checking to see how mum life is going. Have you started weaning yet? Let me know and if you need any advice, I have a few books on baby-led weaning.*

I'll have to message the girls later, when I have time to reply with something meaningful.

I hear the front door open. M is weighed down with sweets, crisps and bottles of fizzy drink. Sadly, none of it is for me.

As if one baby wasn't enough, we're going to visit another. Naila has given birth to another boy, Zayn. She is currently staying with uncle Tariq and auntie Rukhsana, so M, H2 and I are making the once familiar trip to their high-rise flat.

Second time around, there is no cellophane-wrapped gift hamper. Ain't nobody got time for that shit. Instead, I ordered a pack of three baby grows with matching bibs and have put them in a shiny red gift bag.

We've barely got through the door of uncle Tariq's flat and I'm already pissed off. The last time I saw a postpartum Naila, she looked exhausted and fed up. Truth be told, I preferred her that way. It was the opposite of the highly polished, highly filtered avatar she posts online.

Today, having only recently left the labour ward, she looks fantastic. You wouldn't guess she's had a baby and she certainly doesn't look like she's losing any sleep. Or dealing with the breastfeeding sweats, like I did. Naila is as fresh as a daisy. I bet if I ran a tissue under her armpit, it would come back dry. It's not fair.

Maybe it's easier second time round? Maybe once you've had the shock of the first baby out of the way, there are no surprises when you have another.

"How you been, man? It's been time," she says, pulling me in for a hug. She smells of perfume. Expensive perfume.

"It has been a long time. So long that you've had a baby in between."

"Yeah, I thought I better get it over and done with while mum is still young-ish and able to help."

Auntie Rukhsana is currently changing baby Zayn's nappy on their ornate fabric sofa. Would it be rude to ask her to change H2's nappy while we're here?

"Right, let's have a look at her," Naila grabs H2 from me and examines her, as though she's a dress on a hanger. "Yep, still looks like her dad. Not that it's a bad thing!" she says, looking over to M, who is sitting on the other end of the sofa, as far away from the nappy changing activity as possible. He doesn't say anything. He is too busy watching the football on his phone. I think he mentioned something about this visit clashing with the Liverpool game.

Naila puts H2 on her hip. Her nails are really long and painted burgundy. How does she change nappies? I never paint my nails or wear them long and since having H2, I've ditched my wedding and engagement ring. It's too much of a bother. I look in the mirror that's above the throne-like sofas. My nursing tunic is bobbly. I wore my hair in a low-slung mum ponytail, my new style of choice, or circumstance. And, to my horror, there's a white hair poking out behind my ear. The pre-mum me would've freaked out at the sight of it, Googling furiously for natural remedies for grey hair. Now, I just don't have the time. I've let myself go. I wish I got my eyebrows threaded before I came. I wish I'd done something to make myself look a bit more presentable.

"My girl is here. My girl is here." Uncle Tariq comes in, having ended his night shift as a cabbie. "Two girls, now." He strokes H2's face with his nicotine-stained fingers. He then places a hand on my head. "I got chocolate for little one. Shall I give her this now?"

"Oh, she's hardly eating solids, so probably best not to give her sweets yet."

Uncle Tariq pulls a fun-sized Snickers bar out of his pocket. "Are you sure? She can have small taste, maybe?"

"Dad, you can't give that to a baby!" Naila yells. "We shouldn't even have that in the house. You know Ibrahim is allergic to peanuts."

Uncle Tariq shrugs. "What silliness! That's nothing. We all had peanut growing up. In Bangladesh, they sell chilli peanuts on every corner."

"We've talked about this, dad. It's not Bangladesh here. Your grandson is allergic. I'm not messing about. He has EpiPens for a reason."

Blimey, Naila's eldest is severely allergic to peanuts. I must speak to her about this in more detail, as I still have the lingering worry about H2's reaction to the porridge. But given that it's gone 2.30pm and I'm ravenous, I head to the kitchen to see what auntie Rukhsana is doing.

She is adding freshly chopped coriander to a platter of roast chicken.

"Auntie, there's no need to do all this. It's just us."

"Nonsense! I need to feed you up. You be looking so skinny now. Make me sad."

"I have lost a bit of weight. You should come round. I miss seeing you. And the baby would like to see my only auntie in London." I don't mean to lay on the guilt trip so heavily, or for the desperation to come through in my tone.

"Sorry, my dear. Now Naila has had baby, I haven't had chance to breathe. Before that, for past six months I had older one three days a week as she go work. Honestly..." auntie Rukhsana leans in, "you think you get rid of them when they get married. But they keep coming back. Like boomerang..."

She turns back to the cooker and switches the heat off what looks to be meat and potato curry. M will be delighted.

Auntie Rukhsana hands over a bowl of water for M to wash his hands, as he is far too important to go in their tiny kitchen like the rest of us.

"Oh and we have special guest today." She grabs the roast chicken platter to take through to the dining room. "Naila husband coming, and your cousin, Rashel. I asked his brother, Rashid, to come also but he got plans this weekend."

I haven't seen Naila's brothers for years. And I've never seen Darren at my uncle's house. This is going to be quite the lunch party.

THE THING WITH HAVING a six-month-old that doesn't want to be held by strangers, means that M and I must eat in shifts. This is in spite of uncle Tariq's insistence that we put her down on the sofa, squashed between cushions. I tried this approach but H2 was having none of it. She was already unsure of her surroundings on arrival and didn't want to be palmed off so her mum and dad could have a decent meal together for the first time in months.

In accordance with Bengali patriarchy, the men are seated first. It's not fair. I'm the one that's lactating and I'm starving.

I'm half listening to Naila talk about the benefits of micro-blading and half ear-wigging the conversation amongst the men.

Naila's older brother, Rashel, is talking tech. "It's definitely worth getting one of those hands-free kits. Now I'm not living in London, I have to drive a lot for work and mum calls me like, every hour, to make sure I've eaten and check what I'm up to. With hands-free, I can do my son duty and speak to her while travelling between client visits."

"What do you do?" asks M.

What commences is what I would call brown noise, where Rashel explains, in great detail, what he does but I don't understand any of it. I can't blame it on mum brain either, as M looks just as confused. Some kind of travelling salesman, I think?

"And what about you?" M asks Darren, who so far has been quiet at the table, tentatively feeding baby Ibrahim rice with a spoon, whilst having forkfuls of his own dinner. That's right, Darren is using a knife and fork to eat curry and rice. How blasphemous. I wonder what he makes of everyone else around him, scooping up little mounds with their hands?

I can't see Darren as he's got his back towards me but I notice him shake his shoulders, nonchalantly. "Nothing much. This and that. Naila uses up most of my time, getting me to take her photos."

Naila sits up, having heard her name in vain. "You love it really, babe. It keeps things fun. Like that time we took a picture on top of the Burj Khalifa and we had to elbow those other influencers out of the way to get the best shot."

Darren turns around, cheeks flushed from either embarrassment, or too spicy a curry. "That was a good trip, mashallah. We should go again soon, inshallah."

"Fat chance with these two little ones." Naila snorts, whilst looking down at baby Zayn.

"You never know. At this age, they're easily transportable, mashallah," says Darren.

M looks at me and smirks. I reciprocate. Gosh, I think that's the first time we've shared a joke together, and it's all thanks to Darren's many blessings.

Auntie Rukhsana comes in with a replenished bowl of roast chicken.

"You want?" she asks Darren.

He puts his hands up and shakes his head. "No, not for me."

"Come on, have some!" She loads his plate with a chicken leg. "You need to get bigger, like this *damand*." She nods towards M, who sits up straight in his chair, inhaling to pull his stomach in.

"Eat more rice?" uncle Tariq says to Darren, with a scooping motion to his mouth, even though he's speaking in perfect English. There's no need for accompanying gestures.

Darren puts his hand to his chest. "No, thanks, dad. I eat enough, alhamdulillah." He rubs his flat stomach to emphasise his point, just in case it gets lost in translation.

Uncle Tariq smirks and says to M, in Bengali: "He's a good man, mashallah. Even if English."

M nods back. "Mashallah."

I always wondered what it would be like when Darren eats at uncle Tariq's house. Now I know.

My tummy is rumbling and so is my daughter's, apparently, judging by the way she's tugging at my tunic. It might be worth taking H2 into a bedroom for a feed, given that I won't be eating lunch any time soon.

Naila follows me with baby Zayn.

"You're so good for breastfeeding. I couldn't hack it," says Naila, offering Zayn a bottle.

"It was hard at first," I say, "but now it feels easier than having to take formula everywhere. Believe me, this is one of the few easy things about motherhood."

"I know, right?" Naila sits cross-legged and puts Zayn down on the bed. She continues feeding him, then slowly lowers the bottle onto a pillow next to Zayn, while he's still sucking on it at an angle. I've never seen that before. "Nobody prepares you for how bad it's gonna be. I thought I was losing my mind half the time. It's the lack of sleep."

"And anxiety," I add. "I'm always worried about something or other. The latest one is whether she's allergic to dairy."

H2 senses that we're talking about her as she pulls up the feeding apron I'm wearing. Oh well, it's only Naila. It's okay to flash another mother.

"If you think she might be allergic, push to get her tested. Go to your GP. I found out that Ibrahim was allergic to dairy and peanuts after we started weaning him."

"And what was his reaction?" I ask.

"Swelling. His lips got bumpy and his eyes puffed up. It was scary shit, man. Now, I have to be extra vigilant with everything he eats. I make sure there are no peanuts in my house. Obviously, when I come here, dad pretty much forgets all the time. But that's a Bengali dad thing. Allergies weren't really heard of when we were growing up, were they? I don't think our parents had half the worries we do."

I shrug. "I guess it was a different time."

Naila checks herself out in the mirror. She needn't. I can tell her she looks immaculate. "We just lived our lives. None of us had much but we were okay. We played outside all hours. Even here, in east London, everything felt safe. Now you've got online bullying, gangs, all sorts. It's like the worry won't end, even when they're not babies." Naila sighs. "Mum and dad had different worries. Like who we'll marry. Will they be the right person? Appropriate for the community? They still got that worry now..." she lowers her voice to a whisper, "with my brothers."

"I didn't want to ask but are either of them looking to get married?" I'm surprising myself with how old-fashioned I sound.

Naila pushes her hair behind her ear. "Who knows? Neither of them live at home so we hardly see them apart from a quick visit on Eid. Plus, they don't tell us anything. Mum and dad know better than to ask. I guess it was a shock enough when I ended up marrying a white guy. I don't think they can cope with any more surprises. If they don't ask, they don't need to know. Like I say, they have different worries. Theirs is more around society. I tell mum to just be grateful if they even bring a girl home, regardless of race or religion. In this day and age, even that's not guaranteed."

H2 has fallen asleep mid-feed. I unlatch her and she rests her face against my chest. She's so peaceful, with milk remnants around her mouth. In years to come, I'll be worrying about her finding someone, just like mum worried about me. It's impossible to imagine now. It seems so far away.

"I guess, no matter what age our kids are, we'll always worry," I conclude.

Naila rolls her eyes. "Welcome to motherhood."

I lay H2 on the bed, far enough from baby Zayn that she can't roll onto him. "You seem really settled second time round," I tell Naila.

"That's coz I've been there, done it and got the t-shirt. I know what to expect. When Ibrahim was born, I was a total wreck. I swear I had depression or something."

"Really?"

Naila shrugs. "Probably. Or the baby blues. I dunno. It was just a lot, you know."

I nod. "Did you do anything about it? Like get help?"

Naila looks at me as though I've asked the unthinkable. "What, like, antidepressants or therapy? Nah, man. I didn't fancy that. I just got on with it and before I knew it I was back to normal. Why? Are you feeling depressed?"

Naila leans forward, like she wants the gossip. I lean back and build my wall up. "No, I'm fine. I was just wondering, that's all."

ON THE DRIVE HOME, H2 falls asleep, leaving me the opportunity to reply to the messages from earlier.

First of all, I respond to Julia's text:

Hey, would love to know about the wedding venue. I'm sure it'll be very swanky, knowing you! I'm free to chat whenever.

Damn, I didn't mean to sound as if I've got literally nothing going on. I send a follow-on message:

PS. we might be interrupted by a small person, who barely gives me a chance to get a word in edgeways, but yeah, let's try and speak.

Next, I reply to Sophia:

Hey, I just knew you'd have all the books. Maybe I can catch you when I'm up north again?

Must ask something about her, so it doesn't seem like it's all about me.

P.S. How are you guys doing?

Finally, it's the turn of Bushra. As her married, responsible mum friend, I have to share some words of wisdom. I need to offer a considered response, something that will guide her on this very important next stage in her life, and help her decide whether or not Ahmed is the one. My fingers start typing...

Come on now, Bushra. It's been ages that you've been seeing Ahmed. Didn't he also get you a gold pendant, or so I saw on Instagram? If you don't know if he's the one by now, then I don't think you should be leading him on any longer, as he's obviously very keen on you.

Damn, that was blunt of me. Has motherhood made me horribly unfiltered?

I am about to write a follow-on message to soften the blow but Bushra beats me to it and replies with:

Does it seem like I'm leading him on?

I remove my dangerously fast fingers from the keypad. Mustn't reply to Bushra until I've had some time to think this through. The only problem is, with mum-brain being a real affliction, it will take me a while to curate a considered reply. I think I'll need to sleep on it. That's assuming I get any sleep tonight, which is unlikely.

20th October, Bragging

"I was so shocked to find out that Kenzo has a learning delay," says Akari, one of the mums at the playgroup. "They found out during his two-year health check because he apparently wasn't saying enough words in a sentence. I hadn't even realised there was a problem. That's the thing when you have an older child to look after as well, the second baby doesn't get the same level of attention."

"Don't beat yourself up," says Chandni. "I find it hard enough looking after one. I couldn't imagine managing two, especially with such a close age gap as yours."

Akari exhales with relief.

"They said the same about my Daniel," says another mum, Melody. I'm glad she's joined us, otherwise it would've been an Indian, a Bengali and a Japanese woman all sat together, segregated in a room full of white women. Not intentionally, of course, but I'd still worry about the optics. "Daniel didn't start talking until he started school. The health visitor was freaking me out, saying they'll refer him to speech and language therapy but it all turned out okay in the end. Now Daniel won't shut up and he doesn't let his baby sister get a word in edgeways!"

Daniel's baby sister is chewing on her fist, as she's in the throes of teething. I imagine she doesn't have many words yet.

Ruhela, the supermum, chimes in: "It's definitely hard juggling two and it always feels like one isn't getting enough attention. But they're all so different. As you know, Akari, my Jennifer was talking at six months old. Aadam's not talking much but he walked before all the other toddlers his age. They're all so different."

Akari smiles tightly, her face echoing my thoughts. Why did Ruhela's words sound more like bragging than empathic? Also, her daughter was talking at six months? Does she mean goo-goo-ga-ga, or was she reciting Shakespeare?

Chandni gives me a glance which suggests she's thinking the same thing.

Talking at six months... pfft.

28th October, An unexpected venue

"**B**race yourself... I've found my dream location and it's a..." Julia pauses.

"Should I do a drum roll?" I ask.

"Pah! Don't make me snort my coffee. I'm out in public. Among other boring, sensible, trouser-suit wearing people."

"I thought you were outside. It sounds busy."

Julia sighs. "Yes, this city never stops, does it? Anyway, the clock is ticking so I won't keep you in suspense any longer. I'm getting married in a barn!"

I say nothing.

"H-hello? Are you still there?" Julia asks.

"Yeah, sorry. I'm still here. I'm just processing. Did you say barn?"

"That's right. But not as in an Old McDonald type of barn."

"What other type is there?" I ask.

"Okay, so it is a farmyard barn. But it's not like it sounds. It's very chic. And rustic. I just fell in love with it." Julia pauses. "Is that a terrible idea?"

"No! No, it's lovely. Ignore me, I've only ever been to weddings in banqueting halls or school gymnasiums. I once ate a tandoori chicken under a basketball hoop, so I'm not very good at visualising weddings in... alternative places...

but it sounds like you've made good progress if you've got a venue."

Julia scoffs. "About bloody time, too. We spent ages being engaged and doing absolutely nothing, thinking we had all the time in the world. Now, we've only got a few months until the wedding and there's everything left to do!"

"Take it from a girl who got engaged and married within a few short months, it's doable. If I can manage a wedding with 600 guests, not to mention the extra parties to go with it, you'll be just fine."

"I'm not so sure. With our weddings, there are unreasonably long waiting lists for everything. You wouldn't believe... I had a bridal fitting up north and found the perfect dress, only for the boutique to say they wouldn't be able to do alterations for another six months! How long does it take to sew something together?"

"Perhaps there's some sense in that. I remember discovering that my wedding lehenga was massively oversized just days before the wedding. Clearly, they hadn't altered anything. Maybe they need those few months to figure out how to stitch and sew."

Julia sighs. "Maybe. Anyway, when am I going to see you again? I'm missing your little one's chubby little cheeks. How is she doing?"

I look over to H2. She was my little acrobat in the womb and she's just as active on the outside. I grab her by the underarms and lift her away from the coffee table she keeps getting stuck under.

"She's doing great," I say. "Now that she's mastered sitting, she's into rolling around on the floor. She tries to get herself up into a crawling position, her hands wobble and then she falls back down. She doesn't give up, though. I've been watching her work at this for half an hour. Not that I can complain, it means she's on me less. Though she decides she needs mummy cuddles when I'm eating or need to go to the toilet."

"Make the most of the cuddles. It will be over in the blink of an eye," says Julia.

"Why does everyone keep telling me that? I've been blinking non-stop since she was born!"

We both laugh. I hear someone singing a song about falafel on the other end of the line. "Julia, where are you?"

"Well, it's incredibly sad but I'm at our usual spot on Chancery Lane, without you. I'm even having an all you can fill Tupperware in your honour."

"Awww, it's been ages since I've been there. I hope you filled your container. Remember, they don't charge you per item, so fill that box right up!"

"I can't. Wedding diet and all that."

"You don't need to lose any weight, Julia," I say.

"In a few months, all eyes are going to be on me, including photographers capturing the moment forever. So I damn well do need to get in shape. I want a waist like yours in time for the wedding."

"Julia, you do not want my waist as it is right now. I have just birthed a baby. Anyway, how's the rest of the wedding planning going?"

"It's fine. I'm debating whether to go for a sponge or traditional fruit cake for the big day. I also need to factor in allergies, because Miles' mum is gluten intolerant and his dad has a nut allergy. It's massively inconvenient. On top of that, I don't know if my sister will make it back to be maid of honour at the wedding. She's said she's going to come but with her having just had a baby on the other side of the world, I'm not so sure. She's such a free spirit. I don't know how she is managing over there. I know how much you've struggled and you have a husband to help. And then there's the small matter of fittings. How do I get an outfit ready for her if she's not even here? You can't just buy something off the rack..."

All of this is white noise. I don't mean it to be but I think being a new mum is like having a constant ringing in your ears which drown out everything else. I manage to catch bits about her sister and allergies. That reminds me...

"Oh Julia, I'm so sorry, I'm meant to be calling the GP surgery because I need to get the results of H2's skin prick test. You know, the one for allergies?"

"Oh yeah, God yeah. I remember you saying about it. Gosh, sorry, that was really insensitive of me when I complained about Miles' parents' food intolerances. I didn't mean it to be. Truthfully, I'm not sure they're really allergies. I think it's just something they say. I've seen his mum eat a croissant and his dad had a Ferrero Rocher at my engagement party. Or maybe it was a Lindt chocolate? No worries, anyway. Before you go, I wanted to ask one thing."

I check the time. I'm getting late for my call. "Go on..."

"It's just... as my oldest friend... and I know you've got your hands full with H2 and you're crazy busy and all the rest of it. But I was wondering if you'd be free to come into town to meet me one day, as I've arranged a fitting at a bridal store on Bond Street."

"Bond Street? That is posh!"

"Yes, it will probably cost a year's salary. It's one of Miles' mum's recommendations. I'm just going to please her. I'm not that bothered to be there but, for a little support and an extra pair of eyes, I'd love you to be there. I even booked it on a weekday. I'll be going on my lunch break so it's easier for you, as the Tubes can be horrendous on the weekend. That way you can bring the baby, as I know it's hard for you to leave her."

Thoughts come at me, thick and fast. Logistically, how would I do that? What's the route to Bond Street? I can't even remember, it's been so long. Do I have to change Tubes? Are there lots of stairs to negotiate? What if I get separated from the pram?

A journey that I would previously take without even thinking twice seems impossible now. So far, I've avoided Tube journeys by myself. I only ever go with M, and that's on the occasional weekend. Everything else is by foot. I'm getting flashbacks of the London Underground, where hordes of passengers push past either side of me. The Underground is dark. The tunnels are windy. The carriages rush past noisily. How would I do it? I can't even ask M to drive me if it's a weekday.

I can't tell Julia all this, can I? It's pathetic. I'm pathetic! Mums have been taking the Tube forever. I've witnessed it firsthand. Mums with double buggies, carrying twins, climbing the stairs and relying on the kindness of strangers. I was always an independent boss woman. I have to be now. And I have to do this for Julia. She's my best friend.

"Sure," I say. "Send me the details."

"Brilliant." Julia exhales, as though she was expecting an inevitable no from me. "And good luck with the allergy call. Also, are we still calling your baby H2, or should I start using her proper name?"

I look at my daughter, who's rolled her way to the kitchen cabinet. Somehow, she knows to tug at the cupboard containing crisps. "H2 is fine."

"JUST BEAR WITH ME ONE second, mum," says the receptionist on the other end of the line. "I'll bring up the doctor's notes."

I pray under my breath. H2 is now on all fours, pushing herself forwards and backward, like she's gyrating.

"Sorry, mum, bear with me. I'm just going to scan through the results."

"No worries," I say. *And also, could you please, please, stop calling me mum! I'm my own person.*

"Right, I'm scanning through..." This receptionist is really keeping me in suspense as I hear her mumbling words to herself. "Okay, so it says that everything is fine-"

"Oh, thank goodness!"

"No, sorry, mum. I was just about to say, everything is fine, except it looks like she's allergic to dairy, egg and peanut."

I nearly drop the phone out of my hand.

"Peanut? She's never even had peanuts!"

"I understand that, mum. But this blood test determines what she's allergic to, and it doesn't matter if she's not tried it."

"Are they accurate?" I ask. "I mean, sorry, but can we be certain she is definitely allergic?"

"These are the results. Would you like me to book an appointment with the doctor so you can discuss it?"

"Yes, please."

Fuck. Fuck. Fuck. Fuck.

I hang up. I pick up H2 and look at her. This time, I *properly* look at her. Her skin isn't as smooth as the other babies I've seen. Even without the random rashes and bumps, her skin is dryer, as though she needs extra moisturiser. She's beautiful, just not silky smooth. I heard somewhere that eczema and allergies go hand in hand.

Have the signs always been there? Is that why she was crying so much when she was a newborn? Is that why she kept vomiting up the formula milk? Is that why she would writhe in pain while crying helplessly, leaving M and I unsure of how to console her? Has she been suffering all this time?

H2 throws her head back, showing me a gummy grin. She doesn't look like she's suffering now but, in those early days, did I let her down? H2 bends her knees and bobs up and down. She wants to get on the floor again. I shouldn't complain. I've spent most of her life moaning about how much she wants to be attached to me.

I settle back into the sofa, my heart hits the floor. What does this mean? Aren't peanut allergies really severe? Are they fatal? Random thoughts flood my mind. Like the news article I once read about a teenager who had an allergic reaction by accidentally eating a peanut biscuit. She died instant-ly. That's another thing. Is H2's allergy a lifelong thing? Will she grow out of it? If not, would I ever be able to let her out of my sight? And the dairy and egg allergy? How serious is it? Will she need to avoid cakes? Cheese?

Shit.

I lived away at university. Will I be able to let H2 go? Knowing that she has this potentially life-threatening aller-gy? My God, I was lucky to move away given the patriarchal society in which I grew up, where girls were expected to stay at home during their studies. I broke that glass ceiling. I nev-er, ever, for a second thought that I'd be holding my daugh-ter back, for a reason I never saw coming.

My heart races. My fingers tremble. I can't believe this.

I look at H2. She seems happy but I can't keep these thoughts at bay. I ring middle sis as I need to speak to some-one.

"Oh, no," says middle sis as I tell her the news. Maybe she wasn't the best person to call. "Does that mean she'll never be able to have peanuts?"

"I don't know."

"Will she need an EpiPen?"

"I don't know. I'll have to find out from the doctor."

"And how bad is the dairy allergy? Is it just milk or is it things that have got milk in them, like biscuits and stuff?"

"I don't know!" I shout down the phone. "I'm trying to figure all this out. I called you for some big sisterly words of reassurance."

"Awww okay, don't worry," middle sis finally utters the words I needed to hear. "It might just be a childhood thing. I've heard of other people growing out of their allergies."

"Really?"

"Well... I don't know anyone personally but I think I have heard that. Surely it happens?"

"I hope so."

"The main thing is, make sure you don't have any peanuts around. Now that she's more mobile, she'll be able to grab things and start eating them off the floor."

As if I didn't have enough worries, middle sis piles on even more.

"DON'T WORRY ABOUT IT, babe," says M when he's home from work. It's the first time he's called me 'babe' in a while.

"It's hard not to. I just hope it doesn't affect her for the rest of her life."

H2 rolls over to M. He picks her up by the underarms and launches her forward like an aeroplane. She giggles, releasing drool onto his work shirt at the same time.

"Look at her. Does she really look like she'll be negatively impacted by anything in life? Plenty of people have allergies and live with them. It's not the end of the world. Anyway, let's see what the doctor says and take it from there. Then we'll know what to do."

M continues playing with H2. He uses her like a dumbbell, lifting her up and down. She laughs every time she goes towards him, their noses touching. They're so playful together. M can only see the good, the positive. I wish I was the same.

M then looks towards the kitchen, where there is nothing to be had. "What shall we have for iftar tonight?"

"Well, given that I'm not fasting, I've already eaten chip shop chips but what do you fancy? I could maybe do some..." I mentally recollect what's inside our cupboards, "pesto pasta?"

M sighs. "You're alright. I'll just order something in."

We've had a few too many takeaways this Ramadan but, given my inability to do a full food shop, let alone cook a decent meal, I don't protest.

2nd November, The diagnosis

I haven't slept much of late. That's nothing new.

The doctor confirmed H2's allergies and was very nonchalant about the whole thing. She said my baby will be referred to an allergist but warned that there is a long waiting list. She also mentioned something about a milk ladder, where I try items that have a low percentage of dairy, increasing slowly as she manages to eat each one. Or at least I hope she manages to eat each one. The peanut one is less straightforward. I've been told to avoid it at all costs, as the doctor said, rather casually, peanut allergies can be fatal. I'm not sure I liked her bedside manner.

My phone beeps. It's Melanie, one of the NCT mums. She's sharing a picture of a neat square of shepherd's pie. Apparently, this is baby Jasper's brunch. He is having three meals a day now. I, meanwhile, have so far managed to get H2 to have half a toast finger this morning.

Okay, let's keep comparison-itis at bay.

H2's sleep is still shit but in the 15-minute window that she does nap, I'm trying to write. It will help sharpen my brain. After all, I have to get back to work soon. I can't keep my freelancer, Vanessa, on forever. I need to know that my mind is still working. After what seems like terminal mum brain, I must make sure I can string proper sentences together and I still remember how to spell.

Journalling seems like a good place to start. I do sometimes use big words when manifesting. There you go - manifesting - that's a big word in itself.

Grateful-

- I'm grateful that I can still spell manifesting
- I'm grateful that we...

Need to think of two more things-

- I'm grateful H2 is so smart, alert and happy.
- I'm grateful I have the chance to meet my good friend later.

That'll do it.

I'm being super brave today. I'm taking the tube to meet Julia. From Aldgate, it's pretty simple. I need to get the District Line to Westminster, where there is lift access, then I will hop onto the Jubilee line to get to Bond Street. Easy. At least it feels that way in my head.

As I exit our building and head towards the Tube station, H2 starts wincing. Surely she's not doing a poo now, is she? Come to think of it, she might be a bit cold. I should've packed a blanket. I'm an idiot. I thought her coat would do the trick.

I'm already running late to meet Julia but shall I just run back and get her blanket? Yes, let's do that.

TEN MINUTES LATER (I needed a wee once I got back to the flat) and I'm on my way again. My heartbeat quickens as I get to the Tube station and face my nemesis- stairs. I wait for some good Samaritan to help me with the pram. A girl with a spiky fringe covering her eyes and ear defenders plugged in, waltzes past me and skips down the stairs. Rude. Another man, in a shiny grey suit, does the same, without even a second glance. Wanker.

Then he turns on his heel a few steps down. "Sorry, do you need any help?"

"Oh, yes, please. If that's okay?" I say, feeling bad for calling him a wanker and super weirded out having to accept help. It makes me feel vulnerable.

"Of course. Sorry, I didn't see you at first."

He valiantly grabs the bottom of the bulky pram and starts taking it down the stairs, while I hold the handles. H2's pram is heavier than I thought, even with the help of a stranger.

Once we get to the bottom, he lunges it down, offers me a smile and goes on his way, having restored my faith in men in suits at the London Underground. I glide through the wheelchair and buggy access barrier without issue. So far, so good.

Oh damn, of course. There are more stairs. Loads of them. My shiny-suited helper is already on the platform as the Tube arrives. I can't expect him to come back. He probably hasn't even noticed me. It's silly, really, why would you help someone down one flight of stairs, knowing that there's another set just a few metres away and then not hang around to help? What's the point?

I wait at the top of the next set of stairs. A mum in a long cardigan walks past with two small children. Clearly she can't help me, she's got her hands full herself. A skinny boy goes past with his headphones in. I don't think he even noticed me.

H2 starts scratching around at her head. Oh no, don't make yourself bleed now. Please don't scratch your skin. She's getting restless. I rock the pram forwards and backwards. Oh dear. Come on, someone, anyone. Help a mama out.

Another man rushes past, glancing at me through the corner of his eye. He quickly looks away, perhaps feeling conflicted about not helping. He jumps down the steps, two at a time. He must be in a hurry. I can't begrudge that.

More people go past. Really? No one is going to help me?

I walk back to one of the Tube staff, who looks tall, broad and strong, so should have no trouble helping me with the pram.

"Excuse me, could you help with the pram?" I say, my voice as small as possible, so nobody else can hear me begging.

"What?" she replies gruffly.

"I, erm… I was just wondering if you could help me with the pram. Down the stairs?"

She looks away. "I can't. Got a bad back."

I walk away, with a familiar feeling of rejection coming to the fore. This is layered with embarrassment and self-pity. Like the time I was racially abused on the way to the train station in my premarital days. Or the time Fiona at work, asked loudly, across the office, whether I'd have an arranged marriage. All those times I felt uncomfortable, I thought I'd got over it. But, at my rawest, it's still there. I'm still that little girl, feeling awkward.

At least half a dozen people walk straight past me and head down to the platform. One guy stares at the pram, not at me. A woman smiles awkwardly as she goes past, carrying a laptop case and shopping bag. She's wearing a tight pencil skirt. I guess she'd struggle to help me with the pram, anyway. Where is everyone going in such a hurry in the middle of the day? It's not like it's rush-hour. I've been stood waiting for what feels like hours.

"Do you need a hand?" Finally, a silver-haired man offers some assistance.

He struggles to lift the pram from the front. "It's one of those chunky ones, isn't it?"

"It is, I'm afraid."

He laughs, breathlessly. "My kids had them. They're a pain in the neck for the Tubes. Thankfully, my pram pushing days are over."

Or so he thought.

There are a lot of stairs to go down. I grip tightly to the handlebar of H2's pram. I feel my feet wobble. From my vantage point, the stairs look scarily steep. One slip of the handle and the pram would go tumbling down, taking H2 and the poor man with it. It could be fatal. This wasn't a good idea. Why did I agree to meet Julia at Bond Street? What was I thinking? It's too much. I should've just told her I can't do these things anymore. Not until H2 is older. Possibly school-age.

We get to platform level. I thank the man as he puts his bag back on his shoulder. He looks out of puff. He must be in his late fifties. I imagine he wishes he never offered. I wish I hadn't accepted.

I catch my breath just as the train arrives. There is no time to be polite. All etiquette goes out of the window as I push the pram into the carriage. The door slams shut just as I get in, catching my hair in the process. I wrestle some of it back but I feel some strands get pulled off.

Okay, deep breath. Deep breath. Deep breath. I'm on the homestretch now. This is the easy bit. This should take me directly to Westminster, where there are lifts. I won't have to worry about negotiating stairs until the journey back. Then, when I get to Bond Street, I can use the escalator. Oh my God, how am I going to get this pram on the escalator? Is it safe? I didn't think to check.

Crap. Crap. Crap.

I don't even bother to look for a seat on the Tube. Instead, I stay near the doorway, counting down the stops. H2 seems to be enjoying herself. She is looking around at the commuters. A couple of people smile at her, which is most unusual for London. She giggles at them, animatedly. She is very sociable.

The carriage judders. The light flicks off, then on, then off again. Then on again. Bloody hell, what is this! Stay calm. Stay calm. Don't project my anxieties onto the baby.

I look at H2.... her bottom lip is wobbling. Oh no, please don't have a meltdown on the Tube!

I check to see what other people make of this. Apart from a few unperturbed, most are looking around, wondering what is going on. I can't deal with this. We stop between Cannon Street and Monument. I'm not sure why. The train is suspended for longer than usual at the station.

I don't like this. I have to distract myself by messaging Julia. She's probably wondering where I am.

I unlock my phone to see a message from her:

Hey, are you on your way? I'm just at the boutique now. I wanted to wait for you but I've tried on a dress as I've only got my lunch hour. See you shortly X

I hate being late for anything. I definitely didn't want to be late for this. Why isn't the train moving? People are huffing and puffing around me. I can feel the eye rolls.

Julia can't be angry with me, can she? If it's a public transport issue, it's out of my hands. It doesn't matter that I took a bit longer getting to the Tube station because I had to get H2's blanket. Surely she'll understand. I'm a mum now. I'm not as footloose and fancy-free as I used to be.

The train still isn't moving. The carriage is unusually busy for the middle of the day. I feel sticky. I wish I hadn't worn my long coat but it was cold outside. I wonder if H2 is hot? I take her hat off and remove the blanket, letting her kick her legs freely. Then, she rests a foot on the pram handle, as if she's showing off her pink shoes to the other commuters. She's a sassy one, I'll give her that.

I need something to focus on. I look at the adverts on top of the carriages. One is for a laxative. There is another one about iron levels. On the far left, I can see an advert for a new play in the West End. One that I will never get to see now that I'm a parent.

Then I hear a wail. Oh no, the tears have started. Is H2 hungry? Overtired? I was hoping she'd nap on the journey but there's no chance as she is too damn inquisitive nowadays. I pat and shush her, just like the books said. It doesn't work. She's holding her arms out, wanting to be picked up. I couldn't possibly hold her now. The Tube will leave any minute and I will topple over.

I feel eyes on me. Lots of eyes. A guy next to me, in navy blue chinos and a pink top, rolls his eyes. The bastard. As a mum, do I not deserve to travel on the Tube? I paid for my fare just like anyone else. Is my money no longer good enough, now that I've got a child?

H2 is still crying. Panicked and flustered, I pick her up. The Tube pulls away. I realise I forgot to put the brakes on the pram and it slides across into a lady who's too busy looking at her phone to see the buggy career towards her.

"I'm so sorry," I say, steadying myself by holding onto the bar whilst simultaneously holding my baby. H2 is throwing her neck back now in a fit of anger.

The lady frowns. "You should put that in the buggy bay."

"There's a buggy bay?" I ask.

The woman shakes her head and looks back down at her phone.

I pull the pram back and put H2 in. She is now crying more because I've not been able to soothe her. She's kicking her legs now. How the hell am I supposed to endure a bridal fitting when H2 is hysterical? How am I supposed to do any of this? The Tube grinds to a halt at Monument. I get out and walk back home, my own tears matching that of H2's.

I am a wimp. I am the worst.

I can't even do these basic things. I can't even be there for my friend. I can't even manage what most mums do. Living my life whilst having a baby. It shouldn't be that hard. Why is it? I'm angry at myself for being such a wet lettuce. Deep down, I'm ashamed to admit, I'm angry and resentful towards my daughter, as I can't seem to do anything now she's in my world. The thought is dark, crushing and unforgivable but it's there, resting inside me.

Julia will hate me and I can't blame her. She's been there for most of my milestones. I simply can't do the same for her.

I stumble into the flat. H2 is still in the pram, crying. She'll have to wait for a minute.

I get out my phone to message Julia and see she's beaten me to it:

I had to leave as my lunch break was over. Didn't find anything there, anyway.

I throw my phone on the sofa. H2 is still crying but I want, no, I *need* a moment to myself. I go to the bathroom and shut the door.

M IS WORKING LATE TODAY. Once he gets home and cuddles H2, he says: "Babe, I'm just going to have a poop and shower and then I'll take this little monkey."

I don't respond.

"Are you okay?" he asks.

I look down at our cold, laminate floor, which feels even frostier as I forgot to turn the heating on today. "No, I'm really struggling. I think I need to speak to someone. I need help."

20th November, The night before Eid

"We first found out when I was trying to wean her, and she kept getting reactions after eating porridge. Actually, I had a feeling before that. She's always been slightly sickie and uncomfortable. That's probably why she was unsettled and we were mixed-feeding. It was the formula that was upsetting her stomach. The things I blamed it on... colic, unsettledness, her just being a difficult baby. I feel so bad now. Also, to be on the safe side, can we keep things out of reach? Like peanut butter and milk? Just while we're here. She can grab things now. Is that okay, mum? Mum?"

My mother-in-law looks stony faced. She must be devastated. Allergies were unheard of in her time. Then she says: "What you need to do..." she comes in closer, "is cut four, maybe five onions. We got lots of work today if it is Eid tomorrow. Your big sister-in-law is coming later but may not be able to do as much because she be fasting. And you're not fasting, are you? Because you give baby breast? You could think about maybe getting bottle now that she's older. Cow's milk better for her. More filling. You'll see she sleep better and give you more break."

I bite my lip and grab some onions from the orange net sack by the radiator. I shouldn't have expected much of a response from my mother-in-law, especially on such an auspicious occasion. It's potentially the night before Eid. We'll know for sure later on. M's mum has gone into ninja mode, preparing all manner of savoury pastries in anticipation.

H2 is sitting in front of the TV with cushions surrounding her. I check every so often to see if she's toppled over. So far, she seems fine. She is a steady one. I, meanwhile, am less fine. I have tears in my eyes. Though thankfully, this time, not emotional ones. It's the damn onions. They get me every time.

As I coarsely slice the onions, I hear fireworks exploding outside. Are they someone's leftover fireworks from Bonfire Night? Or early Eid celebrations? Not that it matters to me. Whenever I'm over at my in-laws on Bonfire night, New Year's Eve, or even the Wimbledon ladies final, I never get to see the event. I'm always too busy in the kitchen, making whatever is the order of the day. Today is no exception. Oh well, I'll listen to the explosions and imagine what they look like.

Fingers crossed it's Eid tomorrow so I can get this ordeal over with. Otherwise, my mother-in-law will just use the opportunity to make yet more dishes for the many guests we will be expecting.

PRAISE BE, THE MOON has been sighted in Saudi Arabia, signifying that it is indeed Eid ul-Fitr tomorrow.

M's big brother and family arrive around 8.30pm.

"So much traffic! More traffic than you believe!" says M's sister-in-law. I bet they stopped off at a service station to feed the kids/stretch their legs/delay coming over. "It's a nice tradition, all of us sitting around the table, folding samosas."

Despite my grumbling about the arduous prep the night before Eid, there is some warmth when gathering around my in-laws' kitchen table. It's a team effort, with M's younger siblings, us two daughter-in-laws and, of course, the matriarch of the family, creating hundreds, *literally hundreds*, of deep fried snacks.

The two people missing, as ever, are the older men of the family, M's dad and big brother. I'm not sure why the latter gets away with it but he always seems to find some excuse – tonight he's going to the barber to get his beard trimmed, as though there aren't any barbers where they live.

H2 is in the capable hands of the TV and M's nephew and niece, who absolutely adore her. I can hear them clapping for her, as she giggles excitedly. I'm trying not to think of the fact that it's nearly 10pm and I really ought to get my baby to bed. It's one night, so I'll let it go.

"Your samosa rolling is getting better," I say to M's little sister.

"You think so? It's still a bit more Australia-shaped, rather than a full circle."

"It's got character," I say.

"*Heh!* Roll faster! And don't just fill everything with chicken keema. You need to do the beef samosas, too. And the daal," shouts my mother-in-law. "I be the old one and I so much quicker than all you young people."

M's sister-in-law smirks at me. She takes all this in her stride as she's had more years to get used to it. I'm still a little offended by all the micromanaging.

The kitchen is now choked with the heady aroma of oil and spices. I'm going to demand a long shower tomorrow morning. M will have to look after H2. I do not want to hear about any poos, or that she needs a feed, anything. It's my first Eid since becoming a mum and I would like to feel somewhat put together.

"Auntie..." M's niece comes into the room, looking concerned. "I gave her a cookie, and now she's really itchy and bumpy."

I jump from my chair, pushing the seat back. "What happened?"

"She was staring at a cookie I was having, so I gave it to her. Only a small crumb. I thought she was able to have solids now."

I grab H2 from her. My baby's eyes are bloodshot and she has bumps around her left cheek. "What was in it? Is it a peanut biscuit?"

M's nephew comes into the kitchen, looking like he's about to cry. "I don't think it's peanut."

M's sister-in-law goes over to him. "Why did you give her something without checking first? Honestly, these kids. Now, did you wash your hands before you eat? And, have you been to the toilet? You need to go to bed soon."

Is she serious? She's worried about her son's bedtime when my baby has been given something dangerous.

"Show me the packet," I demand. M's nephew and niece look at each other with unsure faces. "I said show me the packet! Bring it here!"

M's nephew runs to the living room and comes back with the cookie packet. I comb through the ingredients, something I've been doing since finding out about H2's allergies. It contains wheat and milk. It must be the milk that set her off.

"Go get the antihistamine," I tell M.

I pat H2's cheek with some tap water. She is still scratching and making some of the bumps bleed. Her poor delicate skin. I can't tell if the bumps have got bigger. Where is M with the antihistamine? For God's sake, everyone's useless.

"Are you getting it?" I shout from the living room.

"*Heh?*" My father-in-law looks up. He's been sat there all this time watching TV, oblivious to what is going on.

"Which section of the bag is it in?" asks M.

"Give it here." I grab the bag from him. I take out the medicine and M, with a shaky hand, gets the spoon ready as I pour out 5mls. H2 refuses to take it, moving her head from side to side. I grab her by the cheeks and squeeze, forcing her mouth open. I manage to get it into her.

"Give her some honey. *Inshallah,* one drop on her lips and she be okay," says my father-in-law.

"You can't give honey to babies under one. It's dangerous!" I say.

"Who say it be dangerous?"

"Everyone!" I run into the back room and offer her a breastfeed, which is my default answer to everything. M follows closely behind.

Please be okay. Please be okay. Please be okay.

"Shall we take her to the hospital?" I ask M.

"No, she'll be fine."

"You always say that. Everyone here is so half-arsed about this. I told your mum about her allergies and you know what she said? She told me to chop some onions! She doesn't even care. It's like nobody even cares. These things could kill her!" I shout, unbothered about who can hear me. I've not even closed the door.

M goes into the kitchen. "Don't give her anything without checking with us!" he says to whom I believe is his nephew and niece. "And that goes for all of you! She can't have any old thing. She's allergic to dairy and peanuts and egg. So don't give her any snacks, okay?" His voice is loud, trying to convey the necessary authority. He then translates into Bengali, even louder this time, for the benefit of his mum.

I hear tears. I'm not sure if it's his nephew or niece. I don't care, for that matter. I look down at H2. The redness in her eyes has lessened slightly. She is still bumpy but it's not worsened. My heartbeat settles. That was a close call.

M comes back into the room. "Is she okay?"

Even though it looks like she's fine, I'm still angry. I need him and everyone to realise the gravity of the situation. "It could've been really bad. If your family can't take this seriously, I don't want to keep coming over so often. It's not safe."

"It looks like the bumps have settled." M puts his hand on my shoulder and I nudge it away. "What do you want to do?" he asks.

H2 has fallen asleep whilst feeding. "I want to take her to bed. And go to sleep myself. You can all manage without me."

I don't ask for permission and instead walk out of the kitchen, to the sound of my mother-in-law going: "*My, my, my... nobody told me she had allergies.*"

1st December, Talking therapy

I hope M and H2 are okay. I'm used to him taking her in the mornings on the weekend while I'm trying and failing to sleep. What I'm not so used to is him taking her out for the afternoon while I have a call with a therapist. I'm not even sure where they're going. M fleetingly mentioned something about going to B&Q to get some supplies and grabbing a coffee after. He's got himself an inbuilt date for life now.

I hope he doesn't let her roam around on the floor in a busy shop. Now that she's crawling, she wants to get everywhere on her hands and knees and M is a lot more cavalier about these things than I am.

Anyway, mustn't stress about H2. That's the reason I'm in this position in the first place. But God bless the NHS. Courtesy of being a new mum, therefore deemed vulnerable, I was fast-tracked for an appointment with the talking therapist. My health visitor, Marianne, played a big part in making it happen.

She asked me a series of questions and, if I'm honest, I don't think I answered them with full transparency. How could I? There's always that worry that they may take H2 away if I reveal to them how much of a nervous shell of a person I have become. I couldn't risk that. Regardless, my filtered answers were still enough to have me deemed as someone suffering a touch of postnatal anxiety.

As if I needed a form to determine that.

My phone rings and I brace myself for another session of playing down my true state of mind.

"Is that Helena?"

The first thing I notice is that I've been called by my name. I've been referred to as mum for so long, I've forgotten what it feels like to be me. I feel acknowledged.

The second thing I notice is that it's a male voice on the other end of the line. I wasn't expecting that. Not that it necessarily matters but I assumed for maternal mental health, I'd get another woman. Never mind, I'll work with it.

"It is Helena. Thanks for calling."

"No problem at all. My name is Ravi and I'll be holding the sessions with you. They're basically conversational and I'll give you some actions at the end. I believe you've reached out because you're feeling slightly anxious? Would you like to tell me more about that?"

Really? No pleasantries to ease me in? Where do I even start?

Ravi must notice my hesitation, as he interjects: "Or perhaps you could share some scenarios where you've had bouts of anxiety. It could be around your daughter, or it could be separate to that. It'll help give me a picture of how you're feeling."

I take a deep breath. If I really want to fix myself, if I really want to be the best mum I can be, I have to be honest. Nothing but the ugly truth will do. For most of my life, I've worn a PR hat. Now, it's slipping off. I have to accept that. I have to be my real self in order to heal.

"Okay... I think I've always been a slightly anxious person. I'm a worrier, you see. My mum is a worrier, too. I've tried to work on it over the years but I think having a baby has sent me over the edge and I've got worse. I worry about everything now. For example, I've always hated the London Underground. I've always felt nervous when we stop at red lights. It makes me claustrophobic and uncomfortable. But I had to do it before because of work. Now, I can't even bring myself to go on the Tube with my daughter. I know that's ridiculous-"

"Why is that ridiculous?" Ravi asks, interrupting my train of thought.

"Well, it's just stupid, isn't it? Everyone can do these things?"

Ravi doesn't say anything. This would be a good time for him to add some words of reassurance but I get nothing.

Oh, I get it. He's doing that therapist thing when he goes really quiet, so I ramble on.

"So that's the public transport thing. I'm also nervous in lifts, too. I'm always praying under my breath, hoping the lift doesn't break down, or crash. Now I have a big pram with me, the lift to our apartment feels tiny. It makes me feel hot. On top of that, I'm anxious when I'm out and about with her in general. I'm always scared of the next cry. I feel flustered and worried that people will judge me. I worry that she's not eating as much as she should. All the other babies that were born the same time as her are really well established on solids, whereas mine is still attached to me." I avoid saying the word 'breast' to a man. "Oh, and I'm weird about going in taxis by myself. I'm always scared the taxi driver might kidnap me. I saw that on a TV programme once. It was a drama but it must have also happened in real life, right? So it's everything. Oh, and she's not sleeping properly. I worry about that. My husband and I have argued about how to get her to sleep through the night and-"

Oops, I said too much.

Ravi is still quiet as a mouse, waiting for me to divulge more word salad.

"I think one of the fundamental things and, it's a bit dark... I hope you don't mind but, I basically worry that I'm not going to be able to do a good job as a mum. Heck, I'm scared I won't even be able to keep her alive." As soon as I say that I regret it but I can't stop myself rambling. "And sometimes, I find myself getting anxious, then frustrated, then even more anxious. I get annoyed with her and think, why isn't she sleeping through like the other babies? Why isn't she eating properly? Now I found out that she's allergic to dairy and peanuts and it's just like, oh my God, another thing I have to deal with. Why do I have all this on my head?"

Stop it. Stop with the word vomit. He is an NHS worker. He might tell social services I'm a mum on the brink of a break-down.

Ravi exhales. He's about to say something. "You know everything you describe? You're not alone."

My mouth trembles. "Really?"

"Yes. Lots of mums go through the same thing. The dark thoughts about worrying that your baby will die? The bit about getting so frustrated with your baby? And angry? That's completely normal too. As long as they're just thoughts. From the sounds of it, you are slightly on the anxious side but it is all completely normal."

I feel a weight slip off my shoulders. "People don't really talk about it. That's why you never really know what's normal and what's not. We're all just trying to get on with it. Is that a British thing? I don't know, it's just I'm always being told to enjoy every moment. Motherhood is an absolute dream, they say. The nights are long but the years are short. You'll only have... God, what was the latest, 18 summers or something? What a load of rubbish. It's just all that kind of stuff is designed to make you feel guilty for not feeling in the moment all the time. For not enjoying every single second, because in the blink of an eye, she'll be grown up. I've never blinked so much in my life!"

Ravi laughs, easing the tension. "When I had my daughter, my wife would always whinge to me about people telling her the exact same things. Everyone was like, 'they'll be grown before you know it'. But it doesn't help when you're in that moment, exhausted and sleep deprived."

"It really doesn't," I say. "I'm on the mums' WhatsApp group and all of them seem to have babies that nap on schedule and they're sleeping for long chunks. My girl's not doing anything like that. And to be honest, it's caused a bit of friction between my husband and I as we have different parenting styles."

Ravi says nothing. I wish he'd interrupt me, as I'm sharing way too much now.

He finally speaks. "You're not the only couple that have fallen out once they've had a baby. The truth is, kids are hard. They're an absolute life-changer. It would be weird if you had a handle on all of it but, let's take things one at a time because we have got a few sessions. Does that sound okay?"

"Yes," I reply, feeling slightly embarrassed for cramming in as much as I can in this first session.

"Now, one of the things you mentioned is being anxious to go out on your own because you're worried that she'll start crying or have a meltdown in public, right?"

It sounds silly when it's said back to me. "Yeah, that's right."

"I have to ask, what's the issue? If your little girl needed something, who would be the best person to meet that need?"

"Me."

"And who is she most comfortable with?"

"Me. My husband, too, but mostly me."

"And who is the person that will do anything for her?"

"Me." My voice quivers.

"So... you have to remember, when you're out and about, nobody can settle her better than you can. Nobody knows her better than you. Nobody can tend to her needs better than you. Therefore, when you're outside with her, she's actually in the safest hands with you. You can manage her better than everyone else," says Ravi. "That's another thing, kids pick up on tension."

"That's what I keep being told."

"It's true. Even though it seems like babies don't know much, they're very perceptive. They can pick up on anxiety and nervous energy. If you're flapping around and losing your cool, she will as well. It'll become a vicious cycle. You'll get stressed out. She'll then get stressed out and act up more.

And then you'll get even more stressed out and it will go on." Ravi pauses. I hear the sound of papers rustling. "I'm going to share a document with you. It's a triangle. It demonstrates what happens when you worry about something before it's even happened. That worry becomes an actuality, and then you react to it. Then, you worry more. It's almost like you worry about things and sort of engineer them to happen, without trying."

"What can I do to stop the worry in the first place?" I ask.

"When you're out, just be mindful. It sounds really cheesy but focus on your little girl. Focus on her hair. Look at a piece of clothing she's wearing. And just listen to the birds."

"I live in central London. Not too many birds here." Right on cue, I hear drilling outside. More dreaded building works.

"Well, anything else, then," says Ravi. "When it comes to mindfulness, you don't actually need specific tools or objects. It's about taking in the environment around you. It's healthier to focus on that, rather than pre-empting a meltdown. Just go out with your head held high and think, you've got this. The day is great, your baby is adorable and you can handle anything that comes your way."

"I'll give it a go," I say, knowing full well that this goes against my very nature.

I CAN'T RELAX. MY CALL with Ravi ended half an hour ago and I'm still waiting for M and H2 to come home. I feel better when she's nearer. How messed up is that? When she's around, I can't wait to palm her off. Or get her to sleep. I always dream of my next break. When I do get a break, like now, all I can think about is her. Motherhood is so weird.

I hear the door twist open. I try my very best to not fly through the hallway to my baby. M walks into the room with H2. He places her on the bed and she crawls over towards me, reaching her arms out for a cuddle. I scoop her up and sniff her hair, which smells of orange blossom shampoo.

"Did you guys have fun?" I ask.

"We had the best time! Look at this." M shows me a series of photos. In one, they're sat at a cafe. She is in the high-chair holding a paper coffee cup.

"You didn't give her any, did you? She can't have dairy," I say.

M tuts. "Obviously not. Even if she could have dairy, I don't think an eight-month-old should be having coffee." M pinches H2's cheek. "How did your call go?"

"It was alright. He let me ramble on, mostly. It was nice to speaking to someone and not worry that they might judge."

"Good. I'm glad you're doing this."

"Me too. Also, I wanted to say, I know we've disagreed over how to get H2 to sleep through the night and, I don't mean to disregard your tough-love approach. I'm thinking maybe we could compromise. I've looked into things like a no-cry sleep consultant."

M looks blankly. "What's one of them?"

"It's exactly as the name suggests. Someone who teaches your kids to sleep through, without having to leave them to cry. It sounds like the ideal compromise, right?"

M comes and sits next to me. "I'll try anything."

"Good. I've found a lady. She's a former nanny. I'll have a call with her first, to see what it's about. Then we can take it from there?"

M pulls me in for a squeeze and H2, not wanting to be left out, brings her head in for a nuzzle. "Sounds like a plan, Batman."

18th December, Solo-parenting

"Will you be okay, babe?" asks M, with one hand resting on my parents' front door.

There's no point in bloody asking me now, is there? It's a bit late for a welfare check, given that you're about to go on a boys' holiday in celebration of your friend getting married. Meanwhile, I have had zero sleep and I could expect it to only get shitter as I'll be solo-parenting at my parents' house while you're living it up in Germany. On top of that, I've now got a wretched cold and I'm coughing like a chain smoker. I obviously didn't get the memo saying that there's no point being ill when you're a mum, as you get no sympathy. And you, dear husband, obviously didn't get the memo that you're a dad, so not only should you stay put and do your share of parenting, you should be nursing me back to full health, too.

Of course, these are dark, inner thoughts. "Yeah, I'll be fine," I reply. "Have fun."

Have fun? Why did I say that? God, I hate myself sometimes.

Dad comes down the stairs just as M is about to leave. "You going back to London already?"

M looks sheepish. "No, not to London."

"Ah... you go to your parents, then? In Droylsden?" asks dad.

"No, I'm going to... erm." He looks to me.

"Germany. He is going to Germany," I add.

"German? What in German?"

M turns to me again, fearfully.

"His friend is getting married," I reply.

Dad blinks. "In Germany? Strange place to get married. Is that where bride from?"

"No," I reply. "They're having a party before the wedding."

This time, M looks at me with a furrowed brow as if I said the wrong thing. But that's what it is, isn't it? He's going on a stag do and leaving me at my parents' with baby H2.

M bows his head, as though he's ready for a spanking from my dad. Instead, he gets: "*Acha acha*. Very good. I think Germany nice now. Not too racist after war. Some Bengalis live there but not too many. Not lots of halal chicken shops like here. We have too much. Make place messy and cause rats to come. And you no worry, we look after them," dad says.

With that crucial bit of intelligence, M bolts out of the door before further interrogation.

I sit down with H2 in the front room and offer her some sleep-inducing breast milk. I feel like I might cry, though I'm not sure if I have any right to. I told M he could go to Germany with Jam but, at the same time, it felt like I couldn't say no. The new dynamic is that M is out and about, while I stay put with the baby.

I didn't expect it to be like this.

My little sister walks in, interrupting yet another bout of tears.

"Sorry, are you feeding her?" she asks, slowly backing out of the door.

"It's fine. You can come in. My boobs are out all the time these days. You'll have to get used to it."

Little sis sits as far away from my lactating bosom as she possibly can.

"Where is *dulabhai*?" she asks.

"He's going to Germany for a stag party. His friend is getting married."

Little sis looks worried. "How long for?"

"A couple of nights."

"Will you be okay?"

I look down at H2. She's fallen asleep. "I'll have to be. Plus, I'm staying here, so I've got mum to help."

"Yeah." Little sis nods. "I wonder what would happen if you went on holiday and left the baby. What would your mother-in-law say?"

"I can tell you now, without a shadow of doubt, that would go down like a lead balloon. Both his mum and mine would have a fit."

Little sis sighs. "It doesn't seem fair."

"That's because it isn't."

"YOU KNOW, YOUR HUSBAND be a dad now, he need to make priority," says mum as she comes into her room - which H2 and I have taken over - and grabs a pillow. "He can't go away with boy friends like he used to."

"I know," I reply. "I just wasn't sure how to say no without him resenting me."

"Yes, it be difficult. And he good husband in so many ways. Maybe next time tell him no."

"Next time? I hope the next time he goes on holiday, it's with his wife and daughter! Anyway, maybe I'll go somewhere and leave her with him."

Mum leans against the radiator, as if she's about to have a funny turn. "*Yalla!* What you mean? Leave baby?"

"My friend Julia is getting married in a few months. I'm sure she'll have a hen party. I'll be definitely going to that. M insisted."

"And who will look after baby?"

"Erm... her dad, who is her other parent?"

Mum looks horrified. "*Nah, nah*. He not be able to look after her all alone."

I slide in next to H2, trying to be stealthy, before a coughing fit attacks my chest. She rustles, I plug in the boob. "Mum, why should he get to go away while I'm at home with H2 all the time?"

Mum chuckles as though I've asked something silly. "It be different for the woman. And you're breastfeeding her. And you never gave her dummy. How you leave her?" She turns to head out of the door.

"Mum, why don't you stay here on the single bed tonight? It won't be very comfortable downstairs on the sofa bed. You'll feel cold."

"*Nah, nah*. It be okay. I better downstairs as I no want to get your cold. I old now. You catch a cold, it get better in few days. I end up in bed for a week with flu."

As mum leaves, my phone pings. It's M:

Hey babe, just waiting at the departure lounge. Will be on the flight soon. How are my two favourite people?

I don't reply. I'm going to settle this issue the only way I know how, with silence, followed by passive aggression.

5th January, Mum and dad meet-up

"**D**o you want to know the latest about Jam's wedding plans?"

Not really, I think to myself. "Sure," I say with a sigh.

Come on now, I could never really be passive aggressive for too long. I spent most of the Christmas break (if you could call it that) at my mum's, and now we are back in London. Back to our flat, which feels draughty during the winter. Back to the noise. The busy streets. The lack of space. Also, now I'm back here, I can't be arsey. I need M's help raising this baby. It's a ridiculous notion that I need M's support, as though he's doing me a favour, rather than being equal partners in parenthood. Yet, here we are.

M leans in, as if he's afraid Jam is in earshot. "His missus wants him to move to Keighley after the wedding. She never mentioned it before but is now saying she doesn't want to be far from her family."

"Could that work?"

M scoffs. "Work-wise, yeah. His company said he could work from home but he assumed she'd come to him, like-"

"Like Bengali girls are supposed to?" I say.

M lifts his hands in the air. "I don't make the rules."

"You just uphold them," I mumble.

M shuffles next to me on the sofa. "Is something wrong?"

Where to begin? It's hard to argue with your husband when you can't exactly pinpoint the root cause of the issue. "No, I'm just tired, that's all."

M rubs my shoulder. "We best wake you up with a cup of tea, as we're going out."

"SHE IS GORGEOUS!" CLAUDIA declares in disbelief as she stares at H2. "I know you're her mum but can you objectively see how cute she is?"

I beam from ear to ear. H2 is gorgeous. Despite what others say, the comparisons with her dad, the asides about her dark skin, she is beautiful. I think, sometimes, in the mashup of motherhood, I forget to appreciate that.

"So is your little guy," I say, as Claudia's son bum shuffles across the shiny floor towards the wooden play area.

I have to say, coming to Claudia's flat is like seeing how the other half live. They're just a couple of miles away from us but it's like a different city. There are hardly any brown faces in Islington and her flat is gorgeous. Don't get me wrong, our apartment in Aldgate is pretty impressive. Uncle Tariq and auntie Rukhsana are always commenting on our concierge and nice, clean lift.

This, however, is another level.

"We are quite lucky that there are not many other buildings in the way," Jean-Patrice says, waving towards the majestic surroundings. "There's a park across the road, so we have a lot of greenery, even though we're in the city."

Now he's just bragging.

Jean-Patrice isn't as dashing as I remember. It must have been hormones making me thirsty when I was pregnant. Now he just looks like M. Tired, and a dad.

Their flat, however, is easier on the eye. It's open like ours but with a proper kitchen island and a dining table. Everything is so neat. The toys occupy a small corner of the living area. There is a changing station in the bathroom, stocked up with fresh nappies and baby vests. Half the time, I can't even find H2's nappies despite having them dotted around the house.

As if their flat wasn't envy-inducing enough, Claudia and Jean-Patrice even have a small outside balcony. What a luxury for central London. I suspect it costs a lot to live here. It's handy, therefore, that they are both back at work.

"I cut my maternity leave short," says Claudia. "They gave me full pay for six months, then after that it dropped drastically. It made more sense to go back, especially now that he's settled with his childminder."

"I'm dreading going back to work," says Melanie. "I'm going to speak to my boss to see if they'll have me for two days in the week. That way, I don't have to leave this little one for too long." She strokes baby Jasper's cheek.

"Is anyone allergic to nuts?" asks Genevieve, laying some peanut puffs on the table.

"I think my little one is," I say, my eyes darting towards H2 to make sure she's as far away from the offending snack as possible. Luckily, she's on M's lap, while he's chatting to Rory. I think they're talking about golf. As if anyone has time for that.

"Oh no." Genevieve gasps. "Have you had her tested? Or did you find out after feeding her?"

"She had a test at the doctors."

"Was it IgG or IgE?" Genevieve asks.

"Erm... I'm not sure. It was a blood test."

"Oh, that'll be the IgE." Genevieve shakes her head. "I found GPs to be terrible when it comes to dealing with allergies. Oliver has dairy, wheat, nuts and an egg allergy. The peanut one isn't severe, which is why I'm giving him small doses. I only knew to do this when I went private. The GPs just tell you to avoid it and leave it at that. Also, you don't keep any peanuts in the house, do you?"

"I don't think so. Actually, we might have a sneaky packet that M keeps for snacks."

Genevieve's eyes widen. "Get rid of them. Make sure you don't keep any in the house. If she is allergic to peanuts, simply having them around can make her allergy worse as it's airborne. Even if she's not eating them and they're lying around, she could still have a reaction." My heart rate quickens. Shit. M has peanuts in the cupboard. I'll have to confiscate them. "It was a nightmare for us because we didn't know half of what he was reacting to," Genevieve continues. "Even a potato waffle would have him projectile vomiting. Now I'm working, I have to know exactly what Oliver eats when I'm not around. Luckily, our nanny is on it."

"You're so brave, leaving her with a nanny," I say, sounding more like my mum than I would like.

Genevieve shrugs. "She's a professional and knows what's she's doing. Plus, I had to go back to work. There was no other way."

These women. All going back to work. Getting on with it. Then there's me. I can't even bring myself to leave H2 for a few hours. Even now, with H2 in her dad's care, I'm still watching like a hawk. I notice when she's crawling towards the cupboards, lurking around the sofa and going between the grown-ups feet, much to their amusement. I need to put a lid on this. I'm barely able to have a conversation with the other mums, as I'm too busy stressing about my daughter.

I go over to M. "She's not eaten anything off the floor, has she?"

"Who?" M asks.

Honestly, this man. "Our daughter."

Rory grimaces as though he's just walked into a domestic. He backs away, making a beeline for the doughnuts Genevieve brought over.

"No, she's fine," says M. "She's just exploring. I'm watching her."

I take a deep breath. Must think about the good things. She's with her daddy. She's in safe hands.

I go to get a glass of water to find Josephine putting the kettle on.

"How's motherhood *really* treating you?" she asks me.

I've not really conversed with Josephine so far. We were never sat near each other during the NCT course and she's been quiet on the mum's group.

I'm taken aback by her question. So far, us mums have discussed, at length, returning to work, sleeping schedules and baby milestones. None of us have actually asked about each other.

"Honestly, it's the hardest thing I've ever done. I'm just about surviving," I say.

"You and me both." Josephine smiles and I notice she's devoid of makeup. In place of eyeliner, she is wearing dark circles. She is waif-like, with a hunched posture synonymous with excessive cradling. I would know, as I am the same. "It was stressful from the start. I didn't want to share this on the WhatsApp group but we had to go to A&E literally the day after being sent home when she was born."

"Me too!" I say with more excitement in my voice than is appropriate. "What happened? Was it around feeding?"

Josephine nods. "The breastfeeding wasn't working and I had no idea. The poor thing must have been starving for 48 hours. I'm now too scared to breastfeed her and she's a fully formula-fed baby."

"I had the exact same thing, so then in the end-" I'm about to share the magic trick I learnt about breastfeeding lying down to make nursing through the night easier. I am about to tell her about the nursing apron, which makes for discreet feeding outdoors. I want to tell her it will get easier after the first few months, once breastfeeding is established. And I want to tell her to absolutely under no circumstances, feel that she has to pump and dump just to increase the supply. Then I see her baby girl. I see all the babies. They are at various stages of development. Most are crawling. Some are sitting and rolling around. Others are bum shuffling. They're not newborns anymore. There is absolutely no benefit in me telling Josephine how to restart breastfeeding. That ship has sailed and it wouldn't be fair to her. She's not looking for tips. I know, I've been there. Having been on the receiving end of so much unwanted advice, I tell Josephine what I wish someone had told me at the time. "I know. It's shit, isn't it? But look at your baby. She looks like she's not doing too bad."

Josephine's mouth trembles. "She's alright. Though we're still fighting the battle of bedtime. How's the sleep on your end?"

I point at my own under-eyes. "Still shit."

We both laugh.

I look around at the mums in the group. Our commonality is we gave birth around the same time. We're like a cross-section of society. Claudia is ready to get back to work. Melanie isn't. And Josephine is struggling just like me, it seems. We all have different opinions, differing ways of parenting and different experiences. While we initially bonded over the lack of sleep and the tears and tantrums, it now feels like I don't have much in common with this group I was messaging through the night. We wouldn't all necessarily be friends had we met any other way. And that's okay. I needed them during this phase in my life. We needed each other. I certainly needed to know that it wasn't just me that was up at 4am at night, debating whether to change a nappy. That it wasn't just me feeling like I was going crazy when the naps weren't coming together. Or it wasn't just me that was feeling lonely. I needed that more than anything.

THE THREE OF US GET home just in time for my call with the 'no cry' sleep consultant. When I mentioned it to

Chandni at the last playgroup, she also raised an eyebrow and asked what the lady's qualifications were. I don't think there is a qualification in getting children to sleep through the night. However, I told Chandni she is a nanny with over 20 years' experience and that more than satisfies me, thank you very much.

I decide to put the sleep consultant, Debbie, on speakerphone, so M can hear for himself and we can decide whether it's the right fit for us. I'm trying to be collaborative, you see.

"I do something quite unique that nobody else does," says Debbie, after explaining something at length about her technique, though I'd missed the bit that was unique. "But I always, always, say that you, as the parent, know your little superstar better than anyone else. Therefore, you're best placed to know what she needs."

H2 is currently under our dining table, picking at something stuck to the carpet. It's probably dried rice. As if I'm best placed to know what this kid needs. She's a law unto herself. That's why I'm considering hiring an expert because, frankly, I have no fucking clue how to do this.

"How does it work exactly?" asks M.

Debbie takes a deep breath. "I'll guide you over the phone. We'll talk at length about what your little superstar's bedtime routine is. We'll start with how you get her to sleep at the moment. And I would suggest strategies that we can pick through to get your little superstar settled at night without needing much intervention from you." Debbie pauses as if she's making notes. "In fact, let's start now. Tell me, how does she fall asleep? On you, mum? Or dad? Or does she nod off in the cot?"

I have to think for a minute, as there is no straight answer. "Sometimes I'll rock her to sleep. Other times I'll breastfeed her and she'll nod off on me. When she's being really tricky, I carry her around the flat. It really depends on what she needs at the time."

Debbie inhales sharply. I can't tell if she's offended or flabbergasted. "Right, how does she actually *finally* fall asleep?"

"That's what I'm trying to say, it varies depending on her mood. There's not one set way for her to sleep. Sometimes it's on the boob. Other times, it will be because I rocked her. Pretty much always, she's on me."

Debbie remains silent on the other end of the line for a little longer than comfortable. "Right... Right. The thing we need to figure out is what the sleep crutch is for your little superstar. The one thing she needs to nod off."

I'm not sure how else to keep repeating the same thing. "Well... I guess she's always on me."

"Is it the being held by you that she needs, or the nursing?"

"Probably a bit of both."

"Hmm..." It sounds as though Debbie is scribbling something down, likely along the lines of: *Hapless parents.* "What is her bedtime routine at the moment?"

"I sort of take her to bed and we lie down, then I'll feed her. Sometimes she won't fall asleep so I'll rock her for a while."

"Have you tried a bedtime story?"

I look at M. He's checked out of the conversation and is playing on his phone.

"Not yet," I reply. "She's a bit small for that, isn't she? I can't imagine she'd pay attention."

"They're never too young for a bedtime story. Anyway, let me explain how this whole 'no cry' sleep method works. I don't want to call it sleep training. It's more like sleep empowering. That's why I call your bubba a little superstar, not a baby. It's empowering you, mum, and you too, dad," Debbie says a little louder.

"Sure, okay..." M springs into action. "Sorry, what was that?"

Debbie clicks her tongue. "I was just explaining, dad, how we'll get your little superstar to sleep. I would put together a plan based on what we've discussed. It'll be like a bedtime routine for your little superstar. You stick to that routine, no matter what. And then, after a few nights, we'll have a call to see how you got on. We can move on from there. I think, from the sounds of it, you're lacking consistency. I don't have any children of my own but as a nanny with over 20 years of experience, the one thing that changes a difficult baby to a little superstar, is consistency."

H2 comes over to M. He picks her up and strokes her hair. He then looks at me and I'm pretty sure we're both thinking the same thing- our daughter isn't difficult.

"I have a question," says M. "If you're doing it over the phone, how will you know what she's like? Or what she needs? This is where I feel like we're going wrong. We don't always know what she needs."

Debbie does another awkwardly long pause. "I truly, truly believe that you are the best person to know what your little superstar wants. Which is why I would rely on you to tell me how she got on through the night. How often you're getting up. What are you noticing when she goes to sleep? What is it that she needs?"

I want to scream at Debbie: *I don't bloody know what she needs! That's the whole point! I am so damn sleep deprived, I don't know what's what. I am the least reliable person to give you an accurate account of how the night went, as it's all one big, exhausting, death-inducing blur. That's the reason we're at your doorstep, figuratively, speaking. We are desperate!*

"Could you not visit in person?" As soon as I ask this, I envision Debbie watching over us, hands on her hips, while we attempt to put H2, sorry, our little superstar, to sleep. That would be so bizarre.

"I could come and see you but I'd literally be saying the same thing in person that I would over the phone for an extra hundred pounds."

M and I exchange glances. I think I've caught his cynicism.

After I end the call with Debbie, we have a cup of tea. Well, I'm about to drink my cup of tea when H2 decides she wants cuddle time. M tries to take her but she won't budge. She wants mummy.

"Shall we just have shit sleep for a bit longer?" I ask.

"Yeah," M replies. "I'm sure she'll start sleeping through when she's a teenager."

8th January, A relief

"**I** watched a Bollywood film for the first time since Rohan was born," Chandni informs me as we walk to a cafe. Oh yeah, we're mates now. "Can you imagine? Sitting down, uninterrupted, for three hours? It was absolute bliss!"

"No, I couldn't imagine that at all," I say.

H2 kicks back her pram shade, which I was hoping would create enough darkness for her to fall asleep. No such luck. She's staring right at us, while baby Rohan is knocked out in his pushchair. Damn weird winter sunshine, keeping her awake.

"Do you like Bollywood films?" Chandni asks.

"I'm not sure. I used to but now I'm conflicted. I hate the colourism, the objectification and how all these Bollywood celebrities, like the Hollywood ones, remain quiet about atrocities around the world. But, at the same time, they provided the soundtrack to my childhood. Being from a white area, it was a rare window into Asian culture. So... I don't know."

Chandni offers a tight smile. I think she wanted a simple yes or no answer. "I'll be getting my fill of Bollywood when we move back to Nottingham."

"You're moving?" I stop pushing the pram. It suddenly feels colder and I'm regretting wearing a thin coat. It felt unseasonably warm when I left the flat.

Chandni adjusts her sunglasses. "Yep, we're leaving London. It's too hard raising a baby here so we're going near my family. Plus, Kishen's family is in Birmingham, so we'd be closer to them, too. I'll be sad to leave this place but it's not fair to keep asking my mum to come over as much as she has. It makes more sense to move near them so this one can grow up surrounded by extended family." She gently places Rohan's dangling leg back in the pram. "I don't think we ever stop needing our mums, do we?"

"That's true."

We spot Ruhela across the road.

"Shall we say hi?" I ask Chandni.

"Mmm... not sure. It looks like she's pretty busy."

Ruhela is wrestling a share bag of Doritos from the clutches of her son, Aadam, while her daughter keeps shouting: "Mummy, I want the iPad! I want the iPad! I need Peppa Pig," while grabbing at her mum's bag.

"You can have it when you're eating your lunch!" Ruhela barks back, shooing her hand away.

"Is that the kid who was talking at seven months old?" I ask, surprising myself at my cattiness.

"I guess she must have become so fluent watching Peppa Pig." Chandni has some shade of her own. "Dare I say, she almost comes across as relatable. It's kind of a..." she searches for the word.

"Relief?" I add.

"That's the word I was looking for. Bloody mum brain."

Ruhela hurries her kids into the nearby greasy spoon cafe, which is full of builders enjoying a midday full English breakfast. She is completely unaware that she has spectators.

"Are we awful people for enjoying this?" Chandni asks.

"Terrible," I reply. "Absolutely the worst. Anyway, shall we get some lunch, at a more kid-friendly cafe?"

15th January, Julia's hen do

Deep breath. Deep breath. I'm only leaving H2 for the day. Actually, the day and evening but it's okay. She's with her dad. The person she's safest with, second only to me, her mother. Of course she'll be fine. I shall ignore what mum says. She's a worrywart. My baby will be fine. I'll be fine. I will make the most of the child-free day because, bugger me, it's overdue. Anyway, why do I worry about these things? M went to bloody Germany! He wasn't fretting about H2. Why am I? Oh yeah, I've got the boobies. And therein lies the elixir for H2.

Luckily, now that we're well into the breastfeeding journey and H2 is closer to being a year old, I don't feel engorged or uncomfortable. I can enjoy the evening.

My foot taps nervously as I sit on the Tube. It's still my least favourite place on earth, especially now that it gets dark early. I'll be travelling back at nighttime. Oh no! Will the Tube be okay on the way home? I saw frost forming on the street before I went underground.

Must distract myself. I'll check my phone.

There's a picture from M. He's holding a tortilla chip next to H2's mouth. Bloody hell! Is he feeding her crisps? Does he not know that's off the table until she's old enough to request it?

I drop him a message:

She's not eating that, is she?

M replies straight away:

No! It's a joke.

I exhale and settle back into the hardness of the fabric seat. Of course it's a joke. I need to lighten up. I'll use the tips the therapist mentioned about being in the moment. Even if this isn't my favourite moment.

Right now, there are there a bunch of teenagers swearing as if it's going out of fashion. A woman is stood nearby, looking out of the window, even though the scene outside is pitch black. There's also a young couple that look like they're in the early days of the relationship, when it's new, exciting. I want to tell them to milk this time for all it's worth. Because, if they choose to have children, everything changes. All of this, the romance, the interlocking fingers, the looking into each other's eyes... it all goes out of the window.

My phone pings...

It's Bushra:

Hey, can you talk?

My God! I never replied back to her? How long has it been? Months? I am an awful, horrible friend. Despite being on the Tube with patchy reception, I have to give her a call.

Before she has a chance to say hello, I launch into my apologies.

"Bushra, I'm glad you called. I'm really sorry but what I said the other day... or was it the other month? Sorry, mum brain. Anyway, what I said about you leading Ahmed on, I didn't mean to be so blunt."

"Don't worry, mate. I get where you're coming from. And it has given me something to think about. The truth is, and you're not gonna like me for it but, I just don't think I can bring myself to see Ahmed that way. I do like him. We get on. He is completely different to what I remember him being like in the office. He's proper keen and he really likes me. I know there's a lot going for him but I just need more. I really feel like I'm settling." Bushra pauses, waiting for a response. I don't give one. "Are you annoyed with me?"

"No!" I reply. "Why would I be annoyed?"

"Because you're always banging on about how I shouldn't be so shallow. I should go beyond looks. That it's about the personality and ticking other boxes. Like, being sensible and not just looking for sexual chemistry-"

"Bushra," I begin, "I highly doubt I used the word sexual. I'm far too Bengali for that. I said a lot of stuff, particularly in the last year, that probably hasn't made a lot of sense. Most of the time I don't know if I'm coming or going but, I get everything you're saying. And if that's how you feel, I don't think you should force it with Ahmed."

"Really?" Bushra sounds disappointed. "I thought you'd tell me to persevere with him. Go on a few more dates to see how I feel."

"From the sounds of it, you have been on a fair few dates and even met the parents! Given that it still doesn't feel right for you, then it probably isn't. If I'm honest, truly honest, I think I've been projecting onto you. I've been saying the things that my mum, my older sisters and every other Asian woman said to me. I was pushing you to make a sensible choice, because it felt like the proper thing to do but that wasn't really fair. Ultimately, I won't be living your life. Whether you marry Ahmed, someone else or no one else, it has to be right for you."

"Do you think I might not marry anyone?"

"What? I didn't say that!"

"You did. You said I might marry someone or no one."

"Oh, it's just a figure of speech. Like I say, nothing I say makes much sense these days. I cannot be trusted with the simplest things, let alone life advice. My point is, Bushra, I've probably been telling you what I think is right but that doesn't necessarily correlate with what you want. Only you can decide. So I'm absolutely not going to bang on about beauty being skin deep or whatever. And, honestly, us women compromise on so many things, bloody good for you for not wanting to compromise on the biggest decision of your life."

Bushra sighs. "I really needed to hear that. You're right but I do worry about ending up alone. I'm 34 now and it just seems to be getting harder and harder to meet someone. I think that's why I was trying to shoehorn Ahmed into the right person."

"I get it. Especially with the pressure we have from family and society but it doesn't mean you should settle. Anyway, 34 is the new 25!"

"Try telling my mum that." Bushra laughs and then the phone crackles. I go under a tunnel and lose reception.

HELEN, MY OLD SCHOOL friend, did her best but I can't help feeling terrible about it. I wish I could have helped. It's not that it's a bad hen do, it's just that when Julia envisaged some R&R with the girls, I don't think a Groupon spa day was what she had in mind.

"It looked nicer in the pictures," says Helen, carefully avoiding a patch of black mould on the steam room wall.

"It's fine!" says Julia with a chuckle. "They even have eucalyptus in the demister. It's quite potent."

Julia is not wrong. The essential oil is giving me a headache.

"I think it's lovely. After years of backpacking, I can tell you that this is a luxury," says Julia's sister, Jemima.

I haven't seen Jemima in years. The last time was probably just after uni, when I went to a barbecue at Julia's house and could only eat the veggie burgers and corn on the cob. I didn't even recognise Jemima, now that she's not a teenager anymore. She is tall and bronzed from years spent in hotter climes. Her hair is swept up into a messy, matted, updo, and she's wearing enough bead necklaces and silver rings to make me wonder how she negotiates such accessories with a small baby. She also, annoyingly, doesn't look like she gave birth five months ago.

I have a ton of questions for her. How is she finding motherhood all the way over in Brazil, away from her family? How is she finding raising a baby without a partner? Has she built a tribe over there? How is she dealing with sleepless nights? Or is her baby sleeping through? What about the feeding situation? She still looks perky, which makes me wonder if she's formula feeding the baby.

However, I keep these nosey questions to myself. This is Julia's day. Plus, my life is so consumed with motherhood, I really need to start changing the subject. At least for today.

Yes, today is for Julia and it's also a chance to resurrect the old me.

As I take a deep breath and inhale the eucalyptus-infused steam, I imagine myself having a rebirth. Coming out of the shell of the woman I've become since having H2 and seeing a semblance of my former self. The ambitious one. The one who ran a business. The one who was somewhat sorted. The one who drove around mum and dad. The one who split the rent with her hubby. The one who was relied upon, instead of relying on, others. I miss her.

There is another lady in the sauna. Of course, we wouldn't get the place to ourselves. There is no such luxury when you get a big discount on a spa day. She has her eyes firmly shut and is trying her best to zone us out.

"Gosh, I can't remember the last time I've done something like this," says Julia. "Work is utter bollocks at the moment. There was me thinking family law would be the easier one of all the sectors. Had I known, I would've just jumped into commercial law and had the big salary along with the crazy hours."

"It won't always be like that, will it?" I ask. "I thought this was the long game towards going in-house and working better hours?"

Julia tuts. "That is the long game but it seems to get longer and longer as time goes on. Miles and I really want to get on the property ladder. His mum and dad have offered to help us with a deposit, which is great. Obviously, when my mum got wind of that, she wanted to match it but I'd rather just do this by ourselves and not be beholden to anyone. At least that's the idea, though the exorbitant London house prices seem to be poo-pooing my plan."

"I don't think renting is such a bad thing," says Jemima. "It's a very British thing, isn't it, to feel entitled to have a piece of land? Having to own something? I'm happy with things the way they are. Living a simple life free of materialism. It means baby Jess and I can see the world. Do what we want to."

Julia snorts.

"What?" asks Jemima.

"It's easy to be a free spirit when you can dip into the bank of mum and dad. And as for the baby, they've been taking care of Jess ever since you got here. I'm all for this discovering yourself, bohemian phase but, come on, I've seen your Instagram posts. It's hardly a commune where you are."

Jemima turns her head away from her sister. "I've only got help from mum and dad since the baby's been born. I did everything by myself before. Anyway, not all of us want to be in the corporate race for the rest of our lives. Paying the big man, helping the rich get richer, while the poor get poorer. It's a lifestyle choice."

Maybe it wasn't a good idea that they both had a glass of Prosecco before coming into the sauna. Helen and I both shuffle along the bench, as far away from this sibling spat as possible.

"I've been renting forever," I say. "Out of circumstance, rather than choice."

Helen shakes her head. "That's where you're all going wrong. I'm quite lucky living at home. I don't have to worry about any of these things."

Julia, Jemima and I throw each other glances. I think we can all agree that Helen living at home with her mum and dad at the age of 35 isn't a lifestyle choice, either.

A girl in a berry-coloured uniform pops her head round the glass door, letting lots of steam escape.

"Ladies, would you like to come through for your massages now?"

We quickly put on our fluffy dressing gowns and follow the lady through the narrow corridor.

The room I am ushered into looks more like the boardroom at my old office. Dated, dark, with wood panelling. I don't feel relaxed. I feel like I'm about to get an appraisal.

"I see you're down for the deep tissue massage," says Lorraine, the therapist.

I shrug. "I'm not sure. I just paid the money and my friend booked it. Though a deep tissue massage sounds good."

"It will be great for you. I can see that you're very knotty."

She can tell that just by looking at me?

"Now, I believe you're lactating?" Lorraine asks.

Did Helen add that in the comments when booking this place? I suddenly turn very Bengali. "Not right now. As in, I'm not leaking but, yes, I am breastfeeding my daughter but I don't get engorged or anything now she's a little older."

Lorraine looks back at her notes. "Don't worry. I can prop you up with some towels for support."

As Lorraine rolls up towels on either side of the bed, I'm reminded of my H2. How I sometimes roll up towels around her to help her sleep better. I wonder what she's doing now.

I wonder if she's missing me. I feel the urge to take out my phone and stroke a picture of her.

"Let's get started," says Lorraine, interrupting my weirdness.

I'm not sure what I was expecting from this massage, but this wasn't it. Lorraine is working hard. Kneading away at the many knots in my back, causing things to pop along the way.

Then she turns psychic. "I can see you hold a lot of worry."

"Well, I have just become a mum. I was a worrier beforehand and it's multiplied now."

"You don't just worry about your daughter, though, do you?"

Huh? What's she on about?

Lorraine divulges. "You see, your back is divided to represent every area of you and your family. And it might sound strange but it says a lot about you as you carry all your worries on your back."

I believe in affirmations and gratitude journalling but this is a bit woo woo even for me.

I close my eyes and let her indulge. "One thing I can sense is that you worry a lot about your mum."

She deduced that from my back? "I guess I do worry about her a bit. And my dad. It's just, for years, I had the most responsibility at home. My older sisters left home long before, which meant I was the one checking the letters. Filling out the forms. Doing the driving. It carried on for a bit after I moved and got married. I resented that slightly, if I'm honest. But I've not been able to do anything like that for the last year. I've been busy enough being a mum myself. Maybe, subconsciously, I do worry." I didn't expect to share my life story with my masseuse.

"You know what they say, the subconscious has a way of becoming conscious. And it's often a more powerful feeling than things that are at the forefront of your mind."

I close my eyes and try to enjoy the rest of the massage. Yes, I probably do worry about mum but doesn't every daughter? In particular, doesn't every immigrant daughter, who has to bridge the gap between the motherland and modernity for their mother?

"I am getting help," I reveal, surprising myself. I don't even know this woman. "I'm talking to a therapist."

"Good for you, darling. I'm so pleased to hear that because, and I hope this doesn't offend you, but I don't think that's a very common thing for South Asian people, is it? Getting help?"

"I guess not. We don't talk about these things but then I've never done things the usual way," I reply.

Lorraine keeps kneading away, slowly breaking down my knots. "Good for you, darling. Good for you."

"I'M REALLY GLAD YOU could make it," says Julia, squeezing my hand at dinner.

"I wouldn't miss it for anything. Even though I did miss other things." I flatten out a crease in the tablecloth with the palm of my hand. "I am sorry about that and I'm sorry I couldn't really help much with organising this hen do."

"Nonsense!" says Julia. "I never asked you to. I wouldn't have expected it."

"That's right. You never asked me to, because you knew I wouldn't be able to but that doesn't make me feel any less guilty. You've been at the forefront of all my milestones."

Julia sips her wine, before noticing that there is a finger mark on the glass. She attempts to brush it off with her thumb but that just makes it worse. The restaurant was also Helen's choice. It is so loud and more like a nightclub than somewhere you could sit and chat. There's a saxophone player that's making my ears hurt. Scores of other women, who are also having hen parties, are wearing sashes, nylon veils and polyester white dresses. One woman is chanting: "I'm getting married, bitches!" while thrusting her finger in the air. I wish I bought Julia a veil at least. It looks like we're having a regular dinner.

"Listen," says Julia. "I've got plenty more milestones to come. Don't forget, I've yet to have a baby and be a raging hormonal wreck. Though I'm not saying that's what you are," she quickly adds. "The point is, there is plenty of time for you to make it up to me."

"And I will." I take a sip of my water. "I am working on myself. It's not necessarily getting easier but I am getting more used to it and muddling my way through. I'm even starting to see light at the end of the tunnel."

I haven't told Julia I'm speaking to the therapist. It's not that it's a secret, it's just that we haven't really spoken much. I planned to call her with a grovelling apology when I missed her dress fitting. Then life, or should I say motherhood, got in the way. I kept remembering to ring her during the 2am night feed, but that would be terribly unsociable. I hope it's not always this way. I hope there doesn't become a divide between me as a mum and my friends who don't have kids. I hope we can still find some commonality and time for each other.

"Anyway, have you got any photos of the little one? I bet she's grown since I last saw her," says Julia.

"I'd love to see her, too," says Helen.

Jemima nods, though perhaps more out of politeness. It's not like she doesn't have the exact same thing at home.

"Ladies, I thought you'd never ask."

I take out my phone, something I've been itching to do most of the day. I bring up my slideshow of H2. I share the video of her first learning to crawl. All wobbly arms and legs as she put one limb in front of the other. The girls melt when seeing pictures of her trying steamed cauliflower and wearing more of it than eating it. They coo at the photo of her in sunglasses while sat on the grass at Victoria Park and they marvel at the video of her climbing onto the top of the sofa to reach the windowsill.

My girl. She is a wonder. It's so much easier to appreciate her from afar, when I've got some breathing space. When it's not all-encompassing. I'm guessing that's why M is so good with her all the time. Because he doesn't have her all the time.

"How are you finding the sleepless nights?" I ask Jemima. Don't judge me. I'm very aware of how absorbed I am right now.

"She sleeps through. Though most of the time, I have her in the sling. That way, she naps on and off on me. It's amazing. I can breastfeed her right in the sling, too. Nobody even notices."

"I never really got the hang of the sling. M usually carries H2 in it when we go for walks. It seems to hurt my back and I'm always scared of her slipping out."

"It probably hasn't been adjusted properly. If you can remember, bring your sling to the wedding and I can give you a little tutorial."

"Thanks, I might do that." I smile at Jemima, then I notice the vacant looks from Julia and Helen. I put my phone away and decide that's the last I'll talk about motherhood tonight.

After dinner, it's time to give Julia some pre-wedding gifts. This is one area where I like to think I've redeemed myself.

After opening Jemima's healing crystals and Helen's bubble bath set, it's my turn. I hand over a duck egg blue gift box.

"You didn't!" Julia's mouth is agape as she unwraps the white ribbon and lifts the lid to reveal a sterling silver bracelet. "What were you thinking? That's way too expensive!"

"Yeah," Helen chimes in. "Don't you know it's meant to be a fun, novelty gift at a hen do. I thought your style would be more of a penis straw."

I nearly snort my water. "That was done at my hen do. We're over that now." I turn to Julia. "I wanted to get you something you could keep. Plus, you deserve it. Also, the next time I flake on one of your milestones, you can wear the bracelet and I'll be there in spirit."

Julia gives me a hug. I know you can't buy yourself back into someone's favour but an expensive present does make things a little better.

I GET THE TUBE HOME. Despite being oiled up like a baby, I'm feeling lighter. I had no emergency call from M. He sent me several photo updates for my reassurance. One of him and H2 at the park, then eating pasta and then her sleeping in his arms.

For the first time since I became a mum, I feel like I can get through this. More than that, I feel I can do this. I feel like it's okay. Everyone tells you it gets easier. And you know it will. Of course it will. I'm obviously not going to have a teenager that doesn't sleep through the night, am I? Yet, when you're in the trenches, it's hard to fathom how things could improve. When you're knee-deep in sleep deprivation, it doesn't feel like there's a way out. But today, having had a precious few hours to be the old me, I'm starting to feel like it's okay. I'm starting to feel like myself.

The Tube stops at a red light. As I don't want to ruin my zen with worry, I call mum.

"Hello lady," says big sis upon answering the landline.

"Hey, I didn't know you were at mum's."

"Oh, it's only a short visit. What are you up to?"

"I'm on my way home from Julia's hen do. You know, my old school friend?"

"That sounds nice. Did you take the little one with you?"

"Erm, no. It was a spa day, followed by dinner. It was hardly something appropriate for someone under the age of one."

"Blimey. Where did you leave her?"

"With her father? The other care giver?"

"That's ever so good, isn't it?" says big sis. "Did he manage?"

"He managed fine. Just as I have all this time. Anyway, is it the school holidays already?"

Big sis hesitates. "No, not yet."

"Oh. Then what about the kids? Did they miss school?"

"No, they're with their dad. I'll only be here for another day and I didn't want to take them out of school. They really clamp down these days on absences. You get fined for taking your own children anywhere. Gone are the long trips to Bangladesh during term time."

The Tube goes through a tunnel and I momentarily lose reception.

Once I can hear big sis again, I ask: "How come you've come up by yourself? You never do."

"Mum had an appointment, that's all. She wanted someone to go with her to help translate."

"Oh, okay. What was it? A dentist appointment?" I'm not sure why little sis couldn't have taken mum. It seems unnecessary for big sis to come all the way from Bristol for an appointment.

"No, not the dentist. A hospital appointment. I guess nobody's told you yet."

"Told me what?"

Big sis hesitates.

"What? Just tell me."

"Well, nobody wanted to bother you as you've had your hands full with the little one. I know you've been all over the place after having the baby and-"

"Right, could you just tell me what you're on about? I don't understand."

Big sis gulps hard. "It's mum. You know she's always been forgetful but it's gradually got worse."

"Has it? I hadn't noticed."

Big sis sighs. "Like I say, you've been busy with the baby. Anyway, we wanted to see what the issue was, so... she had a few tests...and then they wanted to do a brain scan, which is why I came up."

I lurch forward, holding my stomach. "A brain scan? What for? Has she got a tumour?"

"No, no, nothing like that. But... well... you'll find out sooner or later... it's looking like it's dementia."

"Looking like? What does that mean?"

"We're waiting on the results of the brain scan but, from what the doctor said and, given the results for her other tests, it's most likely that's the cause."

I say nothing.

"Lady, are you still there?"

My mouth is trembling. I have words to say but I can't let them out.

"Lady... I think the line has gone funny. Are you still there? Can you hear me?"

"Yeah, I'm still here. What did you say? Mum has got dementia?"

"Yeah lady, I know it's a bit of a shock-"

"Mum's got dementia? Are you sure?"

"As sure as the doctors are, little lady."

"No, that doesn't make any sense. I speak to her all the time, at least every few days. She seems fine. Since when has she had this?"

"That's the bit we don't know, lady. She might have had it in a mild form for years. It still is mild. When it gets quite bad, people stop recognising their own children."

My stomach is in knots.

"Lady, the phone is very crackly. Hello? Hello, can you hear me?"

Big sis says hello a few more times before I go through another tunnel on the Underground, which kills the call.

16th January, My soulmate

According to the mum forums, a baby is more of a soulmate than a partner. They are born of you. They are literally part of your soul. H2 is part of my soul. I am a part of my mum's soul. She is a part of her mum's soul.

I wish my soulmate would sleep better. H2 still gets up frequently. Sometimes she needs rocking, sometimes she wants walking. I know it'll get easier, but when? In two, three, four, five or six years' time?

It's gone 3am. M is snoring like a foghorn. I know better than to wake him. We're in a good place. Let's not argue about how to settle H2.

M has been a rock after I shared the news about mum. He managed the not-so-easy feat of holding both me and H2 in his arms, as I crumpled like a tissue.

The thing is, mum is everything. She is the glue that holds the family together. It's her home we all congregate at. Granted, it's dad's, too, but mum makes the house a home. She is the constant in my life, the one that I speak to the most. Annoying though she is at the best of times, she is everything. And I can't bear to lose parts of her. I can't see her disintegrate into nothing.

I only know basic bits about dementia that I learnt from my work in healthcare PR. I know people start to lose their memory. They can slowly stop recognising their children and grandchildren. They can even think they are younger and living in the past. I don't know much more than that. How quickly does it escalate? One day, will she suddenly not recognise me? Or H2?

Were the signs always there? How long has she been like this? I remember seeing Mrs Barker, mum and dad's neighbour, for the first time in ages. She was clutching a teddy at the front doorstep, like a child waiting to be picked up from nursery. It was strange. Mrs Barker used to be so strong. She'd walk for miles and seemed to be one of those out-and-about old ladies. To see her like a child, it was bizarre. Heartbreaking, even.

Mum has always been forgetful. I mean, she's always flip-flopping when it comes to auntie Jusna, or forgetting she's got letters that need to be opened, read and translated. However, at what point did mum transition from being a little dizzy, to having dementia?

If I'm honest, truly, truly honest, I didn't expect this to happen to mum. I would've been less surprised if it was dad that had dementia. I know that sounds terribly cruel but dad is the one who's more resigned. He's the one that keeps himself to himself, burrowing away when we visit. He's a man of few words and he does his own thing. I didn't expect this of mum. She can't be the one that gets ill. It's her job to stay strong for us. She's our mum. She is the one that makes things happen. She is the one responsible for getting us all together during the Christmas holidays, the Easter holidays, summer holidays. She can't disappear. She can't. I need her.

4th February, Jam's big fat Bangladeshi wedding

I try my best not to look at mum with pity but I'm not sure I'm doing a very good job of it.

"You can not just sit there, you need to get ready, no?" Mum ushers me off the sofa, which is a difficult job as I've got H2 latched on, having an 11am comfort feed.

"There's a bit of time. He's not coming over until 12.30pm. Then again, that'll probably mean closer to 2 'o'clock." I'm referring to M, obviously. Who else do I call 'he'?

"Okay but no leave it too late. Your hair is all leggy. You need give it good comb. You should've done haircut before you came. This be your time to be nice. Also... I wanted to speak with you." Mum sits next to me. She squeezes H2's chubby foot. Is she going to tell me about her dementia diagnosis? I haven't let on that I know anything. I was waiting for her to bring it up to me. Maybe now she will.

"The thing is..." Mum leans in. "Your eyebrows look very bushy. You want your little sister to do them before you leave?"

I raise a hand to my eyebrows. They do seem like they've doubled in size over the last month. The curse of being blessed with thick, coarse hair means that I have thick, coarse hair everywhere. I can't go longer than three weeks without getting my eyebrows threaded. Now that I'm a mum, however, such treatments are a luxury. I tend to leave a couple of months between each threading session. I totally should've got them done.

"If she can do them," I say. "You might have to watch this one, though." I look down at H2, who is slowly getting milk drunk as her eyes roll to the back of her head. Maybe she'll nap for longer than half an hour this time to enable me to get my eyebrows done and look wedding ready.

I put her down with the experienced help of my mother, who places a soft fleece blanket under H2's arms.

"Mum... big sis, told me about your hospital appointment."

Mum's eyes dart from side to side. "*Oh ho*! That be nothing! Doctor think maybe I be losing memory *lit-ool* bit but I don't know. I think maybe I just old."

"Do you find you are getting more forgetful? Do you feel any different?"

"How can I explain how my head feels? Sometimes good, sometimes not so good. What else is there to say?" Mum huffs. "Anyway, there's no worry for you. You've got a bigger thing to think about. Not crazy old mum."

"Don't say that, mum."

"*Acha,* no crying! We had too much of your tears already. I just be making joke. Can mum not make joke? Anyway, you go get ready. I watch this monkey."

I slowly make my way upstairs but leave the door open so I can spring to action if H2, or mum, needs me.

"WHO'S GETTING MARRIED?" asks little sis as she attacks my eyebrows with a piece of thread.

"It's M's best mate, Jam. He's been looking for ages and at one point he thought it wouldn't happen. M had written him off as well."

"Are all your friends married now?"

"Not all of them. Julia is getting married next month, and a couple of my old workmates are still single."

"Are any of them Asian?" asks little sis.

You guessed it, the old aunties view, that brown girls should be married before the age of 30, has filtered down to little sis. What can I say? It's ingrained in our souls.

"Bushra is Pakistani. There was a guy at work she started seeing but she didn't fancy him, so that didn't work." I'm not sure if I should be saying this much to little sis. Talking about fancying and whatnot. I feel I need to be more big sisterly and explain to her about boundaries, keeping things halal and not worrying about fancying them until you get married.

Little sis moves the thread from my eyebrows to my upper lip. "I'll just go over the patch where you've got some long hairs."

Ouch. I mean that figuratively and literally.

"How is mum doing?"

Little sis exhales. "Don't know, really. It's weird because generally she's okay and normal. A bit moodier than usual but then there's been times when she's been so forgetful. Sometimes it's little things like going to the shop and forgetting what she went for, which we all do now and then. Other times, she's super repetitive, which I thought was just a bit annoying. Occasionally, it's more than that. She seems a little lost. Now, when she goes out on her own, I sneak a letter into her pocket that's got her name and address on it."

Little sis continues pulling the thread across my facial hair, while my eyes prick with tears.

"Sorry, is it hurting you? The middle of the moustache is always painful."

"Yeah, it is a bit uncomfortable," I say.

Little sis was always the little shit. She was the lazy one that didn't do much. She was the youngest one, the entitled one. To hear that she's been covertly stuffing envelopes in mum's clothing as a form of identification, having to do something so big, so grown-up, for a situation that is potentially quite serious, saddens me. I'm glad she's stepped up to the plate but I'm heartbroken that these are the circumstances under which she's needed to grow up.

"I do worry about the future, though," little sis adds. "Like, I'm the only one at home now. What happens when she gets worse?"

"If she gets worse," I interject. "She might stay the way she is."

"That's the most optimistic version but it's likely she will get worse. Most people do. And dad's no help, either. He just keeps himself to himself as usual."

"Dad's always been like that but, anyway, you don't have to do it on your own. I'll be around. We come every month."

"Yeah but it's not the same. You don't live here. I know you've got your own baby. You'll be like big sis and middle sis. They can't do much from far away. In a few years, I'll have to get married, too. Then I'll move away. Mum and dad will be on their own. It would be nice if we had a brother that could've taken care of mum and dad."

"Times are changing," I say. "Jam is moving to where his fiancé lives. The girl doesn't always have to go near the boy's family these days."

Little sis wipes her eyes.

"Hey," I rub her arm. "It's okay. Remember, I'm your big sister. I'll always be here to help. And I've still got a responsibility towards you and mum and dad. I know I've not been very good recently but things are getting better. Actually, that's not quite true, it's still pretty shit but, I believe things will get easier. My baby is nearly one now. I'll have more free time. You won't be going through this alone."

"I hope not."

A stray tear rolls down my cheek and gets intertwined in the thread. "You won't," I say, trying to believe my own words.

"I'M GLAD TO BE AT A Bengali wedding," says M, unbuttoning his jacket to make way for food. "It's been a while."

"I know. And it's her first time." I look at H2, who is banging on the table with a fork. "They won't serve nuts here, would they? You know how half-arsed Bengalis can be."

"It's unlikely. Nuts aren't a common thing in our curries but anything we're unsure about, we won't feed her. Did you get the food pouches?"

I tap on my oversized changing bag. "Of course. I've got the antihistamine at the ready, too."

Having waited patiently for 10 minutes, M unwraps a beautifully packaged box. Wedding favours have come a long way since our big day, where we had little mesh bags containing Quality Street chocolates. This box is personalised with the initials J and J.

"Let's hope there's something to eat here," says M. "I'm starving."

"Yes, it's tough, with you being the one breastfeeding and all." I poke him in the belly. "Wait a minute! That's a bloody peanut brittle! Don't they care about allergies? Does Jam not know H2 can't have peanuts?"

"I don't know, to be honest with ya. I think his Mrs was in charge of the favours. He probably didn't have a say in it." M quickly stuffs the sweet in his mouth, crunching vigorously.

I glare at him.

"What? It's better if I eat it, then it's out of H2's reach."

I can't argue with that logic. "Let's take them all off the table," I say. "Quick! Before other people sit here and start chomping on peanut brittles around my baby."

"Wouldn't that be a bit rude?" asks M.

"I don't think there's any room for politeness when it comes to possibly fatal allergies."

M puts all the favour boxes in a pile, while H2 attempts to grasp at their ribbons.

"How about I put them in your bag?" says M. "That way, we can eat them later, when she's asleep."

"No!"

"Alright, worth a try." M puts his hands in the air. "God, I miss peanuts. I haven't had Bombay mix in ages." H2 puts her nose towards M. "But she's worth the sacrifice."

It's nice to have H2 dressed up. Since birth, she's been gifted playsuits, party dresses and the like but I've always chosen comfort over fashion. She's usually in a baby grow or leggings.

Today, seeing her in a black and white striped dress with a puffy skirt, is wonderful. She's getting endless gazes from the many guests, with some stopping to stroke her cheek. I don't blame them. She looks like a brown, mini Audrey Hepburn, complete with a pixie haircut.

There is no partition at this event. No segregation for men and women. Instead, we find ourselves on a table with some young lads, likely no older than 30.

"I'm not gonna leave any seekh kebabs behind. It's every man for himself," says one of the group, patting his stomach.

"Yeah, with you around, we'll be starving, ya beast!" says another.

One of the boys unwraps a favour box. Damn M, I thought he got rid of them all. The boy takes out the peanut brittle and bites it with his side teeth. My heart races. What if H2's allergies are airborne? What if she has a reaction right now? I wouldn't even know what to do.

"Shall we move?" I ask M.

He looks around. "I don't think there is anywhere to move."

He's right. Every single table is taken up by groups of eight. Every seat has a bum on it. They're even rolling out more tables, which suggests they have an unexpected number of guests. Typical Bengalis, never RSVP properly to say who will be coming and then decide on the day that the entire family of eight will rock up.

I take a deep breath to settle my anxiety.

"Are you okay?" asks M.

I take another deep breath. "Yeah, I'm fine."

M puts his hand on my knee. "It's okay. She's fine. See?"

H2 cranes her neck back to have a good look at her surroundings. She marvels at the enormous banqueting hall, which is a decadent mix of red, white and gold. It's not dissimilar to where I got married. They have gold pillars, creating a fake altar, a red carpet which is slightly creased and round tables with white tablecloths as far as the eye can see. I would guess that this wedding will host hundreds.

Observing H2 as she looks around with wide eyes and a gummy grin, helps ease my nerves. The therapist is right, being in the moment, practising mindfulness and observing my daughter, does bring me back from a panic attack. I stroke her hair. She grabs my finger and grips it tightly. She then tries to eat it.

She will be okay. She's fine. Luckily, the peanut brittle is quickly consumed, leading to more piss-taking from the other boys at the expense of the beast.

The starters are tossed onto our table like frisbees. There is a plate of seekh kebabs, a silver tray of samosas, some chicken tikka, yoghurt, chutney and a bowl of salad.

The boys in our company, despite threatening to demolish all the food in sight, gesture for us to start first.

"No, it's fine. You guys go ahead," says M.

"You're alright, brother," says a spiky-haired member of the group. "There'll be nothing left, what with beast and his growling belly."

I wonder how beast feels about having such a nickname?

H2 nibbles on a piece of neon red chicken tikka. Her cheek becomes flushed.

"Is that a reaction?" I ask M.

M looks at H2's rosy left cheek. "I don't know. She seems fine in herself. Let's see how she gets on. Maybe give her some water."

After a minute, H2's redness settles and she's only lightly itching her cheek. I need to calm down. I can't carry on like this, being a nervous wreck. I turn my attention to the table-cloth. There is a dyed-in oil stain from a previous wedding. I look at the napkin arrangement. They are all laid out in fans. Someone had to fold all of these ahead of the wedding. What craftsmanship.

"Babe, let me hold her for a bit. You try to eat or you won't get a chance."

M's right, I've had her in my lap since the food arrived, on account of the fact that there are no high chairs at this venue. That was a miscalculation on their part. Bengali weddings are never short of a baby or two.

No sooner has M put his arms out, that H2 climbs on board and starts bending her knees as if she wants to take off. I think she wants to practise walking.

The place is bursting with children running crazily between tables, manoeuvring in and out at speed. I'm nervous they'll bump into my baby.

Must distract myself.

I look down at my salwaar kameez, which has golden embellishments on pink fabric. I bought it before H2 was born and I'm glad it still fits. It's not nursing friendly, so I'm hoping that the pouches and whatever H2 can eat here will suffice for a couple of hours at least.

M patiently escorts H2 around the venue, hunched over so he can reach her raised arms. He is so good with her. I need to give him more credit. I have to start letting go and trusting him. He is her dad, after all. Why do I find it so hard to relinquish control? Why do I, dare I say, look for issues? Why do I look to rescue the situation? Maybe I'll bring that up with my therapist next time we speak.

Once the mains arrive, I eat in my usual indigestion-inducing way, as I'm readying myself to have to hold H2 or deal with a meltdown. She is happily chewing on a piece of naan bread, which is all the more laborious as she doesn't have any teeth yet. M sneaks in some bites of food while he holds H2.

"Here, hand her over. I'm done now."

"Nah, you've still got food on your plate. Make sure you eat properly. I'm managing to get some food in between this one," says M as he reaches for a mound of rice coated in curry sauce.

A drop of oil falls on H2's dress. Never mind, she'll be perfectly imperfect, just like me.

"Once we've eaten," says M, sounding like a man with a plan, "we'll go over and say hi to Jam. Hopefully his Mrs won't be long joining him. Then we can make our escape."

I've not even looked up at the main stage. Jam is sitting there, wearing a gaudy gold sherwani with diamanté embellishments. He even has a novelty sword, which seems a little

much. He's not going into battle. His red turban has a ruby centrepiece surrounded by feathers. If this is his get up, I
can't wait to see the bride.

"Congratulations man," M shakes Jam's hand. "Welcome
to the club." Jam clasps his hands and they have a brotherly
moment, leaving H2 and I feeling like third and fourth
wheels.

"It took me long enough to get here," says Jam. "How's
the little one?" He turns to H2, putting his hands out for her.

My daughter leans in to get a cuddle from her pseudo
uncle. I try not to focus on the many sharp embellishments
on Jam's outfit that could easily scratch my daughter. H2 is
less concerned and is busy trying to grab his ruby hat jewel.

"Did you get enough food?" Jam asks the most important question of all when it comes to Bengali weddings and
life in general.

"Yeah, we ate plenty," says M. "Though we had to wolf it
down as this one wants to walk around. It's her bid for free-
dom before nap time."

Jam leans back as H2 makes a grab for his feather.
"You've got a magpie on your hands here, mate. Try and
stretch out her nap if you can and stay for dessert. It's gulab
jam and ice cream. Plus, you need to meet the Missus. In
fact..." Jam looks over M's shoulder. "It looks like she's coming now."

I turn around to witness a scene that takes me back to
my own wedding day. A nervous-looking bride, head down,
adorned with jewels and feathery lashes. A cohort of
women- aunties, nieces, cousins, all wearing a pastel shade of
orange. The slow procession walks towards us. M and I de-

cide that now is the time to get off the stage but H2 has other ideas. She refuses to disentangle herself from Jam's cuddles and instead pulls at his hat, determined to release the ruby from its claw. Jam laughs, as that's all he can do, then he lifts H2 in the air by her underarms. She shrieks hysterically, throwing her head back, kicking her legs. While she is distracted, Jam passes H2 to M.

Once she spots the glittery bride, H2 stands on ceremony, along with all of us, as she makes her way towards the stage.

Jam's bride shuffles towards him, the long skirt of her lehengha brushing against the red carpet. Then she looks up and I see her catch the gaze of her husband. Jam returns the look. I can see he's absolutely smitten. They are smitten. It goes to show, the pre-marital disagreements over money or living arrangements pale against the bigger picture. After a long search, Jam has found his person. And, having known M's best friend for nearly six years, I am truly, truly happy for him.

M, on the other hand, is probably low-key heartbroken. After all, Jam is his best mate, his wing man, his ride or die. He'll have to get used to sharing him now. Maybe I won't be the third wheel anymore.

7th February, Apologies

One of the major pluses of having a clingy baby is that I am forced to lie down with her when she naps.

As I'm currently at my mother-in-law's, I am happy to be tethered to H2. I silence any feelings of guilt for not helping prepare lunch downstairs. I try to forget M's mum's queries about whether I brought the baby monitor with me so I can leave her upstairs. I ignore M's sister-in-law's surprise that H2 is not sleeping for longer without me. Oh yes, she regaled me with an anecdote of how her kids used to sleep anywhere, even in the noisiest of circumstances, without her. They'd apparently stay on the sofa in the living room, while she'd be cooking away with our mother-in-law in the kitchen. I smiled when she mentioned this and said something about how all children are different. On this occasion, on this rare occasion, I am glad I've got the one who is clingy.

If only I could fall asleep. I wonder if this is my new normal, a constant state of alert.

I close my eyes and try to shut out the muffle I can hear downstairs. There is the sound of M's nephew and niece playing in the hallway. Then I hear little footsteps making their way up the flight of stairs. I look to H2. She starts moving. Oh no, don't get up. I'm enjoying this lying down and not being able to sleep. I plug in a boob to settle her. Almost a year in, it still works like a charm.

The door twists open. M's nephew and niece burst into the room and, upon seeing me, tiptoe backwards.

"Don't come in!" I say. "I'm trying to get her to sleep."

"Sorry," his niece says, avoiding looking at H2's face as it's attached to my nipple. "We're playing hide and seek and I've run out of good spaces."

After nearly making her cry the last time I saw her, when she gave H2 a cookie that triggered an allergic reaction, she must hate me. I bet both of them think I'm an evil auntie, ruining their fun. Must rectify that. "Try under the stairs," I advise.

I turn to H2, who's looking straight back up at me, big brown eyes framed with huge eyelashes. Damn, my lactating efforts failed. She climbs onto all fours and lowers her legs off the bed, landing with a thud.

The minx.

Never mind, I guess I'll go downstairs and see what everyone is up to.

"CAN YOU GIVE HER TO her dad?" My mother-in-law asks, keen for my input in the kitchen.

"Of course."

I go to the front room, where M is watching the football with his brothers. His nephew and niece come in and jostle over who gets to hold her.

"What do you think is the cutest part of her?" M's niece asks.

"Well, duh," his nephew scoffs. "Obviously it's her hands."

As I leave them to admire my daughter, I just have one instruction: "Remember... don't-"

"Feed her anything without asking you or uncle," M's nephew and niece say in unison. I've trained them well.

M's big brother smiles at his children, then turns to me: "I'll put all the snacks away."

Back in my mother-in-law's kitchen, there are various pots and pans bubbling away. One smells pungent. It must be fish. I'm relieved to see some chicken curry being stirred by M's sister-in-law.

"I go pray now. You ladies keep eye on food, yes?" says my mother-in-law, hobbling into the downstairs bathroom.

My sister-in-law is stirring some rice in a pool of oil and onions.

"Are you making pulao?" I ask.

"Yes," she replies. "You know what mum is like. She loves to make special food when there is no special occasion."

"I know that all too well. Though I'm not doing as much these days as I'm usually breastfeeding or napping the baby."

"Did you not find breastfeeding painful? I found it hurt a lot with mine," says M's sister-in-law.

"At the beginning, it hurt a lot because I wasn't doing it properly. It was only when I went to my mum's that I established breastfeeding. She really encouraged me to keep on trying. If it wasn't for that, I probably would've given up."

M's sister-in-law sighs. "I guess I wasn't doing it properly. I used to find it so painful, like my babies were biting. That's why I gave up way too soon. It felt so hard. Plus, being in the

UK, living with my in-laws, there wasn't any encouragement to carry on with it. You're lucky you have your mum here for support. With my mum in Bangladesh, I didn't have that."

M's sister-in-law adjusts her spice-infused headscarf and expertly pours the exact amount of boiling water to the pot of sautéed rice.

"You're right. I am very lucky to have my mum."

"What you say?" My mother-in-law appears behind us.

"Nothing *maa*," says M's sister-in-law. "Have you finished praying? If so, I'll go up."

With that, the ladies do a little switcheroo and my mother-in-law joins me in the kitchen.

For the record, I can't pray today. H2 must be drinking less during her feeds, as my period has come back with a vengeance.

My mother-in-law boils some water. "You want tea?"

"No thanks, mum."

"I missed you. House been quiet without you and baby."

Dare I say, I've missed my mother-in-law, too. I've missed her comforting meals and, most of all, I've missed the way she dotes on H2. I was so angry with how dismissive she was about H2's allergies. Now, with the benefit of time, I realise that my mother-in-law just doesn't get it. She's never dealt with things like that before. And while I will protect my daughter at all costs, I will try to have more patience with M's mum.

I go over to hold her hand but realise that's way too much PDA for her liking. Instead, I'll talk from a polite distance. "Mum, I'm sorry I've not been very good recently."

M's mum looks startled. "What do you mean?"

"I've not been able to help much. You've had to do all the cooking and preparing because I've been too busy with the baby. I'm sorry about that."

My mother-in-law looks offended. "What you talk about? Rubbish. Absolute rubbish! I can do all these things, I still young lady!" She laughs. "Most important thing is that you and baby are okay. I manage just fine. When she be older, you can help more."

"I will."

She returns to her tea making and I have no doubt my mother-in-law will hold me to my word in years to come.

3rd March, Back in the driving seat

"I don't know if I should do this," I say to mum. "Let's leave it. I'm getting a headache. Anyway, why do I need to drive? In London, I don't even use the car."

"*Dooro!* You all ready, now. Your baby be ready to go out in her cute jumper dress. I think it be good for you to practice. After all, why have car sitting here if you no use it? Time you got some independence back."

I smirk at mum. "Are you sure it's not just so I can take you to the supermarket and do your errands when I come up north?"

"*Nah,* I got your little sister to do those jobs now. And, I could still get bus sometimes with your dad. Your mum not that old. Now, go get your baby. Where she gone? That baby crawl so fast, no keeping up with her. You'll have to watch her when she be big. Too fast for anyone."

I go into the dining room to find dad cradling baby H2 as though she's a newborn. It's funny, she never lets me hold her like that anymore, now that she is an independent woman that can pull herself up by holding furniture. Yet, for dad, she happily becomes a little baby again, playing with his prayer hat and trying it on for size.

"Dad, give her to me. I'm going for a drive now."

"*Eh heh*, where you go? You need me to come?"

"If you want," I say, though, on second thoughts, I'd rather he didn't. Having mum as a backseat driver makes me nervous enough as it is. Combine mum with dad and I'll be a jittering mess.

"Actually, no. I go for walk later," dad decides.

"Okay but you're not going to get a KFC again, are you?" I ask.

Dad looks to the ground. "I like the *seef*."

It's hard to chastise dad when he's so cute. "They are good chips."

"Right, you want to go today or tomorrow?" mum asks, hand on her hip, all ready for the outdoors in her camel-coloured fur trim coat.

THIS IS THE FIRST TIME I've driven since H2 was born. Actually, scratch that. This is the first time I've been in the driving seat since I was about four months pregnant. I feel like a learner driver all over again. It takes me around 15 minutes to plug in the car seat's Isofix, delayed further by mum's incessant commentary.

"Maybe use seat belt instead. Why you no check on internet? YouTube tell you everything!"

I ignore her. All this clipping, fastening and adjusting is getting me hot and bothered. I want to go back inside. When did I become such a feeble woman? How many basic things have I delegated to my husband since becoming a mum? How much of myself have I lost in the process of gaining another human?

Just as I'm about to yank the car seat out, something magically clicks into place. I finally strap H2 in, feeling satisfied I've passed the first stage of getting on the road. I slide into the driving seat. I clip in my seatbelt, check my mirrors, which have been adjusted to my younger sister's shorter height. I push the seat back, which has also been altered to little sis' spec. She pretty much owns my car now. I'm more of a custodian.

"What you keep doing with your fingers on the steering wheel?" asks mum.

"I'm saying *Allahu Akbar* 10 times, counting on each finger," I reply. "It's an old habit."

Mum nods in satisfaction. "Good. Very good. Anyway, I do all praying for us while you drive. Or it be nighttime before we get started."

I take a deep breath and reverse. Then, I move off, making sure I don't hit next door's Volkswagen Polo in the process. My gear change is slightly jerky and my clutch control is a little off but, that aside, I'm okay. I look in the rearview mirror to see H2 peering out of the window. She seems to be enjoying this journey so far.

"Right, mum, we're on the road. Where do you want to go?"

"If it not be too much trouble, I wouldn't mind going to cash-and-carry to get some ground rice."

"The one near the park? They drive horribly there. All those Asian drivers, thinking they own the road."

"*Acha*, let's not do that if you be too wimpy. Why not just drive round for *lit-ool* bit?"

Upon mum's instruction, I drive down to Wellington Road North and head towards Levenshulme. Traffic is busy on the A6, with cars cutting me up from either side.

"It be a bit tricky here. Shall we turn back?" says mum, her default nervousness kicking in.

"Yeah, let's turn back," I reply, glad that it's not my suggestion.

I feel a small sense of achievement. For the first time ever, I am driving my car with H2 in the back. She's not had a screaming fit, I haven't had an anxiety-induced meltdown and, so far, we are all alive and well.

On the way back, our side of the road is blocked due to roadworks. I didn't notice that coming this way. I was so focused on the journey ahead. The diversion takes me to unfamiliar territory. I don't like it.

"I'm a bit lost, mum. Do you know where we are?"

"Me? I be worst person to ask! I never been here. You no worry, just keep going. Then, inshallah, you'll get back to main road."

I keep driving but feel like I'm getting deeper into unknown territory. There's a parade of shops I've never seen before. The road then takes me onto a dual carriageway.

"Shit! There's a sign for the bloody motorway! I'll end up going back to London!" I feel myself getting hotter, my heartbeat quickening. Crap, crap, where am I going?

Luckily, there is a left turn, allowing me to pull up on the side street. I take out my phone, hands shaking and check my map for directions. There is no damn internet! My phone decides that now is the time to be useless.

"Bloody hell! This is why I don't want to go out driving. I told you, mum!"

"Don't worry, keep going forward and eventually you find something familiar."

"It doesn't work like that, mum! Why are you offering to help when you don't even know the way yourself?"

Mum looks away from me. "Okay, you do what's best."

I exhale. "Sorry, mum. I don't mean to shout. I just don't want to be getting lost and far from home. She'll start crying in the back, then I won't know what to do."

Mum smiles. "Look at her. No, really. *Look* at her. She look like she about to cry to you?"

H2 is kicking her legs against the seat and winding her hands up. "She usually does," I say.

"Her stress be your stress," says mum. "If you fine, she be fine."

It's ironic coming from mum, the one who makes me the most stressed.

I take a deep breath and get back on the road. I take a right turn, then another right turn and thankfully, end up back on familiar road.

The traffic is slow and we find ourselves stopping and starting but we are making progress. H2 is okay and so am I. I can do this.

"I went to shop one day and got lost." Mum's voice is barely audible.

"What?"

"I went to shop because I think I needed milk or eggs, or something. I forget. I couldn't remember the way. It's just the usual shop. You know, one round the corner, five minute walk. Then, I thought maybe I need post office? I walk *lit-ool* bit further and then I got scared. Couldn't remember if I needed stamps or envelopes or eggs. So I came back home.

Except, I didn't go straight home. I went past our house to the country park."

"Mum, you never go to the country park by yourself! You've always said it's not safe and it's way too quiet."

"Exactly! I no know why I end up there. Funny thing be, I live in front of country park for all these years, yet I never, ever go there. We never do, do we? It feel scary. You never see people walking. Only occasionally man with dog. It be far too quiet there but, that day, I really, really want-ed to go. Something about country park reminds me of back home. The grass is long, like in Bangladesh. The trees are overgrown. It be so green and fresh and when it rains, every-thing smell good. I like the noise of trees and the leaves when it be windy. I always look from my bedroom window and al-ways think it be so close, why am I scared? So I went there. That day I felt brave for *lit-ool* bit. After that, I came back home. Then I remember, I needed eggs. It be scary how mind can be so tricky."

"I wish you told me, mum."

"What you do? You be so far away and busy enough."

"I'll never be too busy for you, mum. I'm still going to be the reliable one. Even from London."

Mum giggles. "You know, both your big sisters very reli-able before they had children, too. Everything changes. It be good, not bad thing. It be your turn."

The traffic picks up pace but, instead of going straight home, I drive past our cul-de-sac.

"Hey, you missed turn. I know you not driven for long time but you forget already?"

"No, I didn't forget. We'll go for a little detour."

"Where to?"

"The country park."

FOR ALL MY CURSING of H2's bulky pram that is a nightmare on the narrow London paths, I am grateful for it now. The rugged terrain of the country park is exactly what this pram was made for. It rolls over the wood chips with ease and makes short work of the many mud puddles. I can't imagine doing this with one of those sleek silver pushchairs with leather trim handles.

Mum looks delighted, like she's a young girl again. She giggles as she avoids the puddles with her mesh trainers. I wish she'd do this more. I wish we didn't have this fear of the quiet countryside. It's a brown person thing, I think. Fear of being alone and isolated without any witnesses around. We are more comfortable squeezed into the city.

"Whenever I see overgrown grass, it reminds me of our village in Bangladesh." That's an anecdote I've heard many times before. I can't tell if it's the dementia, or she just likes sharing the story. Come to think of it, I never really paid attention to these little clues that might have been peppered throughout the last few years. I just thought mum was being mum.

"This long, overgrown grass remind me of our village in Bangladesh," she says again.

"Do you still remember that, mum? You haven't been for years."

"I never forget. Even when I forget everything else, I never forget that." She looks down.

"Mum, why don't you go to Bangladesh in the summer? You haven't been in years."

"I *doh-noh*. Maybe if I can get your *lit-ool* sister to come." She sighs.

H2 is in her element. One thing I've learnt from motherhood is that kids need to be outside. They need the fresh air. They sleep better and they are less restless. It's like a shot of sunshine to their brains. I'm the same. As an adult, if I haven't been out at least once in the day, I go a bit mad.

For all the perks of a cosmopolitan life in London, such open, un-tamed green spaces are scarce. Yes, we've got Victoria Park a short drive away but there's nothing like this country park.

"Your *lit-ool* one is always grabbing at the sofa and lifting herself up. She be walking way before her time."

"I don't think it's before her time, mum," I say, in a rare downplaying of my daughter's abilities. "She's nearly one, so is right on schedule to walk."

Mum gasps. "Really? It been nearly one year? Already? How time fly. What you do for her birthday? Do you want to come here? Maybe we could book nice buffet? Then everyone can see her."

I hadn't even thought about H2's birthday. I've been so busy surviving in the moment that forward planning has been abandoned somewhat. Though mum is right, I should do something.

"I'll look into it. Maybe we can have it at our usual place, where I had my Mehendi and engagement ceremony."

"I think it's a good choice. Food be good there. Your dad like the poppadoms. Yes, you look at it and maybe I can pay."

"Mum, there's no need to pay. I'll sort it!"

"No, no. It be difficult for you as you just started new job and have all that student loan debt."

"What new j-" I stop myself as I realise mum is describing little sis.

We walk on further. The breeze of the trees cools my mind and washes away anxieties about driving, raising my child, living. Seeing mum marvel at the trees, at the leaves, at mother nature untethered, eases my worries about her. It's nice to grab these moments while we can.

Mum steps in a brown puddle. "Think I need to buy wellies, like the English ladies."

"I think you do, mum."

H2, upon seeing mum's dirty shoes, starts giggling incessantly.

She lunges forward as if she wants to get out and get some muddy puddle action.

"Sorry lady, you've not got the right shoes to go out walking and, of course, you can't walk yet."

"She be walking soon. Before her time," says mum.

"Yes, mum, she's a clever one."

7th March, Stepping up

"I really wouldn't call you unless I absolutely had to tell you this. And you're not going to like it, but I just have to let you know," says Vanessa, my freelance cover.

She sounds nervous and I can only assume it to be one thing. My client loves her work and wants to poach her for a much healthier day rate than what she's getting from me. It happens all the time in the PR industry, though it's usually under cloak and dagger. It's nice that Vanessa is being the bigger person by informing me and I can, of course, fight her on it and fight for my client but, honestly, I don't have the energy.

Oh well, it was a good run while it lasted.

"I appreciate you telling me," I say. "I'm glad you can come to me out of courtesy."

"Of course! After all, I invoice you, not the client. If there's any work I can't do, you'd be the first person I'd come to," Vanessa adds.

"Hold on... can't do? What work can't you do?"

Vanessa takes a deep breath. "I'm sure you saw the email you were CC'ed into. I was meant to do a piece around Raymond being the CEO of the company for 10 years..."

I've not checked my email in goodness knows how long, so I say nothing and let Vanessa carry on. "I was all set to write it this week. But it's my boy, Josh. He's got appendicitis. He's going to have his op and he'll need to take time off school to recuperate. That along with the usual motherhood, dealing with home, I just don't know if I'll have the hours. He's not a baby, but they kind of never stop being your babies, do they?"

I need a minute to take all this in and I'm not sure if mum brain is to blame this time. "Do you want me to write the press release?" I ask.

"Gosh, I feel awful asking," says Vanessa. "It's just I wouldn't unless it was absolutely necessary. Don't get me wrong, I probably could squeeze in some writing at bedtime once everyone's asleep, but with Josh being a teenager, that won't be until after 11..."

"Don't worry, Vanessa. I can pick up the press release. It would be good to get me back into things."

"Are you sure? I imagine you've still got your hands full with the baby."

Vanessa makes a good point. I look around my flat. There are clothes draped across the sofa. My half-eaten jacket potato from lunch (which was two hours ago), is still sitting on the kitchen counter. H2 is pulling at the wires behind the TV. I have unopened letters piling up under the coffee table. I can't even get my house in order. When will I find the time to write a press release? More to the point, having been away from the game for so long, can I even string a sentence together? What about my spelling and grammar? Will I be able to produce something legible?

I sit up on the sofa and roll my shoulders back. It's time to step up. "Vanessa, don't worry. I've got this."

10th March, Julia's wedding

"It sounds like you've made great progress," says Ravi on our latest therapy call.

"I'm definitely in a better place. I still worry about things and suffer bouts of anxiety but I think I can sort of settle them better before they get the better of me."

Ravi interjects: "Also, you might be one of those worrying people, so it's not always solely down to anxiety. Sometimes it might just be you."

Whoa, that's a little close to the bone. It's like he knows me too well.

Noting my pause, Ravi smooths over with: "And that's not a bad thing. Some of us are naturally predisposed to worry, while some of us are more relaxed about things. Neither is necessarily better than the other and they both have their pros and cons. You will get these bouts of anxiety. It's inevitable. However, it's how you deal with them that counts. From the sounds of things, you've used mindfulness and you've practised the steps we've discussed about how to bring yourself back into the moment. It seems like you're on the right track."

"Yeah, I think so." I look at the time. I'm supposed to be getting ready any minute now. I can hear M talking to H2 in his baby voice. It sounds like they're pacing up and down the hallway outside. Bless him. In the small, confined flat, there aren't many places to take a private phone call and, as it's chucking it down outside, it wouldn't be fair to take our al-most-toddler out in the rain. We are Asian, after all. We can't go out in all weathers. Instead, the two of them are resigned to walking up and down the corridor outside our flat.

"If there is nothing else, I think this is a suitable time to conclude our talks. We've had four sessions and of course you can have more if you need it but, by the sounds of things, you've got this. There's nothing really more I can add."

"I don't know if I've fully got it but I definitely think I'm starting to cope better and, dare I say, enjoying motherhood. Now she just needs to sleep through." My attempt at a joke is met with consolatory giggles.

"That will come in time. It's not like you'll be waking up in the night when she's a teenager."

I groan under my breath. I've heard that so many times, except I'm trying to figure out how much time between her being one and 13, it will take for sleep to stabilise. Not that it's worth opening that can of worms. Ravi doesn't have the answer. The sleep consultant certainly doesn't have the an-swer. And, despite my mum and mother-in-law having raised multiple children, they don't know, either. My H2 is a law unto herself. She will sleep through the night when she's ready. Meanwhile, I have to grin and bear it.

"If you ever feel like you're perhaps slipping back into your old thought patterns, you can always get back in touch. We can fast track you to get another session. It might not be with me but you'll get another therapist. Does that sound okay?"

"That sounds great. And thank you," I say.

This all feels quite cathartic.

There's a knock on the bedroom door. M pops his head round, while H2 mimics his innocent expression. They are literally twins. "Is it safe to come in?"

"Yeah," I reply. "All done now. That's my last session."

"Blimey." M gasps. "Does that mean you're fixed?"

I laugh. "Not quite. I might be less of a worrier but I've got a shopping list of other issues that are probably beyond the scope of my therapist."

M comes over to the bed and puts H2 down. She crawls to me and starts pawing at my face. I think she missed me while I was on the phone for 30 minutes.

"I'll take you as you are, you weird worrywart," says M. "Shall we start getting ready?"

"Yes, I better get changed. And remember, you need to-"

"I know, I know." M rolls his eyes. "Eat before I go, as I don't know when I will be fed. On that note, shall I make us some beans on toast?"

I stroke the back of his neck. "Beans on toast sounds perfect."

My phone pings. It's Chandni. It reads:

Hi, I was wondering if you're around this week at all? I bought some birthday bits for your little lady. I know you'll be celebrating up north but if I can catch you before you go, I can give you her presents.

"Who's that?" M asks as I type my reply.

"One of the mums from the playgroup. She wants to meet up to give H2 a birthday present."

"Check you out, making mum friends." M elbows me.

"Yeah, it only took a year and she's leaving London."

M tuts. "First the Bengali neighbour went all weird and now your new friend's leaving? You're not doing well holding onto these mum friends." M puts his hand to his mouth. "Sorry babe, I didn't mean that."

"It's okay." I kiss H2, my inbuilt friend for life, on the cheek. "To be fair, I probably came on a bit strong with our neighbour. I was very needy." M looks at me funny. "Okay *needier*. I'm in a better place now."

M grabs a tie from the wardrobe. "Still, it was odd how she made food for us and then ghosted you."

I shrug. "It takes all sorts."

M furrows his brow. "Who are you and what have you done with my worrying, overthinking wife?"

As we exit our flat, we spot our neighbour, Taslima.

"Speak of the devil," mumbles M.

Taslima is with her son, Hamza. He looks like he's grown taller and no longer has to tiptoe to press the lift button.

Just before she steps into the lift, she turns and sees me. She smiles. I smile back and she is pulled into the lift by her son.

JULIA'S WEDDING IS everything I expected it to be, yet nothing like I'd imagined.

That girl can even make a barnyard look classy.

Long, sheer white fabric is draped across the beams and gently swaying in the spring breeze. Between the hay bales are white wooden chairs. The little girls that are part of the bridal party are decked out in pretty white dresses with satin pumps and frilly socks. Their hair is adorned with crowns made of dried flowers. There is a smell of fresh linen, while white roses and wild flowers create a simple, rustic feature across the long table which is covered with a crisp, white tablecloth.

It's only us brownies that are ruining the theme. I wish I hadn't worn my deep red dress with gold embellishments around the bust. I thought I looked classy when I checked in the mirror before we left our flat. Now, I feel garish. I wish Julia had specified a colour theme on the invitation. Had I known, I would have worn a more muted shade.

For the first time ever, Julia's brown fringe is swept to the side. Her hair is up in a neat, plaited bun, which perfectly highlights a pair of pearl drop earrings. She's wearing a high-necked ivory dress with capped sleeves and a full skirt. She is elegance personified and always has been.

Miles has coordinated with an ivory tie and light grey suit. His blonde hair sits in a neat side parting and his even blonder eyebrows look like they've been combed. He's also slightly pink from their pre-wedding trip to Greece.

"Is that the yummy mummy?" I hear someone say.

I turn to see Helen. Next to her is a rather bookish guy, with short grey hair and thick glasses.

"This is James," she says with a smile. "My other half."

"Nice to meet you, other half of Helen," I say, keeping an eye on H2, who is currently pulling out straw from the hay bales, while M is distracted by his phone. "I've heard so much about you."

"All good things, I hope," says James with a chortle, sipping on a flute of champagne. "I've heard lots about you, too. You're old school friends, right?"

"We are. Julia, Helen and I have known each other since primary school."

James gives a lopsided smile. "That's great. I've been to Manchester a couple of times. Mainly to watch the footy. Plus, I studied with a guy, Mohammad, or Mo, as he likes to be called, who's from there. I don't suppose you know him, Mo Baig?"

We don't all know each other, I want to reply but instead, I keep things civil. "Doesn't ring a bell."

A waitress comes over with some canapés.

"Oh good, I'm starving." I reach for a cheese pastry.

"Um... that's a sausage roll," the waitress bites her bottom lip, perhaps unsure if she's being helpful, presumptions or offensive.

I retract my hand. "Ah, not for me. Are there any pescatarian options?"

The waitress takes a pencil out from her neatly styled updo. "There should be some coming round. I'll also make a note so that the good stuff comes your way."

"That was a close call," says James, mopping his brow for effect as the waitress leaves.

"It was," I reply.

"Still, you get preferential treatment with her giving you the best food."

"I suspect she was just saying that to appease me."

"I don't know. From what I've seen in life, it pays to be a bit different."

"Like at job interviews," Helen helpfully adds, biting into her sausage roll. "I'm devastated when I'm up against someone... not from here."

I say nothing.

James wipes his crumb-coated mouth with a napkin. "I've always wondered, what would actually happen if you accidentally ate some pork?"

James isn't laughing this time. He is deadly serious. I mustn't begrudge him. By the sounds of things, apart from Mo, he hasn't had much interaction with many minorities, let alone Muslims. Once again, I am the ambassador for my community, my culture and my religion. With so much Islamophobia, I must answer wisely to make sure he sees us in the best light. I must assure him that Islam is a religion of kindness, fairness and, most of all, mercy.

"Well, James," I begin, "I'd burst into flames. Anyway, must dash. I've just spotted Julia."

I walk towards the blushing bride, who is being greeted by another well-wisher. Julia notices me, smiles and shrugs her shoulders. We both know we won't be able to get a word in edgeways when everybody wants to see the star of the show. I remember it well from my own wedding.

H2 has taken to putting the straw in her mouth and has garnered quite some attention.

"She is so cute! Can I keep her?" asks a woman with a brown bob and chocolate coloured hat. I guess I'm not the only one standing out in this muted colour scheme.

"Careful what you ask for," I say.

"I'd love to relive it all again. Mine are all teenagers now and I tell you, this is the easy bit."

"Really? I can't imagine it being any harder," I say.

"Trust me, it's a whole new ballgame once they have hormones. Enjoy every second of this while it lasts."

If I had a penny every time...

"What are you doing?" I ask M, which is my polite way of saying: *Why are you on your phone and not looking after our baby?*

"I'm just checking the footy scores," says M.

"Are Liverpool winning?"

"Yeah. 2-1." M grins.

"Good. Does that mean you won't be a grump and we'll be fed tonight?" I joke.

M nods. "I'll even get you dessert." He puts his phone away.

H2 continues pulling out straws and stuffing some in the pocket of her green cotton dress and throwing the rest at passers-by. I'm about to stop her but then I realise that everybody seems to enjoy it. A few more people admire her.

"We have got the cutest kid, haven't we?" says M.

"With all due bias, yes, we have."

There's a long delay between our starter of pea soup (didn't love it) and the mains, so I decide it's best to nip to the loo for a tactical wee.

As I wash my hands, Julia storms in. She doesn't even see me and goes straight to the toilet cubicle. She closes the door and I can hear the gentle, soothing sound of her retching. I pretend I don't notice and continue washing my hands.

She goes to the next sink and washes her hands. Despite me bursting on the inside to say something, I use all my restraint and wait for her to speak first.

"Don't say anything," she mumbles, rubbing her hands with soap.

"About what?"

"Don't! Just don't. You know what."

I smile to myself and continue rinsing my hands longer than necessary. "I haven't got a clue what you're on about. Anyway, James is nice."

"Who?"

"Helen's boyfriend. The one you've invited to your wedding?"

Julia still doesn't make eye contact. "Oh, that James. Yeah, he's fine. A bit provincial. You know, reads the Daily Mail and believes every word of it. But we will forgive him as he is Helen's man."

Julia splashes some water on her forehead. "I've completely ruined my makeup. I bet my lipstick is already gone. Can you still see my lipstick?"

I couldn't see her lipstick to start with. Unlike me on my wedding day and all other Asian brides, Julia's makeup is muted and barely there.

"It looks fine."

"Good, I spent enough money on the makeup artist. You'd think she'd come to the venue with me to touch up my makeup but no such luck. So now I have to look pale and ghastly and all..."

"Morning sickness-y? A little bit pregnant-y?"

Julia looks at me. "I said don't!"

I put my hands up in defence. "Alright, I won't. Anyway, nobody else is here to hear us. It's just exciting, that's all. I think my glass half empty pessimism is rubbing off on you."

"I have bloody good reason to be pessimistic after the last time. Anyway, it's totally unexpected. And to think I had a blooming glass of champagne at my hen do."

"At least it was just the one glass and not a proper bender. That's the good thing about getting Helen to organise the party. You can be sure there won't be a piss-up in the pub."

Julia goes back into the cubicle and collapses on the toilet. "It wasn't part of the plan. I've not even told Miles yet. I'll need to break it to him on the honeymoon. Oh God, what would my mum say?" Julia pulls at the toilet roll and rips off a square. "I don't suppose she'll care actually after free-spirited Jemima. I can't go far wrong. But I'm never going to get a house at this rate. I'll have to stop working for a bit and-"

"Julia..." I walk towards her with trepidation. "Can I give you a hug?"

Julia dabs her mouth with the tissue, taking away whatever was left of the lipstick. "I suppose so." We hold each other for a moment, saying nothing. "I'm scared to do it here all by myself. Miles' mum will be of no help."

I close my eyes and squeeze Julia tighter. I hear her sniff. "You'll be okay."

"How do you know? I've seen how you and M have been with H2. Doing it all by yourselves without support. It all looks so... hard."

"It is hard but you'll be okay. And I know because I'm going to be okay, too. It's just taking a while. But everything will be okay."

My mind sways towards H2. I've been holed up in the bathroom and I'm scared they've served mains and M decides to feed her something without verifying whether it's allergen-free. I release myself from Julia's hug but she pulls me back in.

"I need you to tell me something." Julia's voice is muffled.

"What is it?"

"Tell me what's been your most disgusting experience since being a mum."

"You don't want to know," I say.

Julia burrows her face in my dress, making me grateful I showered this morning. "I do. I need to know it all. I want to be prepared for the worst."

"Right, since you've asked... you know how we're bed-sharing? Well, one night, H2's nappy leaked and she wet the bed but I was so sleep-deprived, I folded over the pissy part of the duvet and went back to sleep."

Julia lifts her head back. "Yeah, I didn't want to know that."

"There you are! Gosh, I've been looking all over for you! We're about to do toasts," says Julia's mum, Gaynor. Then she notices Julia wiping her eyes. "What's the matter?"

Julia shakes her forehead, forgetting that she no longer has a full fringe, at least for today. "Oh, nothing."

"It's a bit late for pre-wedding jitters, if that's what this is." Gaynor laughs. "You're meant to have that before you exchange your vows, not afterwards."

"It's not that. We were talking about how much has changed these last few years," says Julia, looking to me.

"That's right," I concur. "We're both married. I've had a baby. It's something we couldn't imagine years ago."

"I thought it was all part of your plan," says Gaynor. "Don't Asian people have to get married, regardless of whether they want to or not? Like, the whole arranged marriage thing?"

"Mother!" Julia yells.

"Have I put my foot in it again?" Gaynor slaps her forehead. "Honestly, all this political correctness. I don't know if I'm coming or going. Everyone is... what is it they say, awake?"

"I think you mean woke," I reply. "Anyway, we can't miss the toast."

AFTER SOME BAD DAD jokes peppered with a few awkward innuendos, a gushing speech from Miles, and some racially suspect statements about the changing face of London from the best man, I feel it's time to leave.

"You're not going, are you?" asks Miles. "There's going to be a buffet."

M and I abandon our plans of a drive-through on the way home and decide to stay a bit longer. Honestly, I thought the dinner of pea soup and salmon was all we would be fed tonight. If there's a buffet, I'm there.

One of the few good things about having a baby that doesn't sleep is that we're not beholden to a strict schedule. H2 has been awake the entire time, which I'm sure we'll pay for later, when she keeps us up the rest of the night.

OKAY, SO JULIA AND Miles have a very different definition of what constitutes a buffet.

Instead of the usual fare of deep fried goodness I'm accustomed to, we are greeted with a small selection of cheese, grapes, and figs. The wedding cake has also been carved up for us hungry guests.

Though I'm mindful of having dairy around H2, I greedily cut away at the cheese, taking crumbled mouthfuls with the crackers. Don't judge me, I'm a lactating mum.

I spy Julia watching and catch her eye. She's not looking at me with thinly veiled judgement. Instead, it's a look that says: *You'd better keep my secret.*

2nd April, H2's first birthday party

And just like that... my baby's turned one. I have managed to keep H2 alive for an entire year. That is possibly my greatest achievement ever.

Of course, she may be one year older but is no less cheeky. She was up until 5am last night. Mum, who was sleeping next to us, gave up and decided to camp downstairs on the sofa, yet again.

M, on the other hand, having been granted a peaceful night's sleep at his mum's, is the one yawning.

"Jam came over," he says. "It's the first time I've seen him since he got married and moved to Keighley. A couple of the other guys came round, too, and we ended up chatting 'til about 1am. I'm knackered."

I scowl at him.

"Sorry, I know you were kept awake for less fun reasons."

On the plus side, H2 is enjoying being the Belle of the ball. Dressed in a smart navy blue blazer, she looks like she's going for a job interview. I love putting her in grown-up styles now. She's outgrown the baby grow phases, which I'm sort of sad about but I am enjoying this sassy new style.

Her cuteness has not been lost on anyone. She is being passed around, like a chubby prize, since we arrived at the restaurant. She is currently sitting on my eldest brother-in-law's lap. She's looking at him as he's deep in conversation with middle sis' husband. It must all be Bengali gibberish to her. It often is for the rest of us.

M's older brother is leaning over the booth and keeps tapping H2 on her shoulder, then hiding behind his hands when she turns around. He's usually stoic and sensible. H2 has brought out his silly side.

It's not often I mix M's and my family together. In fact, I avoid it where I can, as I don't want there to be any secrets revealed. And there are a lot of secrets. How M and I met, his redundancy, my redundancy... and those are just the ones I can think of off the top of my head. At this stage, I don't know who knows the truth and who's been fed lies.

Also, there's the one-upmanship. My mother-in-law is forever flexing her culinary muscles. I can hear her talking to mum about how many homemade pastry samosas she made last Eid. I turn to see my mum do a lip grimace. She cheats, you see, as she has done for years, by using shop-bought spring roll pastry. Mum looks at the big silver and white clock on the wall, perhaps wondering when this game of *who is the better cook?* will end.

"I can't do much. Hands no longer have same strength," says mum.

"Yes, yes, me too," my mother-in-law agrees, pulling back her saree to reveal her slim forearm, which is adorned with a thin gold bangle. "I got arthritis here now."

This leads to tales of aches and pains and high blood pressure. Mum's been diagnosed with high cholesterol, which is another bit of info I'd missed because I either wasn't told or wasn't paying attention. M's mum matches this with an anecdote about her own dodgy hip, which has been playing up for the last few years. Those matrons will compete over anything.

I wonder if mum has told my mother-in-law about her possible dementia? Has she even been properly diagnosed yet? Mum is still very much trying to keep me not worried about the whole thing, so I hear very little. I also know how healthcare operates, having worked in the sector myself. Diagnosis can take a while but from the last conversation with little sis, the writing is pretty much on the wall.

I shake off that thought and make a beeline for the food counter. I must take full advantage of being hands free while there are so many people to hold H2.

The restaurant has had an upgrade since I last visited. Gone are the pink velvet walls, scroll-back chairs, and typical, old Indian restaurant aesthetic, to make way for dark wood parquet flooring, dining benches and white walls.

I must say, I prefer the way it was before. I had both my mehendi party and our engagement upstairs. I'll have to check it out later to see if that's changed, too.

But first... food.

Having uncovered every single dish on the counter, I return to the table with a plate of spring rolls, chicken drumsticks, chips, pizza, and a side of Russian salad for balance.

I sit next to H2, who is in her highchair, biting on some poppadoms.

"Is she allowed to have that? Did you tell the staff about her allergies?"

M attempts to loosen the poppadom from H2's grip but she wraps her fingers tightly around it, causing it to crumble. "It's a poppadom. What else could there be in it? It won't contain nuts."

"You know, it might do. They're really half-arsed at Asian restaurants."

I take matters into my own hands and head back to the buffet trays.

"Excuse me, are there any nuts in this?" I ask the chef behind the counter, pointing towards a pile of naan bread.

"Sorry sister? Do you want naan bread?"

"No, I'm asking if there are any nuts in there?"

"You mean the naan bread? Why naan bread have nut? You want nuts on your naan bread?"

I realise the idiocy of my question but I'd rather be safe than sorry. "What about dairy?"

The man stops rolling out the nut-free naan bread. "Hold on, I ask manager."

He waves over to a brawny fellow, who ambles over towards me. "How can I help, sister?"

"My daughter has a peanut, egg and dairy allergy, so I wanted to check if the naan is okay to eat?"

The man wobbles his chin from side to side. "Of course, sister. No nuts in here."

"What about dairy? She has a dairy allergy as well."

"Okay, you want nut free or dairy free?"

"Both."

"I see. No dairy in this. Just a little bit... eh... flour, water, butter-"

"Butter is dairy. She can't have that. What about these? Are the chips safe?"

The man chuckles. "Chips is just chips. Potato and oil. What else should chips have?"

Another idiotic question from me but I have to ask these things. Otherwise, who else will? M certainly won't.

I go through each dish with the waiter. I check the fried chicken, the masala fish, the spicy noodles and all the curries. There are only two dishes that contain dairy and another I will avoid because I'm slightly dubious about this manager as things are getting lost in translation. I look at the long line of serving dishes and am relieved. There are more things H2 can have, than she can't. I need to focus on that, rather than fixating on her allergies and feeling like it's the worst thing ever.

I head back to the table to see that big sis has come next to H2 and is patting her on the nose. Despite so many faces crowding my daughter, many that she's seen only a handful of times in her life, she's happy. She's not intimidated or crying or nervous.

"She's ever so good," says big sis. "She's gone to everyone without whingeing. I don't think I've ever seen a baby this friendly."

A smug grin forms across my face. My daughter is so sociable. She loves this. She needs more of this.

"And how are you doing, little lady? Are you a little less wobbly?"

"I am a bit. Actually, I've been receiving some support..." What am I doing, sharing such intimate details with my older, old-fashioned sister in such a public forum? There are family members literally everywhere. However, my mouth keeps flapping. "Not in like, an 'I'm crazy' kind of way but I have been talking to somebody – just on the phone." Some-how, it feels like talking to a therapist over the phone seems a lot less quirky than lying on a couch, pouring my heart out. "They've helped me a bit with my anxiety. It's really common and a lot of people do talking therapy now."

I look to big sis for signs of judgement, disapproval, or cynicism.

Her face is indecipherable as she says: "Good for you, little lady. I didn't have anything like that in my day. Or if it was available, I wouldn't have known. I suppose it was seen as an English thing, having cloudy feelings. We just had to get on with it. And those who couldn't? Well, who knows? It's much better to speak to someone than have things get out of hand."

"Did you have issues?" I dare ask.

Big sis sits up in her chair. "No, no, lady. Not me. But I know you're a bit softer than me, always taking things personally, so I'm glad you're getting yourself sorted."

That's probably the most emphatic big sis will ever be, so I'll take it as a win.

Mum leans over and kisses H2's forehead. She reaches in her bag and brings out a folded £20 note. "This for you, birthday girl but maybe you look after it as she only *lit-ool* and probably drop it in restaurant." She hands the money to me.

H2 reaches out but then pulls away when she realises it's just money. She'd much rather have a colourful toy.

"You already gave her money, mum."

"Did I? When?" Mum furrows her brow.

"Earlier today."

"Then give it back! I don't want to be ripped off by my own granddaughter."

I can't tell if mum is joking or serious but I'm glad she's still got some bite.

Both M's dad and mine seem to be migrating closer and closer to the doorway. I think they want to leave. My dad has his head in his hands. I go over to see what's wrong.

"I be tired," he says. "No sleep well at night."

"Are you worried, dad?" I ask.

Dad looks blankly. "Worry? Why I worry?"

"About m-" I stop myself. I don't know what dad knows. The paperwork round mum's illness would've been handled by my sisters. I don't say anything as it wouldn't surprise me if it's a secret from dad.

ONE YEAR IN AND THE journey from Manchester to London doesn't get any easier. H2's been crying, non-stop, for 15 minutes. My soft heart can't take it anymore and I resort to doing what I've done on most journeys- climbing onto the back seat, taking her out of her car seat and breastfeeding her while M tries his best not to make any sudden brakes on the motorway.

I hate these journeys.

Finally, it looks like she's nodding off. She's quite the vision, with her work blazer and huge 1st birthday badge that big sis bought for her.

"Remember this?" asks M, turning the volume higher on the radio. "This one always reminds me of our first drive in London together, when I proposed."

While Coldplay's *Fix You* hums in the background, I say: "It was more of a pseudo proposal because our families had already set the date."

"Exactly," says M with glee. "There's no way I would get down on one knee if there was a chance you'd say no."

"If memory serves," I add, "you weren't even going to get me a ring at first, were you? Didn't you plan on leaving it to your mum to get a typical Bangladeshi boat-shaped 22ct gold ring?"

I see M in the rear-view mirror, looking sheepish.

"I think I've upped my game on the romantic side now, haven't I?"

I sigh. "You're getting there. I see this as lifelong training, getting you up to scratch as a husband."

"You can talk," says M. "Your reply to my heartfelt proposal was: *'You'll do!'*"

"Oh yeah." The memory comes back to me. "That feels like a lifetime ago. So much has changed since." I stroke H2's cheek. She's sleeping with her mouth agape. "Now you're off the motorway, could you drive a bit slower so I can put her back in the car seat? I don't want to wake her during transfer."

"In that case…" M sounds like a man with a plan, "let's not go straight home. We'll take a little detour to get her into a deep sleep."

"Where to?" I ask.

"Just a little trip down memory lane."

The sky is pitch black, but the night is illuminated by the bright white of Saint Paul's Cathedral. To the right is Millennium Bridge, where M proposed on that fateful night.

We drive towards Tower Bridge (I guess we're having a tour of all the bridges). Even after all these years, having seen it countless times, I still gaze in awe at the centuries-old Tower of London, which contrasts with the modern City Hall just behind it. In a rare moment, the drawbridge of Tower Bridge opens, causing a standstill. Normally, my anxiety would hit the roof as I worry that H2 will wake up and start crying. However, she's fast asleep, leaving me to take in the night. Every time I go to this part of London, I spot something new. I never noticed the thoroughfare of restaurants just near the bridge. I open the window. It's balmy outside and feels much warmer than Manchester, which we left behind hours ago. It must be all the smog from the cars.

Traffic starts moving and M drives on to Spitalfields, where so many young, free and childless people look like they're beginning their night, just as we are about to end ours. Heidi's chip shop has a queue outside, as usual. They do great chips.

We have to drive extra slowly as we make our way through Brick Lane. People have abandoned the pavement and instead are walking in the middle of the cobbled road as if they don't have a care in the world. This part of London seems different to others. There isn't the same sense of rush that commuters have as they go about their daily chores. It's more relaxed, as if people don't have anywhere they particularly need to be. I walked through here so many times. To get a cheeky curry, or to visit the trendier parts of East London. We've trodden these streets until we got bored. We were ready to have a baby. We wanted this next stage of life... I just don't think either of us realised how life altering it would be. I feel so naive now. I really did wonder how hard it could be having a baby in central London. Now I know.

"It was nice getting everyone together back up north, wasn't it?" says M, interrupting my thoughts.

"It was lovely. I think H2 enjoyed having all the extra cuddles. To be fair, I loved it, too, being hands free for a bit."

M nods. "We need more of that, don't we? A bit more help?"

"We do. It's just so hard here finding help. I'm not ready to put her into nursery, either, though I'll have to if I want to start working again."

"It would be so much better back up north," says M. I don't say anything. I want to hear what he has to say, for once. "I've been thinking about this for a while. It's so much harder here. Mostly, it's so much harder for you. I get to go to work every day and spend eight hours not having to do all the stuff that you do. Even the basic things are a nightmare, like booking a dentist appointment. Or, if you're ill, there's no one to look after the baby unless I take a day off."

"That's true. I never expected it to be like this."

"It feels like the right time, babe," says M. "What with our parents getting older and your mum having-"

I stare down into the darkness of the car. "I know."

"And I have been looking for jobs up north."

"You have?" I look back up at him.

"Yeah, on the down-low. To be honest with ya, I've kind of kept my eyes peeled since H2 was born. After everything that happened- the birth, you being unwell, then her being unwell, all of it would have been so much easier if we had family around. Anyway, when I first started looking, there wasn't much. There are always fewer finance jobs in general outside of London. But more recently, I've spotted a few jobs come up in my area." M taps on the steering wheel. "I'm thinking I should apply. I know you're worried about what it will be like going up north. I know you're anxious about what the expectation will be living near my family but we can figure all that out so it works for us. What do you think?"

H2 rustles and I shush and pat her back to sleep. Finally, that bloody technique is working.

M continues: "We don't need to think about it yet but I wanted to let you know." He shrugs, unaware that he has suggested something that's been bubbling along the periphery of my mind.

"Crap!" I shout, leaning forward.

"What is it?" asks M. "Is it H2?"

"No, I just remembered I wrote a press release and sent it to my client on Thursday. I need to check if they've replied."

I go to my phone. There's a message from Sophia. She says:

I'm so proud of you for doing the talking therapy and I can't wait to catch up when you're next up north.

I reply: *Thanks. I'm glad I took that step, for myself and H2. Can't wait to catch up, too!*

I then open my emails. There is a message from Raymond, the CEO:

The press release is great, Helena. And it's lovely to have you back on the account. You've been missed.

I lean back and exhale.

"Is everything okay?" M asks.

"Yeah. They loved the press release."

"I knew they would. You've still got it. I see you and I see how hard you're working to juggle it all. I couldn't do it."

I check myself in the rear-view mirror. There I am. Beneath the milk and the mess, the overgrown eyebrows and untamed hair, I am still there.

M takes another detour, this time a left turn towards Whitechapel. We drive past the hospital where I gave birth. The place where I spent more time than intended. The place which gave me mixed feelings of resentment and gratitude. The place where my life changed completely.

We pass the market stalls, which stand empty as everybody has gone home.

"Do you think she's sleepy enough now for us to go to the flat?" M asks.

"Yes, let's go back," I reply, unable to say the word home.

As we drive back, an ambulance blares past, cutting us up on the road. It's not unusual to see an emergency vehicle on this road, being in such close proximity to the hospital. H2 startles, serving as yet another reminder that where we live is so damn busy.

In the distance, I spy the Gherkin, the giant, impressive structure, so synonymous with the City of London. Then we take a turn towards our flat. People are still walking around, though it's gone 10pm. London never really sleeps. Certainly not in these parts. And, for the longest time, I loved that. I still love it and I still have a great love for London but it's not the same. Everything has changed. Or should I say, the city is the same but I'm the one that's changed. Yes, I still love London but I love this kid, this sleep-stealing kid, more.

M and I have so much to work on. So much was said, by him and me. Most of it hasn't been unpacked. Perhaps it never will. One thing I've learnt from my marriage is that what you choose to hold onto and what you choose to let go of, makes all the difference.

As we get into the car park, I tap M on the shoulder. "I think you're right. We should go home."

M smiles. He knows it. I took a little longer to realise it but, at the end of the day, we have each other and we have our little girl. And it's time to go home.

There's more to the story... free reads and more for you

I hope you enjoyed this story. But wait... there's more. As I mentioned, this isn't your average romcom. It's got people talking, challenged perceptions, and hopefully shown that we're not so different after all. As the series grows I'd like you to be part of my tribe, so I can share exclusive content, free reads, and get your opinion on future book covers, etc. Would you like to join my tribe? If so, sign up to my mailing list https://halimakhatun.co.uk/newsletter-sign-up/

Enjoy this book? Want to read more? The power is in your hands...

Firstly, thanks for taking the time to read my book. It makes my heart happy knowing that people are taking pleasure from my words. It motivates me to write more. I want my book to be read as far and wide as possible, and key to making this happen is having great reviews from readers like you.

Reviews are the most powerful tool in my arsenal when it comes to getting attention for my books. I'm not represented by a global publishing house and I don't have a huge marketing team and endless budget.

But I have something better, that money can't buy – a committed and invested readership. And I rely upon this most important asset, to spread the word.

If you've enjoyed this book, I would be grateful if you could spend just a few minutes leaving a review on the store of your choice. It can be as short or as long as you like.

Books by Halima Khatun – have you read them all?

The Secret Diary of an Arranged Marriage

Winner of the 2021 Bookbrunch Selfie Award for Best Adult Fiction...

A British-Bengali girl looking for Mr Right. A motley crew of men, some hoping it's them. A mum on a mission to match make. And an age-old tradition with a twist. Welcome to the world of the arranged marriage.

The Secret Diary of a Bengali Bridezilla

And I thought finding a husband was hard...

One couple. Three months. 600 guests (most of whom I've never met) and LOTS of opinions. Welcome to my big fat Bangladeshi wedding.

The Secret Diary of a Bengali Newlywed

I found me a man, now I just need to figure out how to live with him...

New husband. New city. New in-laws and new expectations.

Welcome to my life as a Bengali newlywed.

The Secret Diary of a Broody Bengali

FIRST COMES LOVE... then comes marriage... now the nosey aunties are asking when I'm going to have a baby.

In this laugh-out-loud, heartwarming romantic comedy, our strong female protagonist - a British Bengali girl - is contemplating starting a family. But with a blossoming career and a transient life away from family, is she truly ready for the life changing journey of becoming a mum?

The Secret Diary of a Pregnant Bengali

ONE COUPLE. NINE MONTHS. Lots of decisions and even more opinions...

Welcome to my life as a pregnant Bengali lady.

The Secret Diary of a Pregnant Bengali sees our heroine face her greatest challenge yet, negotiating raging hormones, NCT classes, and a whole host of Bengali old wives' tales.

Mother of the Bride

THE SIDE OF THE STORY you never hear...

A mum on a mission to matchmake. A daughter with ideas of her own. A suitor that threatens to tear them apart. When it comes to arranged marriages, you never hear the perspective of the mother of the 'bride'. So now it's time.